Übermensch

A Novel by D. L. Scarpe

Übermensch
Copyright © 2024 by D. L. Scarpe.
dl.scarpe@yahoo.com
dlscarpe.wordpress.com
All rights reserved.

This is a work of fiction. Names, characters, places and incidents are products of the author's imagination or are used fictitiously and should not be construed as real. Any resemblance to actual events, locales, organizations or persons, living or dead, is entirely coincidental.

No part of this book may be used or reproduced in any manner whatsoever without written permission, except in the case of brief quotations embodied in critical articles and reviews. For more information, e-mail all inquiries to info@mindstirmedia.com.

MINDSTIR MEDIA

Published by MindStir Media, LLC
45 Lafayette Rd | Suite 181| North Hampton, NH 03862 | USA
1.800.767.0531 | www.mindstirmedia.com

Printed in the United States of America.
ISBN-Paperback: 978-1-963844-28-3
ISBN-Hardcover: 978-1-963844-73-3

Preface

"Why would you write about two such wicked boys?"

This is the question I asked myself in 2021 when the idea took hold. The answer in a nutshell: Nathan Leopold made me.

I'll elaborate. I had just finished workshopping my third novel. In my never-ending quest for a literary agent to notice me for my manuscripts—which I lovingly refer to as Things One, Two, and Three—the genre that stood out the most was historical fiction.

So, I decided to Google old crimes. Leopold's and Loeb's names popped up as the perpetrators of the Bobby Franks murder, and the names were familiar because of a line in *Seinfeld*, the "Junior Mint" episode. (Doesn't everything in life somehow relate to a *Seinfeld* episode?) The famous-in-my-mind line is, "I can't have this on my conscience. We're like Leopold and Loeb."

Once I began reading about who they were, I was hooked. But their motive and how everything went down made something inside me cry, "Bullshit!" And a novel idea was born. I ordered books, borrowed from my local library, read everything I could find on the subject online, and watched movies about the infamous pair.

I laughingly believed I could complete the novel in a few months. Nope.

Life took over, as it always does, and the birth of my first grandchild drew my attention away from those naughty boys. Oh, I played the game for a few months, bouncing back and forth between writing and cooing but in February of 2022, I conceded defeat and put the half-completed manuscript to rest. I didn't touch it again for a year.

I'm used to delving into the deepest crevices of a mind where dirty things lie in the shadows ready to spring up at the first sign of daylight. My novels number one and three are dark and number two is a twisty pretzel of a read, but this one felt different somehow, and it didn't take me long to figure out why: This is the first time that I've written about real people and dived into a real mind, not one I conjured up in my own. Worse, an actual crime was committed.

My apologies to anyone who might be related to the perpetrators and especially to those related to the victim. My intention was and never will be to hurt anyone, but something (or someone) grabbed ahold of me and wouldn't let go. I changed the names of people and streets, even some towns, but I make no bones about who and what this novel is about.

Many thanks to those who wrote, produced, directed, or starred in everything I read and watched to get a feel for the characters.

Something worthy of note: Clarence Darrow was an attorney like no other. I respectfully and wisely avoided trying to replicate a single word of his closing argument, which reflected his passion for law and his abhorrence for capital punishment. Look it up one day.

Most of all, rest in peace, Bobby Franks. Your mother is said to have been happy that your slayers weren't hanged, because you didn't believe in the death penalty. You sound like you would have been an awesome dude—possibly another Darrow.

D. L. Scarpe

Introduction

ON MAY 21, 1924, in Chicago, Illinois, fourteen-year-old Robert "Bobby" Franks walked home from an after-school baseball game and disappeared. Meanwhile, his parents had been contacted by a man who claimed to have kidnapped their son for ransom. They learned of Bobby's death as they awaited further instructions.

Eight days later, the police were questioning Nathan Leopold Jr., son of a millionaire box manufacturer; and Richard Loeb, whose father was a retired Sears, Roebuck vice president. The Leopold, Loeb, and Franks families all lived within three blocks of each other in the same upscale neighborhood in Chicago.

Certain that "Babe" and "Dickie" could never be involved in something so horrible, the young men's fathers allowed them to be questioned without benefit of counsel. After days of grilling, Loeb confessed to the kidnapping and murder of the Franks boy. Leopold's confession followed. The only reason the unremorseful pair gave for the premeditated kidnapping and murder plot was for "pure love of excitement, or the imaginary love of thrills, doing something different." The country was captivated by the cold, heinous crime.

These are some of the facts. My story is a combination of the truth and my imagination.

D. L. Scarpe

Chapter I

Man is the cruelest animal.

—Friedrich Nietzsche

Wednesday, 21 May 1924 – Chicago, Illinois

I ROLL UP my sleeves and stick my head out the window of the Willys-Knight touring car, hoping for a whisper of wind, but instead I'm assaulted by hot air and the smell of burning petroleum.

Sighing, I drum my fingers on the steering wheel and look around. The red brick building on the opposite end of the alley immediately commands my attention. The Dravah School for Boys. A private academy to prepare boys for college, and my alma mater, the Dravah boasts a tall facade and is located on the parallel street to the one where I'm parked.

A familiar figure comes into my view. Roman. He's walking this way, hands deep in his pockets, long legs carrying him in that carefree manner of his. As I watch him, a trickle of sweat leaks from my hairline, follows the path around my ear, and falls onto my shirt collar.

"Hey, lots of kiddies to snatch," he says, leaning on his elbows through the open passenger window.

"Shhh," I hiss. "Get inside."

"Gee, don't be such a stupe, Noah." He opens the door, folds his legs, and drops into the seat. "No one's anywhere near us."

"I still don't want to take chances." Instead of arguing, I ask about his statement. "So, you saw some viable subjects?"

He glares at me, and in an instant, his brow smooths, and he grins. "Yeah, I went around back to the playground and chatted with a couple of kids." His affable laugh does what it tends to do to my stomach—a not unpleasant rippling. "Ruffled a few heads, sort of like a big brother."

"Okay, well, school lets out soon." I start the car. "I want to go home for my field glasses. It'll be challenging to figure out to whom each child belongs, and we want to pick one whose father's financial situation works best."

Roman's leg bounces up and down. "Sure, sure, but let's pop over to Ballard's Pharmacy first."

"What for?" I turn to him while waiting for an elderly woman to cross the street. An impatient driver toots his horn at me.

Roman gestures to the rude guy in the smoky jalopy behind us and flashes me his brilliant smile again. "Ah, I want to buy more cigs, maybe go to the phone booth and look up Jeremy Levin. He has lots of dough, and his snot kid got a head ruffle. Maybe we can catch him alone. If we grab him, it'll be handy to have his old man's number and address." He winks. "You know, for the call and ransom note."

"All right, but be quick."

"Yes, sir." He salutes, the tips of his fingers brushing the brim of his newsboy cap. His expression hardens, before he leans back in the seat, and I drive us to Ballard's.

When we finally arrive at my house, the family chauffeur is in the side yard.

I get out and walk to the iron fence separating the sidewalk and our property. "Excuse me, Erik," I say, addressing the man who has worked for us since I was six months old.

He turns around. "Oh, good afternoon, Master Babe. I just returned from taking my wife to the doctor, and I'm going down the street to your aunt's house to put air in her tires."

"'El-lo," Roman yells from the car, hanging out the passenger window and flashing his infectious grin. He tips the tweed cap that matches his dark suit. "Pleasant day, hey, chap?"

"Um, yes, Mr. Loewe." Erik looks at me and asks, "Where's your car?"

"In the garage. I'm driving one of Roman's today."

"Is there a problem with yours?"

"Yes, Erik, as a matter of fact, my brakes have been squeaking. Quite an annoyance. Perhaps you can look at them?"

"Of course. I can oil them, and if you drive safely and use your emergency brake, you won't hit anyone."

I shake my head. "No, they've been a nuisance for weeks. Take them apart and fix them, please."

"Yes, I'll work on it right away. I only wish you told me sooner."

"I'm telling you now."

"They'll be done immediately," he promises.

"Thank you," I say, and go inside to get my field glasses.

* * *

"There he is!" Roman exclaims once I park the rental.

"Where?" I scan the boys streaming from the Dravah, unable to place the Levin kid from our vantage point down Essex Avenue, not even with binoculars.

Roman pulls the glasses from me, and the neck strap drags me closer to him. I feel heat from his body. Or maybe it's my own heat.

He looks through the lenses. "Over there, breaking off with a group and heading down the street."

I do see now but don't want to move away from him.

"Let's watch where they go." Grinning, he hands the field glasses back.

Chauffeurs stand outside autos, holding doors open for some children. Others walk off in huddles like the Levin boy does. I pull out into the street, and we follow him. The group turns down an alley, so I drive around the block. By the time we come back, Levin is nowhere. A bunch of kids, however, have started a game of baseball in the vacant lot at the corner.

"Ah, damn!" Roman slams his fist on the dashboard. "Now what?" He points to the ball game in progress as we drive by slowly. "Who knows how long these brats will be playing?"

"We'll go back to my house," I suggest. "The servants are there, but none of the family will be home. There's a perfect view of the lot from my study. We can watch them without being seen, pick one, and wait for an opportunity."

"Yeah, sure. Let's go." He slaps his hand on the outside of the door, loosening his collar with his other. "Gas it, and speed up this machine, will ya?"

When we arrive, we go upstairs to my study, and I pull chairs over to the window so we can watch the kids. Roman and I sit side by side. Our thighs touch. He lowers his binocs and studies me.

"What say you, Noah?" Winking, he presses his thigh tighter against mine. "How about the one with the red cap? I know him. His old man owns a bunch of pharmacies. Wouldn't it be a hoot to make the ransom call from one of Daddy's joints, right in his own phone booth?" He squeezes my leg. I can almost see fireworks behind his eyes, eyes the color of a male *Hylocichla mustelina,* the wood thrush.

"Yes, well, the game's been going on for a while now. We should drive around a bit and be ready for him when he walks home."

"Sure, sure," he agrees.

Back in the car, I head west and turn left down Braxton Boulevard.

Roman's leg resumes its frenetic dance. At Park Street, I turn again and continue for a block before taking Essex Avenue north. He waves out the window when we pass by his house but then slumps back in the seat.

"This is horseshit!" he says after we've gone another couple of blocks. "Let's go back. Why—"

"Hey, look," I say, keeping my voice steady and placing a hand on his knee.

A young boy is walking down Essex on the other side of the road. I slow as we pass him but not enough to be suspicious, although no one else is on the street.

"Sonofabitch! Where did he come from? Do you know who that is, Noah?" Something in the tenor of his voice gives birth to a warm feeling in my stomach. Excitement always thrills Roman, but this is different.

"No."

"Why, it's my brother's friend, good ole Bennie Frisch. He played tennis at my house just the other day. Man, oh, man, is his old man loaded!" He knocks my hand from his knee and grins. "Go back."

By the time I turn the car around, Bennie is about to cross onto Forty-Ninth Street.

"This cocky sonofabitch is perfect." Roman climbs in the back seat as I glide the Willys next to the kid.

He leans forward and calls out the passenger window, "Hey, Bennie, get in and we'll give you a ride."

Chapter 2

Friday, 30 April 1920

I STOOD WITH my friend, Henry, on the sidewalk in front of the University of Chicago's main campus building, one of many Gothic, limestone structures that stretched for blocks, when he called out to someone and waved him over.

"Hey, Henry, how are you doing, chap?" the fella said, slapping Henry on the back.

"Good. I want to introduce you to Babe." He turned to me. "And this guy here is Roman Loewe. I thought you should meet since you eggheads have lots in common."

I wanted to spit out a retort sure to shame Henry Heinz, my intellectual inferior, but the smiling chap stopped the words before they tumbled out. Roman Loewe. I stared at the tall, thin boy I'd never met but had heard about from my mother and aunt. The one who they compared to me, intellectually. I grasped his hand, pumped it fast, and dropped it. Something churned in my stomach, and I averted my eyes from his, uncomfortable about the gleam lurking behind the most interesting shade of brown tinted with red.

"My name's Noah Lieberman," I said instead. Trying my best to look down on Henry as I glared up at him, I rectified his annoying mistake. "My family and close friends call me Babe."

Roman laughed. "After Babe Ruth?"

"No, because I'm the youngest, but if he can put up with the nickname, so can I."

"Yeah, yeah." Henry turned to the other boy. "*Noah* just toured the campus and will be the second anomaly at our illustrious U of Chicago in the fall."

"What do you mean?" I asked.

"Roman graduated high school at fourteen, so when you get here, Noah, you two will be the youngest to matriculate in the college's history. You're not sixteen yet, are you?"

I shook my head. "Not until November."

"Then you're about five months older than Roman," Henry said.

The Loewe boy laughed, but I spotted something behind his eyes, heard something in the sneer he disguised as a laugh.

"Well, glad to meet you, Noah. And my family calls *me* Manny." He pulled a deck of Lucky Strikes from his jacket pocket and tapped one out. "Wanna smoke?" he asked, holding the cigarettes out to me.

I grabbed one, and he lit his and tossed me the lighter. The first draw burned, as it always did since I'd taken up the habit a few months ago. I fought to hold in a cough.

"Butt me too, Roman," Henry said.

"You can afford your own ciggy, you grubber."

Henry's face reddened, and the tips of his fat ears glowed.

Roman bent over, laughing. "Ah, you should see your face! Like a damn tomato. Matches your hair." He plucked out a stick and tossed it at Henry. Turning to me, he winked. "Christ, what do I care? I lifted the pack."

The banter between them amused me, and I sensed that the boy with brown hair verging on blond merely pretended to like pudgy Henry.

"So, what do you think about our campus, eh?" Roman swept an arm out toward the buildings. Young men with books strapped and slung over their shoulders walked around with giggling, silly girls. "Lots of sweet slash hanging about."

"What's your experience with fillies?" Henry said, laughing. "Your brothers say they're taking you to a cathouse for your birthday this summer. Betcha catch a case of the pox!"

Roman dragged on his cigarette and then flicked it onto the grass. He ignored Henry and put his arm around my shoulders, making me stiffen. I didn't, however, wrench myself free as I typically would, because this touch didn't repulse me—rather a strange warmth filled my stomach.

"Lieberman? Your old man owns a few lumber mills, right?" He snapped his fingers, the ones closest to my head, and released me. "Yeah, you live on Greenwick Avenue. I've seen your place."

"Yes." My body felt light and suddenly cold in the mild air.

"Oooh, Roman, think you did well on exams?"

I turned toward the voice. A vapid-looking girl stood on the grass next to the sidewalk.

Roman smiled, widening the cleft between his nose and upper lip, and grabbed her. Laughing, he swung her around before depositing her onto the ground. His light tweed coat swished with the motion.

Clutching a cream-colored cloche in one hand, she waved her other in an exaggerated fashion in front of her face. "You make me dizzy."

He batted his lashes at her. "So, go rest those tootsies, toots!" Winking, he blew her a kiss as she rejoined her tittering friends near the main building. Then he sneered at Henry, and said, "I can handle the fillies."

Henry shook his head and laughed. "Come on, Noah. Tour's over so I'll take you home now." He punched Roman on the shoulder. "What about you, lover boy? Want a ride, or are you going to hang out around here like some drugstore cowboy?"

"Sure, sure," he said. "My dogs are dragging."

We walked in silence until we reached Henry's shiny, yellow Roamer Roadster.

Roman whistled and ran his hand over the curvy fender. "Wow, nice breezer, Henry! This poor man's Rolls is yours?"

"Yes."

"A bit ostentatious don't you think?" I couldn't help asking, but I thought, *More on the line of garish*. "Father's purchasing a new Willys-Knight soon and will turn it over to me on my birthday for my exclusive use. Meanwhile, I drive one of his cars whenever I wish."

"Ole Popsie won't let me behind the wheel anymore," Roman said. "Not since I crashed his Model T at the house in Michigan. Not until I 'reach a particular level of maturation.'"

"Well, you damn near killed yourself and your kid brother," Henry said as he opened the driver's door and got in. "Gettin' drunk and driving Thad around the property."

"Ah, don't worry. Precious Thaddeus is in perfect health despite my giggle-water cruise," Roman stated as he went to the passenger side of the roadster. He hopped onto the running board and jumped in. "Squeeze in, Noah."

I got in, and we started on our way. Roman whooped at a couple of flappers walking down the street. When a Marmon auto passed us, he stood up and tipped his cap.

"Afternoon, coppers!" he said.

"Knock it off," Henry shouted over noisy traffic.

What a child, I thought, conflicted about Roman, who spoke his mind freely—something I myself was a proponent of doing.

"Here we are. Bye, Noah," Henry said.

We're at my house already?

"Uh, thanks, and it was pleasurable to meet you, Roman." Heat rushed to my face at my blunder. Embarrassed, I jumped out of the car.

"Probably see you around next semester," he yelled as they sped off, the car jerking with each gear Henry engaged.

"Henry 'Heinzie' Heinz possesses neither the brains nor the physical dexterity for driving an automobile," I muttered. "However, he's a knowledgeable bird-watcher." I walked through the black iron gate and climbed the steps of the three-story stone structure where I lived. The door opened right before my hand grasped the knob, and there stood Margaret, our head maid.

"Master Babe, I saw you out the window," the tall, stout woman said. "You're home early. I just prepared a sandwich for your brother. Leftovers. Can I make you one?"

When I stepped inside, wafts of last night's chicken made my stomach grumble. "Yes, please. So, Levi's home?"

"No, Saul."

Annoyed, I followed her into the kitchen. Sanctimonious, sarcastic Saul sat at the table with a newspaper sprawled in front of him. Five years my senior, but with fifty more years' worth of arrogance, we barely tolerated each other.

He looked up when I walked in. "That God-hatin' atheist is at it again," he said, and his dark eyes bulged with indignation.

"Who?" I asked, although I didn't care.

"Maurice Milton. Esquire. Savior to the indigent everywhere." He shook his head and slapped the paper. "The man destined to save the guilty from the gallows. Hogwash-spewing heretic!"

"Do you truly wish to debate the existence of God on such an afternoon, Saul?" My impatience slipped out despite my inner resolve to ignore him. "How's Mother today?"

"She's as usual, but why don't you go see for yourself? Of course, she asked after you, her Babe."

"I shall," I snapped, resolve shot like one of my birds, stuffed and on display in my mind—a perpetual reminder that keeping my patience and annoyance under control was not part of my physical composition. Saul didn't say the words—didn't need to say them. I heard them, nonetheless. *You, Noah, are the reason for her delicate constitution. Your birth has been slowly killing our mother.* Not something I wanted to hear either outright or threaded in a tapestry of words. "She was asleep when I checked in on her this morning."

"Here you go, Master Babe." Margaret stood before me with a plate in one hand, a glass in the other. "I poured you milk as well."

"Thank you. If you'll get me a tray, I think I'll eat upstairs with Mother in her rooms."

My brother rolled his eyes. "So, Babe, did you enjoy your tour of the university?"

"Yes, it went well."

"The Heinz chap accompanied you?"

"He did. I look forward to my attendance there." I took the tray offered by Margaret and walked to the door. "Goodbye, Saul, I'm leaving right after lunch. I'm anxious to go to the park this afternoon for a few hours and—"

"You and that damn bird-watching!"

I whirled around. "What's wrong with ornithology? The knowledge gleaned from studying birds is exponentially important to nearly every ecosystem on earth. Why—"

"And I agree with you on the subject, Babe. However, your morbid collection of dead, stuffed birds is creepy. I'll never understand why Father used his substantial influence and standing in the community to arrange city permits for you to shoot birds so you can fill an entire room with your…your—"

"The word you're searching for is *specimens*. I'll accept yours and the rest of the world's gratitude when my collection becomes renowned," I said and stormed off to Mother's suite.

Placing the tray on a small table, I knocked on the door.

Her maid answered. "Oh, Mr. Babe, your mother will be so pleased," the matronly woman said. "She's upset about missing you this morning."

"Is she unwell?"

"Weak, but no more, perhaps, than typical."

I induced my mouth to smile. "You may take leave while I visit."

"As you wish," she said and left. I took my food and walked through the floral-inspired sitting room, hesitating at the entrance to the bedroom.

"May I enter, Mother?" I called out.

"Please do, my precious Babe," came her weak, but swift reply.

* * *

Later, as I lay in bed, I tried to concentrate on my afternoon in the park. I had spotted the spectacular *Zonotrichia querula*; however, I couldn't get close enough to obtain the Harris's sparrow.

I tossed and turned, binding the sheets around my legs. Frustrated, I kicked out until free. Not even birds distracted my mind from the path it longed to take. All-too-familiar feelings melded with new images in my head, and I saw myself, a young man of superior intellect to most, dressed in a raggedy loincloth, each outstretched arm held by savage men. I struggled with them, but they pulled me, making my shoulders ache.

My breaths grew rapid, and perspiration coated me as my body heated up. The brutes pushed me to my knees in front of an ornate throne. A bullwhip cracked and struck my back. Once, twice, three times. I shuddered from pleasure and pain.

"Enough."

The strong command, soft but sinister, made me shiver.

I gazed up at my savior and met his brown, roguish eyes. My release, in fantasy and reality, was monumental.

Chapter 3

Live dangerously.

—Friedrich Nietzsche

Thursday, 29 May 1924

I LEFT THE blasted binocs in here. I'm sure of it, I think, examining everything on the desk in my study. I check my pocket watch and frown. Only ninety minutes until my bird-watching class at Fox Lake. *Where are the damnable things?* A light knock startles and annoys me.

"Yes?"

"Master Babe?"

"Come in, Margaret."

The door opens, and the maid takes a step inside, holding onto the knob with her hand.

"Some gentlemen are here to see you," she says.

"Gentlemen?"

"Two of 'em. They wish to speak with you."

"Very well. Let them know I'll be down momentarily."

"Okay." She backs out of the room, closing the door softly in her wake.

Curious, I walk over to the window. A large, black automobile with both passenger tires on the curb is parked in front of the house.

Not willing to leave my favorite room yet, I turn to my birds. Hundreds of exhibits meet my eyes. Various species of owls adorn the tops of regal, Cherrywood curved-glass china cabinets, five in all. Inside are smaller specimens—Harris's sparrow, Golden crown sparrow, and a Wilson's phalarope seemingly gliding over a shelf. Birds, mounted in flight and resting, are everywhere. I sigh, take one last look, and walk into my bedroom through the connecting door. Everything is as it should be.

As I descend the staircase, I hear male voices interspersing with Margaret's distraught voice.

"Really, sirs, this is highly inappropriate! I told you to wait on the portico and—"

"It's quite fine," I say when I reach the bottom and find her wringing her hands in front of her apron. "I'll speak with the gentlemen."

Two men sporting cheap suits are standing in the foyer, holding their hats at their sides. The Ford belongs to them. Chicago's finest has arrived. Again.

"Mr. Lieberman? Noah Lieberman Jr.?" the taller man asks, beads of sweat forming on his temple.

"Yes, and who might you sirs be?"

"Sheriff's deputies."

I manage to hold in a sneer but still feel my left nostril lift as I demand, "Since you aren't wearing uniforms, I'll require your identification."

The shorter man, although taller than my modest five foot six, points to the star on his blazer. "This is all I need. State's Attorney Bertram Hawke wants to talk to you."

Tilting my head, I respond, "About?"

"That would be for him to disclose, Mr. Lieberman."

"Well if this is regarding the Frisch case, I already spent considerable time discussing the matter with Captain Timothy White this Sunday past. He was speaking with people known to frequent the lakes near the tracks where the poor child was found. I take my bird-watching students out there, and as I explained to him, I was there the previous weekend chasing birds with a friend."

"I have no knowledge of this, Mr. Lieberman. My instructions are simply to escort you to the State's attorney."

"Surely, this can wait. I'm teaching a class soon."

"I'm afraid not."

"Very well, then."

"Do you happen to wear eyeglasses?" the tall one asks.

Of course, I read all about the eyeglasses recovered from the crime scene. Newspaper headlines scream about the spectacles, and every article speculates about their owner.

"I have a pair of cheaters for reading, but I haven't worn them in a long time. Should I look for them?"

"Nah, we better not keep Mr. Hawke waiting."

"All right then, one moment." I go to the door and open it. "Wait outside while I find someone to tell them that I'm leaving." Neither moves, and we stare at each other until one of them nods, and they walk out.

To my immense relief, my eldest brother is home and not Saul. I find him in the library.

"The police are here, Levi. They wish to speak to me about my known presence in Fox Lake, the area where the Frisch boy was found."

He closes the book in his lap and stands up. "What do you mean?"

"It's nothing. They're speaking with everyone seen in the area recently, and I was there with Henry the weekend preceding the matter."

"Should I call Father at work?" His pale skin loses more color, causing his ebony, slicked-back hair to stand out.

"No. No need to concern him with this. However, I won't be able to teach my class in an hour and a half. Would you contact Henry and ask if he can substitute? The students shouldn't suffer too great a loss in my absence. He's a passable instructor."

"Well, Babe, what if he isn't available?"

"Then will you go to Fox Lake and tell the kids that class is canceled today? We meet at the last spur road before the tracks."

"Fine."

* * *

The black Ford, which bears no emblem betraying its identity, has a roomy back seat. I settle into it.

"Mind if I smoke?" I don't wait for their answer, just pull out my cigarettes, tap the end of the pack, and slip one out. Lighting it, I lean back, blow a few rings, and look out the window. After a while, I realize that we're heading in the wrong direction.

"Excuse me, fellas, but isn't the State's attorney's office in the Criminal Court Building on Hubbard? Shall I drive? I hope you two aren't in charge of the Frisch investigation."

"Why you little—"

"Enough, Fred." The taller one in the passenger seat turns around to address me. "Mr. Hawke will be meeting with you at the Hotel Cavalier. He's using a room there."

I raise my almost unibrow, purse my mouth, and give him what Saul calls my "patronizing pout."

Seems the esteemed Mr. Hawke doesn't wish to embarrass the Lieberman family or mar our name. Noble of him.

The car pulls up to the curb. I let the men exit and wait until one of them opens the rear door. Sticky, humid air slaps me in the face.

"This way, Mr. Lieberman."

I step out onto the sidewalk and adjust my black tweed jacket. Placing my hat on my head, I toss my cigarette into the dirty street and gaze at the magnificent building in front of me. Twenty-two stories high and designed after the style of the French Renaissance, the hotel boasts a thousand rooms—one of which is being occupied by the State's attorney.

Once we enter, passing under the hotel's name etched in stone, the bustling pedestrians and noisy honking sounds disappear and are replaced with quiet conversations. We walk through an opulent walnut-paneled lobby with rich green carpeting, dozens of statues, and brass spittoons. Overstuffed chairs surround marble-topped tables where men sit smoking pipes that emanate sweet-smelling apple-and-vanilla tobacco. I glance up at masterfully carved beams crisscrossing high, recessed ceilings, and hanging chandeliers.

The deputies lead me down a corridor—one in front of me, the other behind. Bypassing the elevator, we take the stairs one flight up and go down another hallway to room number eleven.

"Does this mean that the State didn't spring for the roof-top garden suite? Such a disappointment. This is my first occasion to visit the Cavalier, and I hear the garden is sublime."

Neither man responds, but the shorter one turns around, and his dour expression speaks volumes. He opens the door and enters.

I follow him into a room with bold, nautical-inspired wallpaper. The bed, along with an armoire and a walnut highboy dresser, are pushed to one side, making room for a large desk with two chairs in front of it.

"Sir," he says, "this is Noah Lieberman. Junior."

The man behind the desk does not rise. Wavy brown hair, parted on the side, stays in place with the sharp motion of his head when he looks up. He has on thick, round, tortoiseshell glasses which amplify his dark eyes. A square, jutting jaw gives him an arrogant air.

"I'm Bertram Hawke," he says before pointing to a corpulent man sitting in one of the chairs. "This is Assistant State's Attorney Jim Sever." He gestures with his prominent jaw to the empty seat. "Take a seat, Mr. Lieberman."

The larger man nods, making his jowls jiggle. I sit in the proffered chair, take off my hat, place it on my knee, and flick a piece of lint from my trousers.

"Am I to infer by my presence here this afternoon that you're following up on my brief interview with Captain White?" I ask. "I apologized to him for cutting our discussion short, but I didn't wish to be late for my date. The young lady wouldn't have been happy to be kept waiting." I wink at Hawke. "Captain White understood."

"No, Mr. Lieberman. Do you wear eyeglasses?" is his response.

"Your deputies already asked me this question," I say. "As I explained to them, I have reading glasses but haven't worn them in some time. Why?"

"Describe them, please."

"Brown, fake tortoiseshell frames. Not unlike yours, Mr. Hawke. But as far as mine are concerned, the prescription itself is weak."

"When were they prescribed and by whom?"

"Last fall. October or November. Dr. Frederick Dutch recommended them after I complained of mild headaches, annoyances really, caused by eyestrain." I adjust my tie and smile. "In pursuance of my studies, I had taxed my vision with tremendous amounts of reading. Once the headaches ceased, I stopped using them."

"Where did you fill the prescription?"

"At Melar Brothers Company."

"And how many pairs did you purchase?"

"Just the one."

"Can you produce them, Mr. Lieberman?"

"I'm sure they must be at home somewhere. I offered to get them and bring them along; however, your deputies saw fit to deliver me here in a timely manner."

"Then I don't suppose you would mind going back with them to retrieve the glasses."

"Now?"

"Yes, Mr. Lieberman, now."

* * *

"Well, this is puzzling," I say, standing in my bedroom and looking around at the places I just searched. Taller and Shorter, who I learned are Deputies Barney and Melton, loiter in the doorway. The empty eyeglass case is in my hand.

"Let me try another place." I go to the large armoire where I keep my old suits, relegated to birding attire, open it, and check the pockets of the four sack suits remaining inside. I'm wearing the fifth. Is it coincidence that I put on this one today? "Not here. I don't understand."

"At this time, I think a telephone call to our neighbor is in order," Levi speaks up from behind the officers. "Max Ester is a prominent man in the community and a close friend."

"Yes. He's known our family for years," I add. "I'm sure he'll be more than willing to vouch for my veracity."

"I don't think phoning him will hurt," Deputy Barney says.

"I'll go downstairs to the parlor and make the call," Levi volunteers.

The rest of us retire to the sitting room.

"Max isn't home," he says upon his return. "His maid informs me that he is, at present, at the Frisch residence." Levi's eyes won't meet mine. "I'm afraid we'll have to venture the five blocks and speak with him there."

"Then let's proceed quickly," Melton says.

The four of us pile into the black Ford and drive to the Frisch home, an impressive, stately cream-and-white house with a colorful, fragrant garden.

Levi and I are standing at the door, with Barney and Melton behind us, when the maid answers our knock.

"We wish to speak with Mr. Ester," my brother says. "I believe he's visiting with the family. I hate to be a bother during this difficult time, but this is truly a matter of some urgency."

"Who's here?"

The strange man's voice coming from behind the petite woman is filled with a mixture of curiosity, anger, and abominable sorrow. She doesn't answer, simply steps out of the way.

He takes her place at the open door, and I find myself staring into the desolate eyes of Jonah Frisch, father of the murdered boy.

Chapter 4

Saturday, 14 May 1921

"All right, children, follow me. We're trying to spot a Wilson's phalarope this afternoon, but we must be quiet."

Eight ten-year-old birding enthusiasts, wearing rubber boots and sporting field glasses around their necks, waded through the marsh behind me. The sun beamed, and a breeze swirled softly through Bulrush stalks, making tall reeds dance around us. No one spoke, and the air had an electrostatic feel that rang in my ears as we neared the open area. Then I heard something else.

"Shhh," I said, although the boys hadn't spoken. Bending down, I pulled aside pencil reeds and motioned for my students to come forward. "Stay low."

"Eww, it stinks here," someone complained.

"Yes, the mud is pungent today, but pay attention." I put binoculars to my eyes and lowered my voice. "There, at the edge of the weeds on the west side."

"I see," one lad exclaimed in a hushed tone. The rest soon mumbled their discovery.

"Can anyone tell me the sex of this phalarope?"

"Yes, Mr. Noah, it's female."

"Correct. The females are more colorful than their male counterparts during the breeding season. Any other distinctions between the two?"

The red-haired student's eyes scrunched around his lenses. "The black line under the eye going to her neck?"

"Are you asking or answering?"

"A-a-answering, sir."

"You're correct." I stood up, causing the Wilson's to glide across the water before taking to the air. Pulling out my watch, I checked the time. "Let's head back. Our two hours are almost up, and I have a picnic date I don't want to be late for."

A lie, but don't all of us yearn to live in borrowed splendor sometimes?

One-quarter of an hour later we reached the road, having slogged through the swamp and over the railroad tracks. Three automobiles waited in the dirt, two with chauffeurs and the other mine. The drivers chatted with each other and held the doors open for the boys.

"Goodbye, Mr. Noah," they yelled as they climbed inside the cars, half going into each.

"Yes, we'll meet again next week," I said, walking to my automobile.

Both cars kicked up dust and disappeared down the road. A shadow passed over the sun, and I grazed my nose with the field glasses in my haste to look up.

An adult Cooper's hawk. My budding collection of bird specimens included a juvenile female. *I want a full-grown male!*

I reached into the back and grabbed my rifle from the tonneau. Keeping glasses to my eyes, I tramped through grass and brush on the side of the road, gun loaded with dust bullets.

The Cooper's circled above, calling out its distinctive stuttering cry, teasing me, before flying south. I kept up with the elusive raptor, going much farther than I had taken my class, before the hawk slowed and headed toward a stand of trees. Without warning, the large male veered sharply left. A wooden frame-like structure supporting the entrance to a culvert popped into my peripheral vision too late. Tripping, I flailed, dropped the rifle, and tumbled down. Shaken, I extricated myself from mud and water and rose unsteadily. I felt around, patting legs, torso, arms, and head. One hip appeared tender to the touch, but otherwise, I seemed to be unharmed. I looked around for the rifle and didn't find it. It must be on the ground above.

Good place to hide a body, I thought as I climbed out of the drainage ditch, shaking my head at the preposterous notion.

* * *

Back at home, I sat in my study, admiring the birds on display and ruminating. With my first year of college successfully completed, I could declare the decision to skip my senior year of high school a wise one. Wise perhaps, but the past year had been lonely. My superior intelligence, in addition to my younger age, served to alienate me from my fellow undergraduate students. Always willing to debate me—particularly when it came to my Nietzschean philosophies and ideals—I was offered few opportunities to join my peers in non-school-related functions.

"*Der verlust liegt bei ihnen,*" I muttered, adjusting the position of a peregrine falcon. "Yes, the loss is theirs," I translated to the uninterested bird, identified in flight chiefly by its sharp, pointed wings.

A tentative rap on the door diverted my attention.

"Come in."

"Excuse me, Master Babe, but you have a call."

"Who is it, Margaret?"

"Mr. Henry."

"Thank you." I stood up, pulled on each sleeve to adjust my shirt, and went downstairs to the parlor and the small telephone table.

"Hello, Henry," I said into the receiver. "Thanks for returning my call. I spotted an adult male Cooper's earlier near Fox Lake by the tracks. Took a tumble and lost it. Want to ride out there and search for him before darkness falls in case he's still in the area?"

"Gee, I'd like to Noah, but I'm with—"

"Hey who's on the horn? Lieberman? Lemme talk."

The sound of his voice triggered an assault akin to dozens of hummingbirds pushing long, curved bills into the fleshy insides of my stomach.

Muffled noises came through the earpiece before, "Roman here. How about we swing by and pick you up, Noah? Heinzie's accompanying me back to my digs. Mumsie insists on an early dinner tonight, and *I* insist on company so I don't revert to shooting myself or, better yet, everyone else out of sheer boredom. A couple of other fellas can't make it for chow time, but they're coming over later to play cards."

Had I an answer, I still wouldn't be able to form words. Roman Loewe, of substantial intelligence, a boy I spied occasionally on campus, always with a silly girl or two trailing him despite his young age, was inviting me to dine at his house? I spoke to him once when we met last spring, and now he proposed that I share a meal with his family and friends and indulge in a masculine, sociable night of games. Me, intelligent but awkward Noah F. Lieberman Jr.?

I didn't hesitate long. "Yes, um, that'll be fine."

"Cheers, then, we'll be by soon."

I returned the earpiece to its stand and went upstairs to wash and change into an appropriate suit. No one was around other than the servants, so before I left, I slipped into Mother's suite.

"Babe, how handsome you look," she said in her breathy way as soon as I entered her inner chambers. "Do you have an engagement?"

"Yes, I'm having dinner with Henry Heinz over at the Loewe house. Roman invited me. I told you I met him last year."

"Of course. My sister and I have discussed his being a possible friend for you. The Loewes are an upstanding family in the community. Please give them my regards."

"I will, Mother." I bent down and kissed her pale cheek as she lay in bed. She grasped one of my hands in her frail, paper thin ones.

"Now, tomorrow you must tell me everything." She wagged a finger at me. "And don't leave out a description of their home."

"Shall I steal the silverware to show you?" I teased. "Perhaps some china?"

The corners of her mouth twitched, and she fanned her face. "You're incorrigible, Babe. Have a nice evening."

"Good night, Mother."

I waited in the foyer for ten minutes before Henry and Roman pulled up to the curb in Henry's roadster. Donning a bowler hat, I walked outside and spotted our chauffeur standing on the sidewalk next to my aunt's car.

He saw me too, because he came over to me.

"Are you going out, Master Babe?"

"Yes, Erik, please tell Father that I'm dining at Roman Loewe's house and then playing cards with him and some friends. I'll be home late, so he shouldn't wait up for me. I already spoke with Mother and informed her of my plans."

"O-o-of course," he said, looking annoyingly surprised at the word *friends*.

"Come on, Noah. Let's not keep Mumsie waiting. Good day, kind sir!" Roman jumped out of the car, tipped his hat to Erik, and opened the door for me.

I couldn't help laughing as I climbed in.

When the short car ride ended, I stared up at the impressive brick mansion. So near to where I lived, but I'd never paid attention to the house until this past year. It was even grander and larger than ours. Unlike the four-foot iron fence that enclosed our abode, a brick-and-mortar barrier surrounded this mansion. I cemented the images in my mind so I could relay them to Mother since she rarely ventured outside her rooms anymore.

"Well, follow me," Roman said, breaking into an infectious grin as he got out of the auto. I envied him for the easy way his mouth moved so naturally. My own, when attempting to be carefree, invariably twisted into something Saul identified as a condescending sneer.

We walked inside a grand foyer with tall windows that spilled copious amounts of light into the room. Before we advanced into the parlor, an attractive older woman entered.

"Manny, darling, you're on time." She pointed a bejeweled finger at him. "This isn't like you, son. What a great honor for you to bestow this gift upon us!"

"Mumsie, you kid me so. Do you wish to give my new friend a bad impression of me?"

Again, the quick, wide smile revealing a devilish space between his teeth. He turned to me.

"Mumsie, this is Noah. Noah, Mumsie to me, Missus Loewe to you. Henry, you know."

"Nice to see you again, Mrs. Loewe, and thanks for the dinner invitation."

"You're quite welcome, Henry, and I'm pleased to meet you Noah and to have you join us."

"It's my pleasure, and my mother sends her warmest wishes to your family."

She smiled. "How very kind of her." She swept her hand behind her, and said, "Well, come now. We're gathered in the dining room."

We went inside, and Roman introduced me to the rest of his family. His mother and father held court at each end of a long table adorned with a lacy cloth. Henry and I joined Emil, one of Roman's older brothers, on one side of the large table. Before Roman took his seat directly across from us, he kissed the top of his mother's coiffed hair.

"Say, Manny, how'd ya rip your trousers?" Thaddeus, Roman's younger brother, asked when Roman sat down between him and the eldest sibling.

Roman pulled at his pant leg. "This here? Well, Thad, I was hanging around downtown, about to head to the drug store for an ice cream soda." He winked at the boy. "On my way in, I spot this mutt sniffing around a baby pram some inconsiderate girl left all alone while she chatted with friends."

He reached for a tureen and ladled soup into his bowl, not waiting for the maid to do so for him. His mother frowned, and I tried not to smile.

"Well, I couldn't stand there and let this baby get nosed around or chewed up by a dirty old cur now, could I?"

Thad shook his head and stared at his brother, his eyes wide and shiny, a rapt expression on his face.

"I clapped my hands at the mongrel to divert its attention, but it didn't work, so I moved in close with the intention of shoving the beast away."

"Horsefeathers, kid."

"Don't cry horsefeathers to me, Emil!" Roman leaned across the table and glared at him. "Damn dirty mutt grabbed ahold of my pants and didn't want to let go. Why, I'm lucky it didn't catch any skin."

"Enough of that language," Mr. Loewe scolded as the rest of us howled with laughter.

Henry put his napkin to his lips and spoke to me from behind it. "Stray wanted Roman's hot dog, so he kicked at it. Carried on, yelling and screaming, when the mutt ripped his trousers too."

The maid began serving us, and the topic was dropped.

Dinner proved pleasant, despite the inane chatter of Thad, who devoured every preposterous word that came from Roman's mouth. His two older brothers teased him about his stories, and the undercurrent I felt from Roman, despite his amiable countenance, made me curious. Was this how my interactions with my siblings looked from the outside? Could others…could *he* see behind my facade too?

"So, Noah," Mrs. Loewe said as we ate dessert. "I understand you're a bird-watcher like Henry?"

I bristled but didn't stop the spoon on its way to my mouth. The chocolate mousse went down quick, and I dabbed my lips with a monogrammed cloth napkin. "Actually, I'm an ornithologist. However, I enjoy bird-watching as well."

"There is a difference?"

"Gee, Mumsie, Noah here is an expert on birds."

Taken aback, I tilted my head and stared at Roman. Henry must have informed him of my avocation for birding.

"Well, now, my dear, you seem to have embarrassed our guest," Mr. Loewe said.

"Unintentionally, of course, Noah!"

"Nonsense." I sipped my coffee and placed the cup back onto its matching fine china saucer. "The layperson is not aware of the distinction. To put the matter in simplistic terms is to say that a bird-watcher looks at birds to identify them as a curiosity really, whereas a birder, or someone who studies ornithology, actively seeks out birds and does so with the intention of mastering the migratory habits and such of certain species. As it so happens, I've just begun teaching bird-watching classes for children the same age as young Thaddeus here." I nodded toward him. "I'd be happy to add him to my growing list of students if you'd like."

"Birds are bunk," the young boor said.

"Now, Thaddeus—"

"Ah, enough," Roman said, interrupting his mother's admonition. He stood up. "We're going to my rooms. Send the guys upstairs when they get here." Patting Thad on the head, he kissed his mother and turned to Henry and me. "Let's play billiards while we wait."

I rose, placed my napkin on the table, and went over to shake Mr. Loewe's hand. "Your hospitality has been much appreciated." I nodded toward Roman's older brothers. To Thaddeus, I managed to raise the corner of my mouth. I bowed to Mrs. Loewe and walked out of the dining room, Henry at my heels.

On our way to Roman's room, I committed to memory rich, dark wood floors, tall ceilings, and ornate moldings. We passed a fieldstone fireplace that took up an entire wall. Bells chimed before we reached the enormous, curved staircase, and Roman pivoted and headed for the front door.

"I got it," he shouted, although I didn't see anyone. To us, he said, "Must be the guys."

He swung open massive double doors.

"Hey, fellas, perfect timing!" Roman looked around conspiratorially and intoned, "You brought hooch, right?"

One of the chaps patted his jacket.

"Well, c'mon, keep it under wraps and let's get upstairs." Roman looked at me. "Oh, yeah, this is Noah Lieberman. Noah, this is Tony Mason and Jim Felton."

Both said hello and hurried inside. Roman closed the door behind them and sprinted toward the stairs.

Like me, he also possessed more than one room. Whereas I had a study which contained books and my growing specimen collection, his massive second room held a billiard table, a dartboard hanging on more walnut paneling, and a large card table set up in the corner with chairs surrounding it. Open pocket doors revealed the bedchambers with a four-poster bed, and I saw at least three armoires.

"Fellas, you know where to stash those flasks in case Mumsie or Popsie pop in." Roman went to a bookshelf, rummaged behind books, and pulled out three glasses. "Tony and Jim drink from your flasks." He handed Henry and me each a glass, but before he let mine go, he asked, "You can hold your juice, right?"

"Yeah, how about it, Noah?" Tony said, smirking.

"Of course," I replied, annoyed by the condescension in their implications. Levi had been supplying me with cigarettes and booze for over a year now as a "bonus" for exceeding every educational goal I set for myself.

Tony filled my glass to the top. "There, that's half each."

"Well, fair is fair," Roman said, clapping Jim on the back as he held his glass out. "But it leaves the rest of us chumps splitting a third."

"I'm perfectly happy to share mine with you," I offered.

"Nah, I can sneak some from the gardener's stash later."

Henry laughed so hard liquid came out of his mouth, and he slapped his thigh. "Is this how you get your rotgut? Creeping into the garden shed and pilfering off the help?"

Roman's quick laugh and infectious smile followed, but I noted the same activity behind his pupils that I spotted the first time I met him. He did not think much of Henry.

I decided to enlighten Henry about taking charge of one's needs. "As Nietzsche says, 'Were he to wait for opportunities to fall at his feet, he might suffer frostbite on his toes.'" All four chaps looked at me. "The new man, the *Übermensch*, makes and lives by his own rules."

"I believe," Jim said, "that a good argument can be made against Friedrich Nietzsche's superman theory as it relates to moral—"

"Enough of the boring, fellas." Roman took a big sip. "Time for cards." He walked to the table. "We're five tonight, so instead of bridge how about poker?"

Groans met my ears. I had played poker numerous times as it was a favorite in my house, and I'd mastered the game quite proficiently. These guys must prefer bridge. I was the reason for their dissatisfaction.

"Ah, these wet blankets are mad because I win at poker so much." Roman winked at me and sat down. He removed his dinner jacket and ripped off his bowtie. "Close the doors, Jim. Noah, if you didn't bring any cabbage, I can lend you some."

He picked up a deck of cards and began shuffling. "Have a seat, boys. Somebody light me a ciggy while I deal. I'm feeling lucky tonight."

Chapter 5

> Is it better to out-monster the monster or to be quietly devoured?
>
> —Friedrich Nietzsche

Thursday, 29 May 1924

JONAH FRISCH, A man of medium stature and breadth, appears small in the large entranceway. He's holding onto the thick, mahogany door with both hands, and from what I can see, there is nothing substantial under his clothes—as if the outer shell survives but the insides have rotted away leaving air to toss around leaves where organs, blood, and bones once resided. Wild, loose strands of hair crisscross an almost-bald pate. Eyes flit behind round pince-nez glasses with a gold nose piece and a long black cord hanging down one side. The haunted eyes go from Levi to me and then to the two policemen. All four of us have removed our hats and are holding them in our hands.

"I'm sorry to bother you, sir," Levi begins, and Frisch's gaze moves to his face. "Especially now, but as I was telling your maid, we wish to speak with Mr. Max Ester. It's of an urgent matter, or we wouldn't call on him at your residence during such a—"

"Yes, Levi," Max says, appearing behind Mr. Frisch. "How may I be of service?"

Levi gestures toward the expansive portico where we're all standing. "Perhaps we can talk in private?"

Max eyes each of us, giving Chicago's lawmen the longest scrutiny before turning to his friend.

"Jonah, why don't you go sit with your wife, and I'll join you in a few minutes?"

Some interest sparks in Frisch's eyes for an instant, but then they dull over. He nods, and sallow jowls shaking, turns and leaves without a word. Max steps outside and shuts the door behind him.

"What's this matter about?"

"Well, now, Max," Levi says, and the tenor of his voice changes as he tries to inject a gaiety that I suspect he doesn't feel. "The police wish to speak with Noah about a terrible mistake."

Max's eyes dart over to me and then back to Levi. "What kind of mistake?"

"Well, sir, a pair of spectacles, with a rather common prescription to be sure, were found at the scene of little Bennie's tragic demise." Levi looks down at his hat, grasped in both hands in front of him, and taps his thumbs on the rim. "The police are aware that Noah frequents the marshes in his bird-watching endeavors and happened to be in the area the weekend before..."

One deputy coughs, and the other one shuffles his feet.

"Well, the weekend of May seventeenth. He was there with a class on Saturday and with fellow birders on Sunday."

"I'm unclear as to why you are here."

"Well, sir, Noah—"

"My reading glasses are missing," I interject, having grown bored with Levi's fumbling. "The State's attorney is questioning everyone who wears, or as in my case, wore, eyeglasses and has been in the vicinity of the horrible crime." I tuck one hand into my vest and hold it next to my heart. "And, as I stated, my spectacles seem to be misplaced."

Max's thin face darkens, and he turns to the officers who are standing on my left.

"Preposterous! Why, I've known Babe here since he took his first steps, spoke his first words. His father is a fine, honorable man and an upstanding citizen, and Babe's mother, may she be lying in peace, was a good woman. I can vouch for the entire Lieberman family."

A faint noise, one that sounds suspiciously like a sob, comes from somewhere in the house, and Max inclines his head toward the door.

"However," he adds, "considering the seriousness of this unfortunate situation, it's probably best to continue cooperating with the authorities so justice can be served, and the true culprit captured.

"Now, I must return to my friend's side." He looks at Deputy Barney. "I assume you're with the State's attorney's office, so please have someone keep me apprised of any developments."

With that, he turns and goes back into the house.

We put on our hats and walk to the car.

"Would you officers be so kind as to take Levi home? Father is throwing another dinner party tonight to celebrate our brother's engagement, and—"

"Rubbish," Levi insists. "Mr. Hawke can't possibly have cause to hold you much longer. We'll clear up this little matter and return home together."

"Don't worry. I'm sure I won't be much longer." I check the time. "Besides, you couldn't reach Henry, and so you need to leave now to meet my students."

He runs his hands over his face. "Right. Okay, I'll see you soon."

The scene at the Hotel Cavalier is the same as when I left it: Mr. Hawke is sitting at the desk, and Mr. Sever is spilling out of the chair across from him.

"Did you find the glasses?" Hawke's eyes narrow behind his own round frames, and his jaw protrudes until it sticks out past his nose.

I stand in front of the open door with the two deputies flanking me. "No," I reply reluctantly.

Sever rises. "Here, Mr. Lieberman, sit down," he says in what sounds more like a demand than an offer.

Once seated, I place my hat on the desk, cross my legs, and point to a cigarette smoldering in the ashtray. "I presume I can smoke?"

Hawke nods, so I light up. Sever goes over to Barney and Melton, whispers something, and they leave, shutting the door behind them.

"Can these be yours?" Hawke asks, holding up the common pair of eyeglasses displayed over the front page of every newspaper.

Squinting, I lean in closer for a better look. "Well, I suppose they might be, sir, but the same can be said of hundreds, perhaps thousands, of spectacles in the Chicago area alone."

"I'm afraid I have to contradict you," he says. "These glasses can be one of only three pairs."

I sit back, rubbing the butt of the cigarette with my thumb as is my habit, and stare at Hawke.

"As it happens, Noah, the prescription is indeed prevalent, and the frames themselves rather common. The hinge, however, is unusual. A manufacturer in New Jersey produced it, having just recently procured a patent. They sold only three of these tortoiseshell frames with *this* hinge in all of Chicago."

Sever is quiet, teeth clamped on the wet end of a foul-looking stogie, as he walks over and plants his generous bottom in a chair. With all of us puffing away, the room has taken on an eerie, ghostly aura and smells like Saturday night at a speakeasy. No boozing, dancing, or pretty flappers though.

Hawke leans forward, elbows on the desk, and holds up three nicotine-stained fingers, a Pall Mall stuck between two of them. "One pair belongs to a judge who is visiting with relatives in Mississippi. Another to a priest at St. Mary of the Angels." He pauses, undoubtedly to milk drama from the moment. "The third pair was sold to Noah F. Lieberman Jr."

I meet his eyes, and although I read curiosity, perhaps some suspicion in them, I doubt he believes that someone with my intellect and familial position had anything to do with such a sordid matter. He's fishing.

"So, Noah, now that we've established that they are, indeed, your glasses, can you explain how they were found near poor Bennie Frisch's body?"

"I'm sure you're aware of my lengthy conversation with Captain White this Sunday past wherein we discussed this very point. I'm out in the Fox Lake area often. Nary a time comes when I don't wade in swamps and trudge through brush in pursuit of a sighting. The glasses must have slipped out of my jacket pocket."

"I believe I recall you saying you don't use the glasses anymore."

"Correct, Mr. Hawke."

"Then why would they be in the pocket of a suit you wear for wading and trudging?" he demands.

Sever abandons his cigar in the ashtray and says, "And why take reading glasses out birding? I think you'd be more apt to bring binoculars."

I concentrate on keeping my facial muscles under my command, so they give away neither agitation nor stress, and bring the cigarette to my lips, nice and steady. My fingers tremble a bit, but I forgive them this transgression.

"Well, sirs, I'm a practical man. When my suits become too worn and tattered to wear in everyday life, I relegate them to slogging through marshes in pursuit of a migratory bird, or to chase a Cooper's hawk or a pileated woodpecker." The tremor shakes itself out, and I take a draw and hold in smoke for a few seconds before expelling it in controlled O rings. "I retain five such birding suits."

"And the glasses would be in the pocket, why?" Hawke persists.

I shrug. "They must've been in there when the rag made the transfer to the armoire in which my birding togs are stored. Since I stopped using them, I didn't notice their absence."

"Plausible, Mr. Lieberman," Sever says, but his tone tells me that he doesn't believe my explanation. His face and manner remain cordial, however.

"Can you explain how your glasses wound up in the weeds next to the drainage ditch where Bennie's body was found?" Hawke's measured voice is low, but the words ring loud in my head.

I sigh. "I already told you I was at Fox Lake last—"

"Yes, Mr. Lieberman," he interrupts, "but how would the glasses fall from your pocket?"

"I tripped."

"You tripped."

"Yes. We spotted some rather strange shorebirds—"

"Who is we?" Hawke asks.

"Henry Heinz and myself. The birds flew—we chased. We crossed over the railroad tracks. I remember stumbling over something and falling to the ground as we passed by the ditch." I reach over Hawke's desk and grind my cigarette in the ashtray next to Sever's still-burning cigar. "That ditch holds a special place in my memory banks, as I fell into it once around three years prior." I lean back and smile with my mouth closed. "Hunting a Cooper's hawk at the time."

"As I said before," Sever says, "quite a plausible reason for your eyeglasses to be in the area."

"Would you mind demonstrating?"

I look at Mr. Hawke. "Excuse me, sir?"

"I'd like you to illustrate how the glasses might have fallen from your jacket pocket."

My body heats from the inside, making my skin prickle, but I keep my face impassive. "You want me to feign tripping and falling?"

"Yes, please." Hawke hands me the glasses.

"Very well," I say, unable to think of a reasonable excuse for refusing. Sighing, I stand up. Placing the blasted spectacles in the right pocket, I venture a few steps and, with a bit of exaggerated flair, trip over my feet and fall, landing on my hands, face inches from the carpeted floor.

The glasses stay secure in their womb.

No one speaks.

I rise. "I'm quite certain I was running at the time. The velocity—"

"I think there's room in here to get up a little speed," Sever offers.

So, I try to run and fall. Once, twice, three…

"That's enough," Hawke says after the fifth try and the glasses remain glued inside the pocket. "Why don't you take that off and hand it to me? You look sweaty and flushed."

I fume at the implication. *Women* flush. I rip off the garment and hand it over. "I claim to be a scholar, not an athlete. My only physical activity besides chasing skirts"—I wink at the men—"is chasing birds. Perspiration is an unavoidable affliction."

Hawke drops the jacket. Bending, he retrieves it by the hem and hands it back to me, upside down. The glasses unweld themselves from their position and plummet to the floor.

Traitors.

"Could you have removed your jacket, and then picked it up?"

"Mr. Hawke, I would never pick up my clothing in such a manner."

"Maybe it was dark out." Sever's implication hangs in the air.

I snort and shake my head. The State's attorney and his portly assistant are taking their fishing expedition into deeper waters, but I still don't sense danger. Despite the damning coincidence of the spectacles, my explanation cannot be ignored or ruled out.

"All right, Mr. Lieberman," Hawke continues as he picks up the glasses. "Let us assume you dropped the eyeglasses the weekend prior to the, ah, incident with Bennie Frisch. Wouldn't they be dirtier having survived the elements for three or four days? Wait, which day did you trip? Saturday or Sunday?"

"Sunday, I believe."

"Well, then, I should think being exposed to sun, wind, and as the case on Tuesday, light rain would make these glasses much grimier. They look rather well preserved, don't you think?"

"Can I be so bold, sir, to inquire about the method in which the spectacles were obtained? According to the newspaper accounts, a rail worker discovered poor Bennie, and he and a few other men pulled the child's body from the culvert. One of them found the glasses. Isn't it possible that the chap wiped them on his pant leg or shirt sleeve?" I smile with my mouth closed. "I remember adapting a habit of doing such a thing myself during the brief time when I wore the readers. I'm sure you can relate, Mr. Hawke, as you wear eyeglasses and studied law also."

His facial expression never changes, but I read disgust in his eyes.

"Yes, I hear you're a law student."

"Harvard in the fall."

Hawke nods. Sever says nothing.

Someone knocks on the door.

"Come in," Sever barks.

The door opens, and Deputy Melton pops his head inside. "Can I speak with you in the hallway for a minute, Bert?"

I light another Lucky after Hawke gets up and leaves. By the time the State's attorney returns, I've smoked half.

He pulls a watch from his breast pocket, examines it, and states, "It's late, so we're going to pick up some sandwiches and head over to my office to continue this conversation."

We stare at each other, and something moves around in my stomach as he holds my gaze without blinking. A bit of nausea creeps in because genuine suspicion is now evident in his eyes.

Chapter 6

Saturday, 14 May 1921

BY THE TIME we were on our fourth hand of poker, Roman's room had taken on a hazy, surreal quality. We smoked Lucky after Lucky, put down some rotgut, argued over cards, and talked about which girl's eye each of the fellas hoped to catch.

"Ah, one filly's as good as another," Roman said over his cards, that grin on his face.

I looked around at the other guys and saw that I wasn't the only one whose lips curled into a smile when Roman spoke. Something about him and his energy deprived the room of oxygen and left me struggling to breathe.

Or perhaps I drank too much. Mr. Loewe had checked on us only once, and before Emil left to go out for the evening, Mrs. Loewe sent him in to see if we needed anything. Roman kept the study door locked, giving access inside through his bedroom, thereby alerting us to company in time to hide our liquor. The five of us finished the whiskey from the flasks, and Roman made good on his promise to visit the gardener's shed and did so after both his parents were ensconced in their suites. Each of our glasses filled another time, mine was perilously close to being finished. I decided to slow glass-to-mouth motions and instead smoked one cigarette after another.

"What about you, Noah?" Tony asked. He had just thrown down his cards in disgust. Although feeling the effects of the alcohol, I won the last two hands. Even Roman, whom I'd been watching surreptitiously and noticed that he sneaked glances at Jim's cards, hadn't been able to gain momentum on me. He didn't appear bothered by my wins since I was playing with his money anyway. However, Jim and Tony were showing signs of displeasure.

"I beg your pardon, Tony. *What* about me? Royal flush." I put down my cards, face up.

Roman laughed. "Aw, he just wants to know if you're dizzy with a dame is all."

Tony snorted and slapped his thigh. "From what I hear, this bird's too obsessed with birds and Nietzsche to care about dames." He rose, unsteadily, and walked to the billiard table. "Enough poker. Come on, Jim. Wanna let me beat you at eight ball?"

"Sound's Jake."

"Noah has lots of interests outside of ornithology," Henry blurted, before I could formulate a proper response to the boor. "And Marie Turnhill from our philosophy class is enthralled with him. Says she finds his brooding intellect stimulating."

Tony muttered something mostly unintelligible, but I heard the words *flat tire*.

How dare he insinuate that I'm boring? I forgot my promise to keep my glass away from my mouth and tried to drink and smoke at the same time. Embarrassed, I put the glass down and swept the pot toward me with both hands.

"Well, now," Roman said. "I think Marie's friends with the little dish I'm giving time to. Whaddaya say we take the girls out on a double date, eh, Noah?"

Henry got up, grabbed a handful of darts, and started flinging them at the dartboard. I counted out my money and handed over the amount that Roman loaned me.

"Thanks for the advancement. And I'd enjoy a night out with the young ladies as I'm interested in many things." This statement, I aimed at Tony, who was bent over, lining up a shot. He chuckled.

I felt Roman's eyes on me as we sat alone at the card table.

"Nietzsche, huh?" he said.

"Something wrong with Friedrich Nietzsche?"

"Blasted if I'd know. Just wondering what makes a fella read the kind of stuff a fella reads. You know, for fun. Me, I fancy detective stories."

"And what makes you believe that I read Mr. Nietzsche for fun?"

A quick smile graced his face. "Henry here"—he nodded toward Heinzie, who had missed the target and, in fact, missed the dartboard with his last throw and was pulling the projectile from the wall—"he tells me you're known to debate the German philosopher's ideals quite forcefully."

"And the problem is?"

"No problem." He raised his glass. "Here's to living your ideals."

The light behind his eyes drew me in. Aware that I was inebriated or, at the very least, on the road to inebriation, I felt for the first time in my sixteen-and-a-half years on earth that someone understood me.

I drank to the feeling.

"Confound, I juss can't get a break," Tony said, diverting my attention. Most of the balls remained on the billiard table, except the eight ball.

Jim grinned, cue stick in hand, and checked his watch. "Iss well after midnight anyway." He burped, swallowed, and said, "Time t'go, chap."

"We're leavin' too. C'mon, Noah." Henry went to drop the darts on the table but missed, and they fell to the floor. He left them there.

"Ah, you guys are wet. Let's tip a few more," Roman said and rose to his feet. His legs swayed, and he grabbed the edge of the chair. "I can head back out to the shed."

"'Nother night."

"Henry's right. Anyway, thanks for the hospitality, Roman. Nice meeting you, Noah," Jim said.

"Yeah, Roman, thanks. Enjoy that double date, Birdie," Tony said to me, laughing and slapping Jim on the back as the two stumbled through the bedroom toward the hallway.

"Ah, don't worry about him," Roman said.

"Yeah, pay him no attention." Henry looked around and scratched his head. "Now, where'd I leave my hat?"

"Hall tree in the foyer."

"Thanks. All right, well, let's go, Noah. Give regards to your mother again, Roman." Henry waved and walked out.

I got up. "I also wish to reiterate my gratitude to you and your family for—"

"Come back after he drops you home. I'll sneak out. Meet me at the rear of the house in fifteen minutes." The quick smile had a mischievous glow that I should have ignored, but in my altered state, I couldn't resist.

Instead, I said, "Okay," and left on rubbery legs.

Other than Henry's noisy roadster, the south Kensington neighborhood was quiet on the short drive. Streetlights and outdoor lanterns glowed, but most of the homes were dark. Henry pulled to the curb at the apartment building behind our carriage house on Greenwick. I was about to ask why he stopped there instead of at the front gate, when he opened his door and vomited in the street.

I got out of the car. "Gee, Henry, you better get home. Probably not a good idea to be driving around."

"Yeah," he said, wiping his mouth on his sleeve and closing the door. "Shouldn't have had anything to drink since I was feeling sick before dinner."

"Indeed. Well, thanks for the ride. I'll walk from here."

He tooted the horn as he drove away. My shoulders tightened, and I stared at my house for signs that someone had awakened, but no lights came on. Everyone appeared to be tucked inside for the night.

I checked my timepiece. *Morning,* I corrected myself. *Seven minutes left to get back.* I turned around and walked briskly, turning my jacket collar up against a chill that I was determined to believe arose from the late-night air.

When I reached the rear of his house, I didn't find a gate in the brick fence surrounding the manor.

Where do they park their cars? Surely, not on the street?

I looked for an opening in the barrier. Nothing. No way to enter either by foot or vehicle.

"Pssssst, Noah."

A pebble hit the back of my head. I turned around and saw Roman standing at the end of the neighbor's driveway. He held a finger to his lips and waved me over.

Curious if my theory was correct, I blurted out in a hushed tone, "Do you gain access to your home through this property?"

Again, that smile. "Yes, we own it. Garage has doors in the front and rear, so we drive through. This parcel connects with ours." He jerked his head toward the smaller house. "Servants live here. C'mon, let's skedaddle."

He turned and hurried down the street toward South Essex Avenue. I followed, my boozy feeling abating but my excitement rising. When we turned onto South Chicago Avenue, he stopped walking. No cars or people were anywhere on the streets, and the light from the streetlamps gave off an eerie glow.

"Here." Roman handed me a flask, which felt full. "If you don't have one, you can keep it. I nicked it from my brother's friend." He winked and patted his breast pocket. "I have my own."

"Thanks," I muttered, taking a drink. The homemade hooch blazed over my tongue, scorched down my throat, and lit my stomach on fire.

Roman pulled a silver flask from its resting place. As he unscrewed the cap, I attempted to read the initials engraved in between ornate swirls, but he was soon bringing it to his lips. I couldn't make out the letters, but they were not *R* or *L*. Of that, I was certain.

"Did you nick this one too, Roman?"

He threw back his head and howled. A dog barked, and we both bent down on our haunches and put our hands over our mouths. I tried not to laugh.

"Okay," he said, straightening up and wiping his eyes. "Let's go."

"Where?"

"Woodlawn Avenue. Where Tony lives."

"Your friend from tonight?"

"That's the one." Roman started walking, and I tried to keep pace, but his legs were longer than mine. "He was rather rude, don't you think? Calling you 'bird' as an insult."

My face burned from embarrassment, a feeling of which I had some association. Although I had learned long ago not to let the lesser man's ignorance bring me sorrow, I succumbed to the common emotion because Roman had witnessed such treatment. Anger followed, so I sipped from the flask.

"What do you have in mind?"

He didn't answer me, just turned onto Woodlawn and kept walking until we reached a small grassy area between houses. "See that brick bungalow, third from left?" he said, pointing across the residential street.

I nodded.

"Tony lives there with his folks. That's his father's Milburn electric auto parked at the curb. Tony doesn't have a car. Jim takes him everywhere. I bet they drove right to a cat house after my place, unless they stopped at a speakeasy downtown first."

"How do you know?"

Roman tapped his forehead. "Ah, I know those two hounds. They don't like losing money, and not to someone like you." The quick smile, which triggered odd shocks throughout my body, helped temper his *someone-like-you* remark. "They'll need to chase away the Daisy by grabbing skirts. Make 'em feel like men again."

"Well, what of it?"

He pulled something from his trouser pocket and held it up. "I swiped Mumsie's key." We were alone, but he lowered his voice all the same. "She has the same Milburn, a Broughman, so I can handle the steering and speed tillers easily."

"And?"

"I also figured out that one key fits all engines."

"You're not suggesting that we…" I couldn't finish because a bolt of lightning zapped through me.

He took a long swig from his flask. When he finished, he capped the container, stashed it in his pocket, and wiped his mouth with his sleeve.

"What I'm proposing, my dear sir"—he bowed slightly and tipped his hat—"is that we take the elder Mason's Milburn for a spin and leave it smashed in some remote place. When Tony stumbles home ossified again, his pops will think he copied his key." Roman winked. "Like I did with Mumsie's."

The prospect excited me. "How will *we* get home?"

"We'll walk, of course. It'll take the better part of an hour, and the two of us shan't fall into our cozy beds 'til three or so. Popsie wakes at five-thirty every morn. I have his routine down precisely." He smiled and winked again.

I nodded. "My father rises at six, my brothers and cousin shortly after. I, too, shouldn't have a problem reaching my room without running into anyone."

"Even blotto?"

"Let's wish," I said, drinking again.

He laughed. "Swell. Now, follow my lead. Pull your hat low on your head. I'll go to the driver's side, you the passenger, then we open the doors and get in. Be quiet closing the door."

"Sure."

"I'll insert Mumsie's key, start it, and take off!"

I shivered as I crept to the Milburn and slipped in. We looked at each other and closed our doors simultaneously. The engine turning over was quick, and then we were moving down the street, slow at first before we picked up speed. I glanced behind us—no lights illuminated Tony's house or any of the others standing shoulder-to-shoulder with it.

Roman turned the first few corners, narrowly missing parked automobiles of various colors and models.

"Where're we heading?" I held onto my hat as he made another dangerous turn.

"No clue. What say you, Babe? Any suggestions?" He looked over at me and grinned.

"Pay attention to the road so you don't kill us," I said, trying to disguise the thrill I felt at his use of my intimate nickname.

He returned to driving but took one hand off the steering tiller and punched my arm.

"Make the next right, then a left onto Fulton Boulevard. That'll bring you—"

"Yeah, yeah," he said, "toward Indiana."

"Yes, I do a lot of birding out in that area."

"Which Henry's aware of. If Tony suspects you, Henry might convey this bit of information to him."

Roman was correct, but he followed my directions, nonetheless.

"Then we won't go far," I said. "Just drive for now."

He sped up once we got out of town. "How do ya like this, Tony-bird?" he hooted before taking a swig. The compact, boxy auto swerved, and I grabbed the door handle with one hand, my hat with the other.

"Slow down!"

He listened, but before we slowed enough, the tires hit a bump. The tillers slipped from Roman's hands as he bounced in the seat. We veered across the street and crashed into a lamppost marking the entrance to the park. Both of us flew forward, landing on the floor and missing the windshield. Unhurt but jostled, I said, "Are you okay?"

He didn't answer, just leaned his head back and laughed with tears streaming down his face.

"Stop that," I cried, unwilling to give in to the alcohol's influence and let loose. The entire night had been an intense rush of feelings, wonderful, but we had to leave before someone showed up and saw us. "Grab the key and your hat, and let's go!"

"Okay, okay."

I shut my door, but he didn't bother to close his. The lamppost was embedded between the bug-eyed headlights. I started to go back the way we came, but he dashed toward the closed park.

"Hey, what're you doing?"

He continued around the stone gate post and into the wooded area. I caught sight of him on a path and chased after him.

"Roman, where are you going?"

"Let's cut through the woods and walk home from the rear," he called over his shoulder. Then he ran into the trees, forcing me to follow with barely more than a wisp of moonlight.

Branches slapped my face, and I tripped over roots and rocks before he finally stopped in a little grassy clearing.

"What a caper! That was the cat's meow, wasn't it, Babe? We did it," he exalted, bouncing around on his heels. "We showed that Tony."

"Too bad he won't know it was us."

"Ah, even still, Babe. *We* know!"

I finished the rest of my whiskey. The entire experience had my blood sizzling. Being with Roman made me feel other things.

He tipped his own flask, drank, and then stumbled to his knees.

"Gonna lie down," he said before falling onto his back, legs and arms splayed out.

I rushed over. "Hey, are you all right?" Kneeling next to him, I placed both of my hands on either side of his shoulders and stared at his face.

He opened his eyes and grinned up at me, but it wasn't the carefree grin I'd gotten used to seeing. Still, I knew the smile because I'd seen it in my dreams. The king commanding his subject. His slave.

He hit my arms out from under me, and I fell on top of his chest.

"I shall be fine soon, Babe."

Chapter 7

> All things are subject to interpretation. Whichever interpretation prevails at a given time is a function of power and not truth.
>
> —Friedrich Nietzsche

Thursday, 29 May 1924, through Friday, 30 May 1924

"THE CRIMINAL COURT Building offers not a fraction of the ambiance in abundance at the Hotel Cavalier," I say as I look around. Instead of being in Mr. Hawke's office, I'm sitting at a conference table in a dreary room. A large chalkboard, with nothing written on it, fills most of the wall, and the only other furniture is a battered black filing cabinet with a fan on top of it. With me are Mr. Hawke, Assistant State's Attorney Jim Sever, and Chief of Detectives Marvin Harrison, who only moments before, carted away the remnants of thick, roast beef sandwiches and potato salad containers. I sip my water and lean back in a wooden chair with insufficient padding under leather upholstery. A glass ashtray sits in the center of the table, half-full of discarded Lucky Strikes, Pall Malls, and a few stogie butts.

I reach for my deck, tap out a cigarette, and light it with the sterling silver striker engraved with an eagle that Levi gifted me for my eighteenth birthday. After I return the lighter to my pocket, I pull out my watch and look at it.

"The hour has almost reached eleven in the evening, sirs." I cross one dark slacked leg over the other. "For approximately eight hours, I've been answering questions regarding my eyeglasses, which have had the misfortune to be lost in the area where the unfortunate Frisch boy was found." I turn to Detective Harrison. "While I'm always willing to engage in an intellectual debate about Nietzsche's theories on the Übermensch or the 'superman' as you steered the dinner conversation, Detective, I'm tiring." I try not to smirk at the lanky man with a huge nose. "And the frequency with which you ran to the bathroom or to Mr. Hawke's office to make 'telephone calls' leads me to assume that you have a copy of *Thus Spoke Zarathustra* by Mr. Friedrich Nietzsche in the next room."

No one says anything, which amplifies the whirling sound of the fan. Hawke is sitting across from me. Sever is to my right, folds of flab hanging over the sides of the chair, and Detective Harrison is pacing from one end of the room to the other and back, hands in his pockets jingling change.

"Am I to assume the mishap regarding my glasses has been sufficiently explained?"

Hawke leans forward with his forearms on the table. He took his jacket off before dinner and never put it back on. Crisp, white shirtsleeves are folded, revealing a mass of light hairs.

"Yes, Noah, I think we're done with them," he says. "However, we need to discuss what you did that day. We discussed your whereabouts and actions on the Saturday and Sunday before Wednesday, the twenty-first of May, but where were you on *that* day?"

He stares at me. I draw on the cig and let smoke out in measures, taking my time before answering him. Nicotine slips out the end, griming my fingers, so I rub them. A lightbulb flickers overhead, casting eerie shadows in the hazy room. Someone coughs.

"Well, class in the morning, of course."

"Which class?" Sever demands.

"Commercial law with Professor Kamper at eight. My next lecture on agency and torts didn't start for another hour, so I sat in on a lecture about a group of late-nineteenth-century French poets."

"Who gave this lecture?" Hawke asks.

"Professor Dart."

"And your presence in these classes can be verified?" he persists.

"Certainly, sir."

"What next, Noah?"

"I spoke with a lady friend afterward."

Hawke exchanges a look with Sever.

They're holding onto something.

"Who is this lady friend?" Mr. Hawke says, continuing his questioning.

I readjust my position and run a finger under my collar. "I hate to involve her in such a distasteful situation as—"

"Don't worry, kid," Detective Harrison says, sneering over my shoulder. "We'll only talk to her if necessary."

Running my hands over my face, I shift again, stiff from sitting so long. "If you must know, her name is Sally Lord."

Three heads nod as one, although none of the men write anything down. I have no doubt they're keeping detailed notes in their heads, however.

"Do you own an Underwood portable typewriter, Noah?"

"No, sir."

"Are you certain?"

"I should think I would be certain, Mr. Hawke."

"Well," he persists, "do you own or are you in the possession of any typewriter?"

"Yes, a Hammond."

"A portable?"

"No, sir, a Hammond Multiplex." I smile. "Quite a nifty machine wherein you can change the type shuttle and write in Greek, italics, and mathematical symbols."

"What time did you leave campus?" Sever interjects.

"When the last lecture ended, so it must have been eleven."

"What did you do then?" Hawke says.

I pat the deck in my jacket pocket. "Enjoyed a Lucky." Turning to Sever, I say, "Before you ask, I know this because I always have a cig after class."

"Where did you go after you smoked, Noah?"

"Home to study, I imagine, Mr. Hawke, but I can't recall specifically. I've taken multiple final exams in the last couple of weeks, plus my Harvard entrance exams."

"You can't remember?" Sever's eyes widen, and his bushy black eyebrows rise. "You told us at dinner that you're an ornithologist with an article published in *The Aux*, and you speak multiple languages. You'll be attending Harvard Law in the fall. You're saying *you* can't remember what you did one week ago?" Suspicion cloaks every syllable of his words.

"Can you remember what you did that day, Mr. Sever?" I retort.

Color creeps into his fat face and neck, and he opens his mouth to respond, but Hawke throws him a look. When the State's attorney turns back to me, his jaw is protruding even farther than usual, and the tips of his ears are tinged with pink.

Detective Harrison stops pacing and pulls out the chair to my left, turns it around, and straddles it. "Did ya meet up with your lady friend? Sally?"

"No."

"Well, if ya can't remember the day," he says, keeping the pressure on me, "how do ya know for sure?"

"Because we had a date to go dancing on Friday evening. I confirmed our date when I spoke with her after Dart's lecture." I turn away from Harrison and glare at Sever on my other side. He's chomping on the end of his cigar, a nauseating sight. "And, yes, I remember the date."

"I find your inability to recollect all of your whereabouts on that day difficult to swallow," Sever says.

"My memory lapse doesn't begin and end with Wednesday. I haven't a clue what I did the prior day, nor do I have a clue what I did the following day. Other than study, take exams, and go bird-watching."

"Do you own a gun, Noah?"

"Yes, Mr. Hawke." I reach for my water and take another sip to slow the trajectory of his subject change. Three against one is challenging. "I employ a shotgun on birding expeditions."

He nods.

"Shoot birds, do ya?"

I don't bother looking Harrison's way. "I do quite a bit more than that. I've become adept at taxidermy and have an extensive, rare collection of specimens that—"

"I'm sure there's much more to it than shooting and stuffing, Noah," Hawke interrupts, "but—"

"Don't ya think a young guy killin' and stuffin' birds is odd?"

"No, *Detective* Harrison, I do not." For the first time, I let my cool slip. It only slips a fraction, but it slips. "Why, the study of birds will benefit—"

"Enough about birds." Hawke's voice never rises, but the hairs on his forearm stand up. "Try, Noah, to remember what you did and where you went the day and evening of the twenty-first of May."

I can put it off no longer.

"The discussion about birds does remind me of something." I reach over and grind my cigarette in the ashtray. Pressing my hands together and resting my chin atop my fingertips, I take a deep breath and let it out in spurts before addressing Hawke.

"Yes, I remember going out one day. I believe it *was* Wednesday. I ate a light lunch at Edgar's Grill with a friend."

"That the place downtown, the one on Main Avenue? Did ya go with your lady friend, Sally?"

"In answer to Edgar's, yes, Detective. No to Sally."

"What did you do after lunch?" Hawke asks.

During most of the questions being fired at me, I have kept my eyes on Mr. Hawke. It appears that the man's suspicions are growing despite my flawless answers.

"Went to Washington Park. I hoped to spot a heron. Someone gave me a tip about one being in the area."

"And you're sure this occurred one week prior to yesterday?"

"Yes, sir." I pull my timepiece from my vest and look at it. "We are about to cross into Friday, gentlemen, but I'm certain I have the correct day since it was the one night of the week that we neither threw a dinner party nor attended one."

"Must be nice to socialize so much."

"It's not a regular occurrence, Detective. One of my brothers recently announced his engagement."

"Did you find the heron?" Sever asks.

"No."

"Do you know Mark Kurt McConnell, Noah?"

"Yes, Mr. Hawke." I sip more water. "He's an English teacher at The Dravah School for Boys. I read in the newspapers that he's been questioned in relation to the Bennie Frisch matter and released."

"Ever hear stories about him being a pervert?" Harrison asks, leaning in so close I can smell his stale coffee breath.

I don't look at him. "No."

Detective Harrison jumps up and exits the room. Neither Sever nor Hawke comment on his abrupt absence.

"Did Mr. McConnell ever make any"—Hawke clears his throat—"advances while you were a student?"

"If you're referring to what the newspapers are printing about him, then no, I don't recall any untoward overtures."

"Do you own any guns other than your birding rifle?" Sever asks.

I smile around gritted teeth. "My father obtained city licenses on my behalf for three shotguns. I believe he owns a few as well."

"Anyone else in the household own a revolver?"

"One would have to ask them this question, Mr. Sever."

The door opens, and Detective Harrison walks back inside. Voices and footsteps filter in, and the air in the hallway looks clear compared to the perpetual gray cloud residing in this room. Someone rushes by, and the door shuts.

"Busy place," I say.

"Recognize this?" Harrison asks, placing something on the table.

A Remington handgun. Mine.

I reach into my pocket and pull out my cigarettes. Three left. I light one, giving myself time to compose my thoughts. They searched my house, my bedroom, and study. Now I understand what the whispered conversation at the Cavalier between Hawke and Deputy Melton had been about and how they knew about my interest in Nietzsche.

What else did they find?

"I can't help wondering, Mr. Hawke, why you're so concerned with guns? Have the newspapers been fooling the public about Bennie Frisch's cause of death?"

"Who did you lunch with, Noah?" he demands.

Back to this. "A male companion."

"Did you go to Washington Park alone?"

An acrid line of smoke emits from the ashtray. Sever failed to completely grind out his last stogie, and it lay atop the carcasses of more than a dozen discarded butts of all varieties, sending a steady puff of struggling, pungent smoke into the air. Detective Harrison dumped the ashtray twice, and it's due for another purging.

I take a long draw and let it out. Bowing my head, I place the fingers holding the cigarette to my forehead and rub my temple.

"All right, gentlemen, it's time to confess." From my peripheral vision, I see all three men lean forward. I lower my hand, raise my head, and keep my eyes trained on Hawke. "I didn't want to mention my friend's name because…well, after lunch while I searched for the heron, he stayed behind drinking. I joined him when my quest failed. My friend's father is the vice president of Chicago Railways and quite a teetotaler. He wouldn't be pleased with this news."

Hawke's body deflates as he doesn't receive the confession he perhaps wishes, and his eyes narrow behind thick, round spectacles.

"As a parent myself, Noah, I'm positive he'll want his son's name to be cleared of any unpleasantness."

We stare at each other across the table. Seconds tick by.

"And the gentleman's name is?"

"Roman Loewe."

"How long were you fellas at the park?" he asks.

"Oh, well, I'd say four hours or so."

"What time did you leave, and what did you do then, Noah?"

"About five. We headed to The Mango Grove for dinner. After we ate, we drove up and down Sixty-Fifth Street looking for pretty fillies who wanted to go for a ride."

Hawke makes a face. "Whose automobile did you take?"

"Mine. I drove."

"And your car's a Willys-Knight, correct?"

"Yes, a nifty sports model. Red with a tan top." I wink at him. "Girls love it."

"Did ya find any?"

"Yes, Detective Harrison, we found two whose names escape me at the moment, and we drove around."

"For how long?" Sever asks.

"Not sure, but we wound up at the north end of Washington Park. Roman sat in the back with his girl. Mine sat in front with me. They happened to be in possession of…well," I say while tugging on my shirt collar. "I know it's illegal, but they brought some bathtub gin, and we parked and drank."

"Did ya kiss them?"

"I held my own with my lady," I tell Harrison.

"What did you talk about, Noah?" Hawke cuts in.

"Her conversation consisted mostly of giggling, but she liked my car and thought that the way my eyebrows grew across the bridge of my nose was cute. Inane conversation."

"How long were you parked?"

"Oh, an hour and a half must have passed with Roman and me trying to come to some sort of, ah, terms with the ladies. When a proper understanding couldn't be reached, we dropped them off where we found them."

"Can you explain"—Hawke's voice rises—"why on earth two young men who had a 'falling out of cocksuckers' would drive around looking for girls?"

I keep control of my facial muscles, but it takes great effort to do so.

They found the letter.

Chapter 8

Friday, 10 June 1921

"Why do you have your valise? Where are you going, Babe?"

Saul's voice startled me as I stood next to my bed, and I spun around to find him standing in the doorway. Annoyed, I shut the suitcase harder than intended.

"Well, if you must know, I'm taking the rail to the Loewe's vacation home."

"You're going to their huge estate in Michigan? You haven't even been friends with him for long."

My face heated up. "Why're you objecting to me spending time with someone my own age when for years you've been telling me that I spend too much time with older people, birds, or books?"

"Listen, Babe, you don't know the Loewe kid well, that's all."

"I don't appreciate your implication that Roman's a bad influence." I straightened to my fullest height and glared up at him.

"He's celebrating his sixteenth birthday tomorrow, and his parents have invited six of his pals to stay the weekend—"

"Six drunkards, I dare say! Friends of his brother, Emil, tell me Roman has developed quite a taste for liquor. He runs wild, that one, and I don't think it's wise to associate yourself with him so much."

"Nonsense! You and Levi taught me to hold my liquor, and that's of no consequence since Mr. Loewe is a strict abstainer. There will be no alcohol served."

He smirked. "I'll bet."

Of course not, you fool, I thought and resisted the urge to pat the flask in my jacket. Instead, I grabbed the handle of the suitcase and lifted it from the bed. Placing the straw boater that I wore for travel atop my head, I went to the door.

"Now, I have to leave. Roman is picking me up, and his family's chauffeur is taking us to the train depot. If you'll be so kind?" I gestured for him to step out, and then I closed the bedroom door behind us. "Have a pleasant weekend, Saul." I walked down the hallway, and he followed me.

"So, are you traveling in the Loewe's Pullman car?"

"No."

"Why not?"

"Roman doesn't wish to endure the trip in the Pullman with his family and their servants. He prefers first-class accommodations to listening to Thaddeus prattle. I agree and am accompanying him since Mr. Loewe won't allow him to drive such a distance. Besides, the Pullman left earlier this morning."

He descended the stairs behind me. "Aren't you saying goodbye to Mother?" he asked as I bypassed the second floor.

I didn't answer until I reached the wide, curved bottom step. "Rest assured, brother, I visited her suite earlier and bid her my adieu." Unwilling to engage in further conversation sure to lead to more arguments, I crossed the foyer to the front entrance and stepped outside to wait. Walking through the gate of the iron fence and onto the sidewalk, I placed my suitcase on the ground, reached for my pack of cigarettes, plucked one out, and lit it. When I returned the lighter to my pocket, my fingers grazed the flask Roman gave me. Tempted, I resisted indulging now to assuage my irritation with Saul. I brought the gin for the weekend's enjoyment—and the lengthy train ride.

Despite standing under the shade of a black cherry tree, sunlight burned through the leaves, and I began perspiring, causing my shirt to dampen. I removed my jacket, tossed it over my arm, and loosened my collar. Roman and I had yet to speak about what occurred the evening we appropriated Tony Mason's father's car. Or to repeat it. We simply walked home that night in silence after succumbing to drunken frottage and a nap. I never expected to talk to him again.

But Margaret gave me the message that Roman called when I returned from a birding excursion with Henry two days after the park incident. My hand shook as I picked up the receiver and asked the operator to be put through to the Loewe residence.

"Hear about Tony?" Roman had said when he got on the line.

I breathed easier at the sound of his voice. "No. Did something happen?"

"Yeah. Seems he took the old man's Milburn for a joy ride. Walk over here. I'll meet you halfway and tell you all about it."

With that, our friendship grew. He came birding with Henry and me a couple of times, although he didn't care much for it, and the three of us lunched at the grill in Marshall's Department Store. Twice, I sat and read while Henry and Roman played tennis on the Loewe's backyard court. Roman and friends of his, Owen Gregory and Dick Renford, joined me at a special off-semester lecture by the renowned jurist Professor Charles Montgomery.

And here we are.

A horn beeped. I looked up, and my stomach filled with lead. Henry's roadster was idling at the curb. Roman sat on the passenger side, but he got out and opened the door for me.

"Henry's tagging along with us on the train, Noah."

I tossed the butt on the ground, picked up my suitcase, and loaded it into the back of the auto. Disappointment raced through me.

I hate Henry Heinz right about now.

"Yeah," Henry said, "it'll be more comfortable in first class on the train than driving with either Jim and Tony or Dick and Owen."

"So, those are the other guests, Roman?"

He smirked at me. "Sure are. They're driving up. Damn long trip either mode of transportation, but I prefer the comfort of the train."

I got in and shut the door. The upcoming journey loomed, no longer something to look forward to.

After we boarded and the porter took our luggage, we walked through second and third-class carriages toward our first-class car, situated between another first-class section and the dining car. The luxurious carriage sported roomy leather club chairs spaced far enough apart to afford ample leg room. Dark-red velvet curtains, pulled together and held by tasteful gold ribbons, adorned every window. The same shade of red showed up in geometrical designs on thick, black carpeting. I walked behind Roman and managed to procure the seat closest to him when he settled into one of the chairs and stretched out his legs. Henry sat across from someone's sour-looking grandmother. Almost every chair in the car was occupied.

Henry leaned forward. "Too bad I'll be crushed between Dick and Owen on the way home."

His words surprised me, and I ground my teeth together and concentrated on keeping my face from showing delight. "You mean you aren't staying until Monday?"

"No. My sister's visiting with the baby, and the family expects me home Sunday night at the latest."

Roman turned to me. "You don't mind that Henry isn't staying another night, do you Noah? I'll take the train back with you. Mumsie and Thad are staying in Michigan for ten days or so, but I don't want to be stuck there with them. Popsie's returning to Chicago Monday evening, so he agreed to let me go back home."

"Popsie," Henry teased, "won't let Romansie stay in the housey by himselfsie because he doesn't trust—"

"Ah, can it, Heinzie, what do you know?" Roman slumped in his chair, reached into his inside jacket pocket, and withdrew his flask. "I never get into trouble," he swore, eyes shining as he took a nip.

The old woman scowled at us before she turned away and settled in with a knitting project. I sat back and got comfortable.

* * *

On Saturday evening, servants bustled about the formal dining room, clearing away plates and the remnants of dinner, until Mrs. Loewe tapped a fork against the crystal in front of her. They took their cue and left the room.

She stood up and raised her glass high. "Here's to my sweet Manny," she toasted. "Happy birthday, son."

"Hear, hear," came intonations as everyone drank their beverage.

One of Roman's brothers got up and started talking, but I didn't listen. Instead, I fumed over having to share a room with Henry, who snored vociferously.

I glanced around, and my eyes landed on Tony across from me at the massive table. He didn't like or trust me. The snide glares he aimed at me gave testament to his feelings despite Roman's assurances that Tony had been blotto that night.

I paid attention to the conversation when Emil embarked on a story Roman took exception to, and the two began bickering. Mrs. Loewe fanned herself, but Mr. Loewe rose unsteadily to his feet. The oldest son jumped up and assisted his father back into his seat.

"Father's not feeling up to par tonight," he said. "So, stop this nonsense in front of our guests."

Henry kicked me, but I didn't look at him for fear I would laugh.

Roman stood up, clapped his hands, and rubbed them together. "Ah, c'mon, fellas, let's head to the ballroom. The girls will be here soon."

I turned to Henry and whispered, "Girls? What girls?"

"Roman lined up seven fillies, one for each of us to dance with." He winked. "Or anything else we can talk them into."

Why didn't Henry mention this last night? Instead, he blathered on about the odd sparrow he spotted in a tree when we disembarked from the train. No one said anything about girls coming over for a dance. I danced well enough, having gotten an early start on practicing during my years at the Spade Institution—a girls' school. My mother enrolled me there from the ages of five through seven after they began admitting boys. I was one of three. Information I hoped no one ever acquired, especially Tony Mason.

By the time we entered the ballroom, girls stood in front of a large table with a gold tablecloth. A crystal punch bowl sat in the center, surrounded by glasses, and the rest of the table supported fancy finger foods, baked desserts, and candies, each more pleasing to the eye than the next. On one end sat a huge, five-tier birthday cake with swirls of white and blue frosting.

Roman led our group over to the country flappers, who gazed around in awe. Henry slowed his pace to match mine.

"This place is ducky, Roman," gushed a pretty girl with short light hair and wearing a mid-length dress.

"Yeah, that's right, you've only been on the grounds of 'the Grand House,' as Popsie calls it." He nodded at high ceilings. "They finished construction on this place and the farm down the road a couple of years ago. We spent last July and August here, but this is my first birthday gathering."

"I love the stonework," one girl said, and the rest of them nodded together in a synchronized, choreographed movement.

"Mumsie modeled the mansion after some castle in France." He threw a wink their way. "I'll tell her you admired the shack. It'll please her."

The girls wore a variety of drop-waist dresses, stockings, and a corresponding color patent leather party shoe. They also all wore identical expressions of adoration as they gazed at Roman. His words, no matter the subject, became overshadowed by the way in which he spoke them—the movement of his eyes as they danced and flitted, the smile he flashed on and off with such ease.

"It's my party, so I say we snack later and cut a rug now." He strolled over to the phonograph on a marble table and rifled through a pile of albums, opened one, and pulled out a record. "Isham Jones Orchestra!"

The girls squealed when the music played. Henry stood next to me, and he took a small step backward, as did I, although I doubted for the same reason. I shrank back in horror because Roman grabbed the girl with shoulder-length dark hair and the shortest dress and pulled her close.

"I'm dancing with Lilly," he declared, giving her upper arms a squeeze. He ripped off his bowtie and flung it into the punchbowl. Everyone howled. "Girls, these are the guys, Tony, Jim, Owen, Dick, Henry, and Noah."

Each of us nodded when he called out our names.

"Guys, this is Lilly—"

"Lillian," she corrected.

"Lillian to you, Lilly to me. Sorry," he said, dragging her to the middle of the floor. "I don't remember the rest of the dames' names. You tell 'em Lilly."

She giggled them out as they gyrated to the music.

* * *

Monday, 13 June 1921

I woke earlier than necessary for our trip home. Henry left the previous day with the other guys, so peaceful slumber should have been a given. Instead, I spent last night as I had spent Friday and Saturday nights: tossing and turning. Henry's snoring didn't have a thing to do with my insomnia. Images of Roman dancing and laughing with Lilly until the sun rose sent jolts of hurt throughout me that made breathing a chore.

When I went to wash up in one of the private baths in Roman and Emil's section of the house, the face that Frannie, my insipid leech for the night, had stared at with a look of puzzlement and admiration, gazed back at me in the gold lattice-framed mirror. My skin tone lacked a certain healthy glow and resembled floury dough. Too-big eyes sat underneath eyebrows that connected and dipped at the bridge of my nose. Full lips never seemed able to form into a genuine smile.

Look at me, bemoaning my average looks like a girl. No wonder Tony thinks of me as he does.

Disgusted, I returned to my room to dress. At least the evening didn't drag on. Roman insisted on so much dancing it left little time for conversation. However, that didn't stop me from overhearing Tony tell Frannie to be careful of me because "I'm a strange bird and a pompous intellect."

I shook my head as a disturbing thought crept in.

I'm upset because I witnessed Roman kiss Lilly on the mouth.

* * *

By the time Roman and I boarded the train, I was tired.

"What's wrong, Noah, you've been quiet all weekend."

I didn't answer, unwilling to risk embarrassing myself by speaking of an event in the park that clearly hadn't happened except in the wild stirrings of my imagination, so I said nothing.

"Didn't you like Frannie? She told Lilly you were cute in an aloof way." He laughed as we entered the first-class car. I went to sit in a chair, but he said, "Nah, I got us a couple of bunkers so I can lay back and rest." He winked and patted his breast pocket. "And finish off this gin."

Something stirred in me as we went through the dining car. Our destination was wedged between three private bunker carriages accessible by shaky bridge connections. Large side-by-side compartments, with heavy curtains open, revealed spacious beds.

"Not close to the luxury of a Pullman, but without the intrusion of pesky porters," Roman said, and he claimed a bunk. I took the one to the left of his. Each of the bunks on either side of ours had the curtains drawn. Windows lined the opposite side of the train, and the countryside blurred past in a blend of colors.

"This is nice, Roman, thank you. It'll be comfortable to lie down."

"Sure, sure, but first let's stand outside and have a smoke." He turned and headed for the connecting door that led to the next sleeper car.

"Outside?" I asked but followed him, nonetheless. "What do you mean? Where're we going?"

He didn't answer, just continued into the next car and through that one too. When we were outside with the door shut behind us, he stopped and pulled out his Luckies. I did the same, holding onto the railing and swaying with the rapid motion of the train. It took a few tries to light our sticks, but we got them going.

"We don't belong out here, Roman," I yelled over the noise. "Let's go back, return to our carriage."

He took a draw and pointed to the car in front of us. "This is where the porters sleep. Let's have a look around, maybe nick something."

"No, that's not a good idea."

Too late. He opened the door and entered. I waited a second before following him. Every curtain was pulled aside, revealing clothes and personal belongings strewn over beds. The place looked empty, so we walked to the end.

"See anything worth swiping, Babe?"

As he finished speaking, someone crawled out from under a pile of clothes on a bunk. The guy, who looked not much older than we were, stood, shaking, between us and the connecting door.

"Hey!" Roman flicked his cigarette at him. "What're you a stowaway?" He sniffed and wrinkled his nose. "Yeah, smell like one, and look at that greasy hair. Ah, I bet you're the friend of a porter, a dope fiend stealing a free ride." He turned to me. "What do you think? Should we report him?"

The guy stared at us, his eyes wide, then he turned and fled through the door. We followed him outside.

"Don't go in there," Roman said when the stowaway reached for the door to the next sleeper car. "You'll stink up the joint."

I laughed.

"Please leave me alone. I don't want trouble," he begged, and he lifted his leg over the rail.

"Where do you think you're going?" Roman moved closer to him. "You're coming with us to talk to the authorities. Besides, train's moving too fast for jumping off."

The doper got both legs over the thin rail and held on. Before I could ask as to what his intentions might be, he lost his grip and, without a sound, slipped under the wheels.

We stood still, staring at the spot where he disappeared in a mist of blood.

"Wow! That was something, huh, Babe? Let's scram!"

I tossed my cigarette and followed him back to our bunks without encountering anyone else. Roman bounced on his bed, and his eyes held the same look that I remembered from the park. But this one was different, more intense.

Watching the stowaway die excited him. I took a deep, shaky breath. *Me too.*

"Close your curtain and come in here," he commanded in a whisper.

I couldn't refuse my king, nor did I want to refuse him.

Chapter 9

> I would believe only in a God that knows how to dance.
>
> —Friedrich Nietzsche

Early morning, Friday, 30 May 1924

"What does a 'falling out of cocksuckers' mean, Noah?"

I allow not one muscle in my face to break rank from their stiff positions, don't even pause in rubbing the end of my cigarette, when Hawke quotes from my letter to Roman.

"Mr. Hawke, I've no clue what you're referring to." I lean over and flick ash in the vicinity of the receptacle.

"I'm referencing a letter addressed to your friend, Roman Loewe. My men discovered it hidden in a drawer in your bedroom." He makes theater out of opening a file folder and withdrawing a piece of paper that's been folded and unfolded dozens of times. "Is this your handwriting and your signature?" he asks, holding the paper up to my face.

I give it an obligatory glance. "Yes."

"You're an educated fella," Sever spits the words out around another stogie. "A law student, an ornithologist, an intellect." He leans closer, elbows on the armrests. "Can you explain why you blatantly threatened Mr. Loewe's life in this formal, dare I say dramatic, correspondence?"

I take a draw, hold it in, and blow smoke rings in his direction. His nose twitches and his lips purse.

"Well, Mr. Sever, as I now recall, I wrote it last October. At that time, I'd had torts up to my neck, so I penned the letter as a lawyer." I smirk. "Except for the threatening his life part. This was a joke, of course."

"'I will understand if you wish to break our friendship,'" Hawke reads, "'as our misunderstanding turned into something too cumbersome to handle.' What does this mean?"

"I can't recall the specifics, but I believe Roman misconstrued a comment I made to another friend."

"Who?"

"Dick Renford."

"'In the utmost regard to our former relations,'" he continues, "'I suggest that we stand on equal sides of the wide avenue called Law and that any implication otherwise would be foolish.' Can you explain this, Noah?"

"Again, I was absorbed in my schooling." I try for a carefree smile and view the disastrous results on Bertram Hawke's face. "And I'm known among my peers to possess a dramatic flair when demonstrating my point."

"Just tell us what legal issue ya boys were equally guilty of."

"Well, Detective Harrison, because of some inane misinterpretation of a remark I made to Dick on a previous day that I can't even recall at present, Roman became angry and wouldn't permit me to leave his room. He left and locked his bedroom doors and didn't return for hours."

I crush the butt of my cigarette into the overfull ashtray.

"Get that, will you, Marvin?" Sever says.

"Sure thing." Detective Harrison grabs the receptacle and dumps it into the trash can in the corner of the room. When he returns it to its prior spot, it's clean but odoriferous.

"And your illegality against him?" Hawke asks as if no interruption occurred.

"I refused to let Roman out of my car one day after the incident at his house and insisted we discuss matters in my automobile to avoid another childish, distasteful prank."

"So?"

"When he further resisted acknowledging his part in the miscommunication with Dick, I drove around, speeding up when he tried to exit the car."

"Where does the term 'falling out of cocksuckers' originate? What's the significance of it?"

I aim my stare at Hawke, see myself mirrored in his round spectacles, and keep my expression impassive.

"It refers, Mr. Hawke, to perversions of which Roman and I were maliciously accused. A friend of his who disliked me started a nasty rumor after I beat him in a poker game."

"When was this?"

"Nineteen twenty-one. The ridiculous falsehood became so prevalent that the two of us avoided being alone together."

"Did you ever commit any perversions with Roman Loewe?"

"I did not." I resist the urge to loosen my collar and gulp down a glass of water to combat the stale air in the room. Instead, I take a tiny sip.

"I understand that you're Jewish. Do you attend religious services?"

"No, Mr. Hawke, I don't believe in the existence of God. Any God."

"So, what happens when ya die?"

"You die, Detective Harrison."

He stares at me with a quizzical expression. I hold back a Nietzschean retort sure to change the narrative into a more interesting debate, but it's late—or early as is the case—and I'm tiring. However, I need to make myself clear.

"I am, sirs, what is fashionably titled these days as an 'atheist.'"

"'Since two intelligent fellas like ourselves,'" Hawke continues reading, "'cannot come to a proper pact that meets both our terms, I wonder if my only options left are to end our friendship or kill you, which is something I expected to do that day in my car when you accused me of treachery.'" He pauses to study me, but I make sure my face displays nothing.

"'Because we have taken this disagreement to its furthest point, and you insist that I perform an act I refuse to do, I'm leaving the punishment for this refusal up to you. At your discretion, I propose two scenarios for consideration. We continue our relations as prior, and I restrain myself from kidnapping and threatening to kill you, or you can dispose of the friendship and inflict penalties and anything else you conjure.'" Hawke looks at me. "What act did you refuse to do?"

"Roman wanted me to sign an official apology letter declaring that I was the wrongful party in our disagreement."

"'I caution, however,'" he continues reading, "'should you choose to break contact, care must be taken when we meet on the street, at school, or any public function or outing. Pleasant greetings must be afforded to each other, and further breeches are not advisable. It's wise to avoid the impression of a falling out of cocksuckers.'"

"So, I guess ya two kissed and made up, huh?"

I grit my teeth but keep my eyes on Hawke's beady ones as I answer Harrison. "Droll. I was being melodramatic. I don't even remember the original misconception."

Hawke continues, "'I ask one thing, Manny, and it's that you phone me before tomorrow night to apprise me of your decision. You're aware that I'm going on a birding expedition for a few days with Heinzie and some fellow birders…'" He places the letter on top of the folder. "It goes on a bit more, but you signed it 'Babe.'"

"Yes, my family and close friends have used this nickname for years." I sneer at the State's attorney. "And Roman's family calls him 'Manny' in case you're under the delusion that we have pet names for each other."

"Ya gotta admit it sounds strange for two fellas to carry on like ya do."

I glare at the intellectually inferior detective. A sheen of sweat coats his forehead, and he wipes it away with his hand.

"Well, ya must be very close for someone to spread such awful accusations and—"

"As I already informed you, *Detective*, this person made the egregious allegation after taking a dislike to me when I won all his money playing cards."

"If a fella done or said something like that to me, I'da clocked him upside his head."

"We came to terms sometime later after he spoke of his remorse for making up such an untruth." I shift in my seat and adjust my vest, which is riding up on my stomach. "I believe that Roman is still cordial with him, but I'm not and choose to keep my distance from the worm."

A look passes between Sever and Hawke.

"Excuse me." Sever stands up and crushes his stogie in the ashtray. "Call of nature," he says and leaves the room.

"What are these?" Hawke asks, sliding something on the table in front of me. I glance down, and the remains of the sandwich I ate hours earlier hardens in my stomach.

"They look like dope sheets."

"What are dope sheets?" Harrison inquires.

"It's common practice for law students to study in groups, discuss pertinent areas of the law, and then type up doping sheets, a summary, for members to use."

"Well, Noah, do you recognize these as being ones that were typed during your study group?"

"Yes, Mr. Hawke, I do."

"Whose typewriter did you utilize?"

"We met at my house in my rooms on the third floor. My typewriter was utilized. I already informed you that it's a Hammond."

"These particular dope sheets weren't typed on a Hammond."

I glance at them and concede, "Yes, I believe, on occasion, we preferred the warmth of my father's library downstairs. Someone must have brought a portable typewriter on such cold days."

"Give us the names of the boys in ya group."

"Of course. Martin Bergen. Leonard Aaron. Abraham Morris. Hubert Ogdon."

As Detective Harrison is writing down names, the door opens, and Jim Sever walks back in and reclaims his seat.

"Can you remember who brought the portable Underwood into your house?" Hawke continues with his line of questioning.

"How do you know that the mystery typewriter is an Underwood?"

He smiles, and his eyes magnify behind the thick lenses. "Well, Noah, because an expert in such matters already examined your papers."

I raise an eyebrow.

"Before you ask why, a fella, a young reporter who went to the University of Chicago and a friend of one of the guys in your study group, heard that you were being questioned." Hawke taps a finger on the notes. "He got a hold of these dope sheets and checked them against the ransom letter. Now, are you familiar with the ransom note that Mr. Frisch received?"

"If what you mean by 'familiar' is have I read it as published verbatim in the newspapers, then, yes, I'm acquainted with said correspondence."

Someone snickers, whether Harrison or Sever, I can't tell since I keep my eyes on Mr. Hawke's, which are narrowing further behind his spectacles.

"The note appears to have been drafted by a man of intelligence, do you agree, Noah?"

"Yes, sir."

"What act of deviance did this so-called friend accuse you and Mr. Loewe of committing?" Jim Sever says, changing the direction of the narrative.

I don't blink. "I'm unaware of which particular type of perversion the false allegation revolves around." I decide to enlighten their minds. "But, according to Aretino's *I Ragionamenti*, there are thirty-two various modes."

"Who's Aretino?" Hawke asks.

"Pietro Aretino. His erotic works and venomous quill made him quite scandalous in his time."

"And you've studied his work?"

"No, sir, I wouldn't say that I've *studied* his work. For a brief time, I planned to translate some of his writings, but a professor convinced me not to do so."

"So, how many of those perversions are ya aware of?"

"A few, Detective Harrison."

"Sodomy one of them?"

Sneering at him, I say, "If you're referring to the inserting of one's penis into someone else's rectum, then yes, this is one deviant form of behavior of which I am aware. There's also the practice of placing the penis in other areas such as between clenched legs or armpits. Toes even."

"How about in the mouth?"

"Yes, Detective, this is a method. Cunt lapping is another one."

"Does it seem unusual to you that the killers typed the ransom note but handwrote the address on the envelope?"

"I assure you, Mr. Hawke, this is information I didn't possess. However, now that you mention it, why is it relevant?"

He leans back and rocks the chair on its rear legs. "As a student of law, you should know that everything is relevant."

"Fair enough," I concede.

"And your answer to my original question?"

"I have none, sir." I take the opportunity to drink more, which makes another need present itself. "I'd like to visit the water closet, please."

"Down the hall to the right, fourth door on the left."

"Thank you, Mr. Hawke," I say and make a great show of stretching my legs and spine when I stand up. Detective Harrison follows me as far as the door and opens it for me. Relatively fresh air fills my lungs as I turn and head down the hallway. Along the way, I observe bland plaster walls with pocks and dings and floors, which have a distinct walking pattern worn into the maple. The first door on the left is closed, as is the second one, frosted glass obscuring any occupants that may be inside. When I come upon the third door, it opens, and a man hurries out, placing a straw hat atop his head as he moves down the hallway.

"Shut it," someone barks.

A man rises to close the door, and I catch sight of a room much like the one I just left. A large black filing cabinet stands against one wall, and there's a rectangle conference table with a few men sitting at it.

One of the fellas turns around.

I glimpse Roman's smirk as he recognizes me, and then the door shuts.

I hope he sticks to the alibi.

Chapter 10

Monday, 5 September 1921

"You look peaked, Master Babe," Margaret said from the stair landing while her clasped hands wrestled each other in the pleats of her apron. "Perhaps it's best to not visit with your mother this morning. The missus is weaker than usual. Your father is with her now."

I paused on my way past her, gripping the handrail on the wide staircase so as not to sway. "I'm sure I'm well enough to poke my head into her room and wish her a good day," I said, but by the time I reached the second-floor landing, I changed my mind and continued to the third floor.

Instead of going into my bedroom, I entered my study and closed the door behind me. I relieved myself of my jacket, placed it over the back of an overstuffed club chair, and loosened my collar.

I fear Margaret's assessment is correct.

Although I had yet to examine myself in the mirror and couldn't attest to the pallor of my skin, I didn't feel well at all. My throat was scratchy and sore when I swallowed, and my body alternated between chills and sweating.

Gazing around at my specimens, I frowned when my eyes landed on my very first acquisition made at five years old, *Turdus migratorius*. The stuffed American robin, posed upright, chest puffed out with dignity, faced the wrong direction.

"I've told Margaret umpteen times," I griped as I moved the robin back to its original position, "to make sure everything is undisturbed when she dusts in here."

A soft knock caught my attention. Expecting it to be the maid, I walked over and flung open the door.

"Yes?"

Levi stood there. "Here you are, Babe. Margaret says you look ill." He frowned. "I have to say that I agree with her. Go to your room, undress, and get into bed. I'm calling the doctor."

"No need to disturb him, Levi. I'm tired because I spent six hours trudging through the marsh yesterday, and all for naught because the damnable phalarope evaded me the entire day!"

"Nonetheless, with the fever going around, it's wise to err with caution."

"Fine." I turned, stomped into my bedchamber, and slammed the door behind me.

Not until I changed into pajamas and lay on the soft mattress did I allow myself to admit the true reason behind my lethargy. I hadn't slept much in the past week. Not since Roman left.

* * *

"I'm going to Michigan," Roman said last month. We lay gazing at the stars in our private spot in the woods behind Washington

Park, near a favorite birding area of mine. No one came out there at night.

I was confused. He and his family spent all of July and some of August at their vacation house in northern Michigan. In July, I joined Henry and other friends for a week and made a trip by myself in August for four days before going off on a birding expedition. The days were filled with lots of activities when the other fellas were around. Tennis, golf, and swimming with the local girls interested the lot of them, but I merely went through the motions. Often, everyone paired up to go for "walks." Frannie, my habitual companion whenever I went there, seemed as content as I to converse and try, as I told her, to learn about each other. But my thrill, what I craved and *needed*, came in the dead of night when only creatures stirred. That sweet section of dark when drunks gave in to blackness, and the world wasn't ready to awaken. In those moments, those slices of life, I lived. Breathed. Existed. With Roman.

"You just returned from Michigan," I said.

"I mean to the university in Ann Arbor."

Three things had happened simultaneously with his words. My throat closed with no warning, and I couldn't swallow or speak. My lungs tightened, faltered, like they forgot how to push out and pull in air. But the desolation that filled me…

He sat up and began dressing. I watched with envy, as I always did, when socks and undergarments slid onto his skin. How I longed to be his clothes—touching him and pressing against him all day.

"Why?" The word escaped, despite how hard I tried to hold it in.

"Geez, Babe, are you serious?" He stood up and thrust first one, and then his other leg into his trousers. "I told you what that dirty louse, Tony, said to my brother!"

I ran my hands over my face to disguise the treacherous tears welling behind my eyes. Once I gained control of my emotions, I grabbed my pack of Luckies from the ground.

"Want one?" I offered, but Roman, tying his shoes, shook his head. A first for him; he never turned down a smoke. I lit my cigarette. "Tony knows nothing." I concentrated on keeping my voice steady. It would do no good for whininess to infiltrate my tone. "He only implied that we—"

"Implying is enough!" He grabbed a handful of clothes and tossed them to me. "C'mon, let's go home."

"We've been exceedingly careful, Manny. Tony just wants to get rid of me. I told you that I think he's jealous of me, of how close we are."

"Rot! He saw you glaring at Lilly and me necking."

"Maybe if you weren't so enthusiastic in your role-playing, I wouldn't have to glare."

"Forget it, Babe, I'm not debating this again. We agreed that this works because no one knows the truth."

"Truths are illusions which we have forgotten are—"

"Ah, can it with Nietzsche." He kicked at a tree root. "Tony will blab to Jim, Jim will say something to Owen, and everyone will think we're pervs."

"So, you go to Michigan and what?" Tiny, invisible beaks pecked at the inside of my stomach.

Is he really going to leave Chicago, leave me?

"Well, before I go, I'm gonna knock hell out of Tony!"

"I mean, how will you get your enjoyment?" I took a draw on the cig and blew out smoke rings. "And I'm not referring to this." I gestured around at our little clearing. "Who will do your bidding with you?"

Roman had reached down, grabbed my arm, and pulled me up. "I can stay out of trouble," he said. "Now, put on your clothes."

* * *

"Noah? Can you hear me, Noah?"

I opened my eyes, unsure of when I closed them. The last thing I remembered was putting on pajamas and getting into bed. I was still under blankets, but the doctor's long face, cloaked in a cloth mask, had replaced Roman's face.

"Y-y-yes," I said, surprised at how much effort and pain the word caused me.

"Open your mouth so I can look at your throat."

I obliged, and he pushed a dry, wooden depressor down on my tongue.

"It's as I feared." He rose and backed away from my bed. "Scarlet fever."

Someone gasped. I turned my head, and the motion made me dizzy. Levi and Margaret hovered in the doorway.

"I'm afraid there's been a recent wave of such cases," the doctor said.

Margaret made the sign of the cross, to which I almost made a comment sure to send her on her knees praying for my soul. However, I felt too weak and didn't wish to tax my throat.

"What do we do?" Levi's voice trembled.

"This house is now under quarantine. Lead me to your telephone, so I can contact the Health Department forthwith."

The last thing I heard before weariness succumbed to sleep was something about the doctor posting yellow signs on the exterior doors.

* * *

Monday, 10 October 1921

Margaret stood outside my study when I opened the door, her hand poised as if to knock.

"Oh, you startled me, Master Babe. Your father wishes to speak with you. He's in the library."

"Thank you." I walked out of my room, and she backed up as was her custom this past week since I've been permitted to leave my rooms. I scowled. "You're aware that I've been cleared by the Health Department, right? I'm not contagious anymore."

"I'm sorry, but it's been a long confinement."

"Yes, and if I remember properly, *I'm* the only one in the house who became sick. I should think you and the rest of the staff would be grateful that you didn't fall victim as well and stop treating me as some sort of pariah."

I went downstairs to the first floor and walked past the parlor and a formal sitting room to reach the library. There was no door, just a cherrywood archway, cherry being the theme of the expansive room. The rich wood made up the tray ceiling, and the floor-to-ceiling shelves on every wall, which housed thousands of books. A thick, crimson-accented carpet dulled my footfalls as I walked to the reading area in front of a massive stone fireplace. My father sat in a leather club chair, a pipe in the corner of his mouth, a large tome in his lap. He didn't look up, and from my vantage point, I could not see what kept him so engrossed.

"You wish to speak with me, Father?" I asked as he reached for a glass that I guessed by the lemon wedge to be a gin Rickey.

Instead of picking up the drink, he closed the book and removed the pipe from his mouth. "How do you feel, Babe? You gave your mother a fright, you know."

"I'm much better. And stronger. As soon as I'm permitted to see her, I shall reassure Mother myself."

"Yes, well, due to her fragile condition, the nurse from the Health Department thinks it wise for you to wait six weeks after your first symptom's occurrence before visiting with her. That will be in seven days."

I nodded. I understood the need to protect her, but I'd grown tired of confinement. Not only had I been isolated from those in my own home other than my nursemaid, but visitors were forbidden as well. And Roman was gone. Off to the University of Michigan in Ann Arbor.

"Is that all you wanted to ask me, Father? If so, I'm heading out to Washington Park for a few hours of bird-watching this morning."

"No, Babe, I wanted to tell you that I spoke with the appropriate people over at the University of Michigan, and after reviewing your records, they're confident that you'll have no trouble catching up."

"They're approving my transfer then?" Joy crept in. The first I felt since the day Roman told me he was leaving.

"I never believed there would be any doubt that they would take you, Babe. You're a brilliant student. You may move into a double-room dormitory and begin classes two weeks from today." He removed his glasses and pinched the bridge of his nose. "Are you certain that you want to do this, son? It might not be wise to follow a friend three hundred miles when you've never lived away from home before."

I kept my temper under control because I knew this came from Saul. My father didn't care where I went to school, provided I continued with law as was my intention. But Roman's brother told Sanctimonious Saul what Tony inferred.

"Look, kid, your friend already had it out with that blabbermouth," Saul had said from my doorway a few weeks ago. He laughed. "I heard Tony wore a T-bone on his face for days after. But these kinds of stories—"

"It's a filthy lie!"

"I know, but the thing is, well, the way that Roman goes after the fillies, well, no one will believe it about him."

"You're implying, Saul, of course, that people will believe such of me."

"Just stay away from Roman Loewe. He's too wild. Find yourself other friends. Maybe a nice girl."

I erased Saul's face and voice from my mind and addressed my father. "I think that a change of scenery after this difficult illness will do me good. And at least I'll know one person at Michigan."

"Very well, Babe. We'll miss you at home when you leave."

* * *

Monday, 31 October 1921

Even though I arrived in Ann Arbor over a week ago, I didn't get up the nerve to visit Roman until the night of Halloween.

I went to his fraternity house, and someone directed me to the common room.

"Noah, what're you doing here chap?" he said when I approached him. Dressed as a robber, he sat at a table playing cards with a Pierrot clown, a couple of gypsies, and an ugly flapper with a beard. Cigarette smoke filled the air, and they were all blotto.

"I grew bored with the University of Chicago and transferred to Michigan."

His eyes blazed behind his domino mask, and although his smile stayed affable, I recognized anger bubbling under his skin.

"Did you now? Well, pal, I'd introduce you to the fellas, but I don't remember their names at this moment." He howled, and the others laughed and slapped their knees.

My face grew hot, but worse, it felt like a hole opened in my stomach, and my insides spilled out leaving me empty. A barren shell.

"Y-y-yes, I can see that you're busy. I just wanted to say hello, but I'll run into you around campus, I'm sure." I nodded to the smirking, no-name boys, turned around, and left.

* * *

Tuesday, 15 November 1921

I looked around the large classroom filled with pre-law students, all bent over books, scribbling notes, and gazing in awe at the professor as he lectured. Although I generally agreed with him, on this subject, I could not hold my tongue.

"So, Professor," I began, despite the cross look on the face of my only companion in this class—or any other.

"Noah," he hissed and kicked my foot, but I paid him no mind.

"Do you agree that no intellectual man can achieve the level of the Übermensch, or superman, while following the dictates of man?"

"You mean, Mr. Lieberman, by adhering to the laws of man?"

"Yes, sir."

"And by superman," he said, walking out from behind the walnut lectern. "I presume you're speaking of Friedrich Nietzsche's definition of a man who lives by his own rules?"

"Correct."

"Then I guess my older brother has reached Nietzsche's pinnacle," some ridiculous student shouted out. "My mum's always saying he thumbs his nose at the rules of the house!"

"If you're comparing your lazy sibling to Nietzsche's vision of the Übermensch, then you're quite dim," I retorted. "Flouting rules because of idleness and entitlement are the complete opposite! The true superman is of high intelligence and lives by his own rules because regulations and constraints of the mundane do not apply. The true superman rejects the herd instinct to follow the laws of Christianity. The true superman stands outside of the moral laws of ordinary man. The true—"

"All right," the professor said, "enough Nietzsche for now. Let me continue with my lecture on the development of…"

I tuned him out.

Later that afternoon I sat at my desk in the dorm, books and papers surrounding me, including on the floor, and tried to concentrate on studying laws of evidence for an exam the next morning.

"Are you sure you don't want to come to the library with me?" my dormmate asked. "You always study here."

"That's because it's quiet here."

"It's quiet at the library too, Noah."

I stared up at the almost white-haired fella, who, at six three, towered over me even when I wasn't seated. He was a decent guy. Smart and courteous, he went bird-watching with me on a few occasions.

I smirked and raised an eyebrow. "We'll have to debate the quietude of last week."

He laughed. "Oh, not fair. What're the odds a freshman's going to sob over his books the one time you come to the library to study?"

"Sob? Blubbering is more like it."

"Yeah, well, are you sure you don't want to go, Noah?"

I shook my head and returned to my books.

"Okay, see you later." He patted my shoulder and left.

The pencil in my hand snapped. I didn't even realize I was squeezing it. The truth? I would have liked to go to the library. Despite my complaint about the slight ruckus on Friday, it had been refreshing to be in the company of a group for a change.

I threw the splintered pieces of wood onto the desk. Frustrated, I stared at the words in the book closest to me. They were too blurry to read, so I gave up and closed my eyes.

I miss Mother.

I shook my head, still unable to fathom that she had succumbed to her delicate condition on the day I was to visit with her after my convalescence. I had risen early, washed up, and dressed in a proper suit to assure her that I'd recuperated fully. Levi, his eyes red and wet, met me in the hall before I could make my way down one flight to her suite.

"Babe, I'm so sorry to deliver such news, but Mother has died," he'd said, choking on the words. "She passed in her sleep. God's taken his angel back."

Heat spread throughout my body. My legs wobbled, and I grabbed the wall to steady myself. Tears burned and threatened to spill over, but I held them inside and let anger rage instead. Were Saul the one delivering the devastating news, I would have railed, *Gott ist tot!* Your God is dead. The one created by you, by people as a collective. Or rather the idea of what you perceive as God. But I said nothing to Levi.

"Did you hear me? Mother's gone."

"I heard you." I turned around and started back up the stairs.

"Babe, where are you going?"

"Back to my bedroom to grieve alone."

Roman did not call after her death. He must have learned of her passing, but I heard nothing from him.

A loud rap on the door startled me out of my ruminations, and I jumped up in the chair and gazed around the dorm room.

Losing Mother and Roman had made the last few weeks some of the darkest ones of my life, but I needed to focus on my studies.

Someone rapped again and yelled, "Hey, Lieberman, fella's outside looking for you."

"Uh, thanks," I said.

My heart tightened as I walked downstairs.

It can't be him. It won't be him.

But when I went outside, Roman stood in the grass looking like he swallowed the sun, glowing in a light blue pullover. He had an arm draped over the shoulder of a vapid-looking girl wearing a scandalously short dress, her cloche pulled down around chin-length dirty-blonde hair.

"Noah, I'd like you to meet Mary." He leaned into her and rubbed his nose disgustingly against hers, making her giggle. Then he nodded behind them. "And this is Dorothy."

I didn't notice the other girl until he mentioned her.

"What say you, Noah?" he said. "Let's all go grab grub and hooch and have some fun."

He had fun; I just drank. Later, we dropped off the girls and parked on a remote spur road.

"How dare you follow me here when I told you I wanted to get away from that rumor!" he screamed the second he turned off the engine.

"I required a change as well," I said, unwilling to divulge how hurt I'd been by his desire to leave Chicago. And me.

He slammed a fist on the steering wheel. "I oughta shoot you and leave you out here to rot."

I raised my chin and stared at him. "If that's the punishment you wish to mete out, I accept it with fervor."

The hard lines of his face softened and morphed into the infectious grin he threw around so effortlessly. Then the grin transformed into another look I knew well.

"Ah, I think I can come up with something better, Babe."

Chapter 11

> He who cannot put his thoughts on ice should not enter into the heat of dispute.
>
> —Friedrich Nietzsche

Friday, 30 May 1924

DEE, DEE, DEE, dee!

The call of a *Poecile atricapillus* filters into my head, stirring me toward consciousness. Eager to see the compact chickadee with its black cap and bib and contrasting white cheeks, I open my eyes and immediately throw up an arm to shield them. A line of glaring sunlight is shining straight into my face from the one small window near the ceiling.

Sitting up, I yawn and look around. I'm in a cell. Alone. Although I didn't let Hawke or the other men know that I had seen Roman being interrogated in another room, and they never let on about bringing him into the Criminal Court Building, I felt certain that when I woke up, he would be enjoying Chicago's finest accommodations in the cell next to mine. He isn't. I reach into my pocket and pull out my watch: three-thirteen in the afternoon. They put me in here a little after seven this morning. I slept all day.

I stand up and stretch. My shirt is sticking out of my trousers, so I tuck it back in and smooth it. I can't do much with my hair other than run my fingers through it and try to flatten it in spots.

Whistling captures my attention as I'm donning my vest, and I look out the bars.

"Here you go, Lieberman," an unfamiliar deputy says, walking over with a tray in one hand, keys in the other. He fidgets with the lock and opens the door. "Sandwich, potato salad, and coffee. Wash in the basin when you're done eating. Mr. Hawke wants to finish up his questioning."

"How much longer do you think this might be? After all, I've been in his custody for twenty-four hours now."

"Hurry and you can ask him yourself."

Three-quarters of an hour later, the deputy escorts me from the jail to the offices in the Criminal Court Building. I want to look inside the rooms as we pass through the hallway, because I'm positive that Roman is being questioned in one of them, but the doors are shut.

"I trust you're well rested?" Jim Sever asks when I enter the same conference room I was in before.

"Yes. Thank you."

Sever, Bertram Hawke, and Detective Harrison are seated at the large table. They're still in the rumpled suits they wore when I last saw them. Each holds a coffee cup. When Hawke takes a sip of his coffee, it steams up his eyeglasses. Cigarettes smolder in the ashtray, and a manila folder, a couple of newspapers, and three portable typewriters are on the table in front of the men.

"Have a seat, Noah." Hawke points to the chair I sat in earlier. "Would you care for something to drink?"

"Water, please," I say, sitting down and pulling out my cigarettes. Two left. I tap out a Lucky and stick it in the corner of my mouth. "And I guess I'll need more cigs if this nonsense goes on much longer."

My attempt at levity fails. They all have contemptuous looks on their faces, but Hawke sends Harrison out for more. When the detective comes back, he tosses a deck on the table and sits next to me. Hawke and Sever are across from us.

"Now," Hawke says, "these are models, of course, but which of these portable typewriters do you say you used at least once in your father's library? The Underwood, Corona, or Remington?"

I pretend to study them. "The Underwood."

"You're sure of this?"

"I believe so, yes."

"All right. And you recognize these as your dope sheets? They're not dated. Can you tell me when they were created?" Hawke hands me the notes, and I look them over.

"The subject is torts, so it must've been this past November, December." I place them on the table and slide them back to him.

"How did the Underwood, on which these were typed, get into your house, and where is it now?"

"No clue, Mr. Hawke."

"How does a typewriter appear and disappear without ya knowing anything about it?"

I glare at Harrison. "It seems to be a mystery."

"Bring in Mr. Bergen, Marv," Hawke says. Detective Harrison grumbles something unintelligible and rises so fast that his chair scrapes across the floor.

Marty's here? This surprises me, even though I suppose it shouldn't. Mr. Hawke will cover every conceivable base, no doubt.

No one speaks. The only sounds are the quiet crackle of cigarettes burning and the persistent humming of a sad, little desk fan.

The door opens, and Martin Bergen walks inside, Detective Harrison behind him.

Hawke doesn't get up, just points to an empty chair, and says, "Sit down, Mr. Bergen. I'm State's Attorney Bertram Hawke, and I'm going to ask you some questions."

Marty doesn't meet my eyes as he takes the seat between Hawke and Sever.

"Okay, what's your full name and address?"

"M-M-Martin L. Bergen, sir. I live at 3481 Layette Boulevard."

"Where did you attend school last semester and the prior one?"

"The University of Chicago, Chicago, Illinois."

I try not to smirk as Marty squirms in the chair. Tiny beads of sweat form on his forehead.

He's nervous under Hawke's questioning. How will he survive dealing with judges? He'll make a terrible attorney.

"Did you participate in a study group with Mr. Lieberman?"

Martin glances at me before averting his eyes. "Uh, y-y-yes, Mr. Hawke, and with three other boys."

"Their names?"

"Leonard Aaron, Abraham Morris, and Hubert Ogdon, sir."

"And all five of you were present in Mr. Lieberman's house when these dope sheets were typed?" Hawke hands Martin the papers, and Martin scans them.

"Yes, sir."

"Please look at the portable typewriters and tell me which one was utilized to make these preparatory sheets."

"This one, sir." He points to the Underwood.

"Are you certain?"

"Yes, sir."

"Who did the typing?"

"Noah…Mr. Lieberman did."

"Excuse me, Marty," I say, unable to keep quiet any longer. I grind my cig in the ashtray, lean over the stained and scratched wooden table, and stare at the chap until his eyes meet mine. "I seem to recall Hubert typing after I received a telephone call."

"Oh, ah, maybe. Yes, you're right. Hube did type some also."

"How'd the typewriter get to the Lieberman house? Who brought it, and did they take it with them?" Sever asks.

"Uh, I don't know. It was there when I arrived, and I suppose it stayed at the Lieberman house after I left."

"Did ya see anyone take it with them?"

He turns to Detective Harrison. "No, I didn't."

After Hawke, Sever, and Harrison run out of things to ask Martin, Harrison walks him out and returns with Leonard Aaron. When they finish with him, in comes Abraham Morris. Hubert Ogdon moved to Germany in January, so he misses out on the fun.

I wonder if they'll contact him by telegraph.

All three fellas say the same thing: Yes, we used a portable Underwood at the Lieberman house. No, none of them either brought the machine with them or took it when they left, nor did they see anyone else take it.

"So, Noah," Hawke says, "if no one removed the Underwood from your house, then it would still have to be there. Do you agree?"

"Yes, I suppose in theory."

"What d'ya mean, in theory?" Detective Harrison's face reddens as he stands over me. "Did ya get rid of the typewriter?"

"No."

"Then where is it?"

"That is the question, isn't it, Detective?"

Harrison's hands ball into fists.

"Do you need to take a walk, Marv?"

He relaxes his hands and runs them over his head through his sparse hair. "No, Bert."

"All right, then sit down." Hawke turns to me, and his chin is jutting out even farther. "You can understand our frustration, can't you, Noah? After all, your dope sheets and the ransom note to Jonah Frisch were all typed on the same Underwood that drops the *t* and *f* letters."

Of course, the connection has been made, but to hear the words spoken aloud is unsettling. I resist the temptation to roll up my sleeves to try and combat the heat.

"Any more ideas about the Underwood, Noah?" Sever asks.

"Hubert could have brought it and then taken it with him."

"Your friends say he didn't."

"No, Mr. Sever, they said that they never saw him or anyone else take it." I smile. "There's a difference."

"It's a shame that Mr. Ogdon is abroad and can't be here to testify about the—"

"Testify? Is this a trial, Mr. Hawke?"

His eyes darken behind thick lenses, a smoldering cigarette between his fingers on one hand, his other hand tapping the armrest of the chair.

"Allow me to rephrase, Noah. It's a pity Mr. Ogdon isn't in the United States to give his *statement* about the missing typewriter."

Hawke and Sever exchange a look.

I pick up my glass and sip water. When I put it down, I say, "Interestingly, Hubert's the friend who was going to translate Aretino's work with me."

"The project you never did? The one that included translating that perverted book?"

"Yes, Mr. Hawke." I stare at him. "I suppose it's possible that he brought the typewriter with him. Perhaps he left it at my house and forgot about it after our professor strongly suggested that we not pursue the endeavor."

"Well, then," Sever says, "Mr. Ogdon would have made note of his property when he arrived and saw it, or at the very least when he *typed* on it."

"One would assume so."

"Then where is it?"

I shrug. "No idea, Mr. Sever."

"Well, I guess you're not so smart if ya can't remember how a portable Underwood gets in and outta ya house."

When I look back at the detective, I catch Hawke nodding at him. What do they know?

"Did Mr. Ogdon ever visit your house again after that study session, Noah?"

"Not that I recall, Mr. Hawke."

"How many maids do ya have?"

Harrison's getting on my nerves, I think, turning to him again. Before answering, I take my time pulling out my Luckies and lighting the last one. Taking a big draw, I let out the smoke, crumple the pack, and toss it on the table.

"I don't have any maids, Detective, but my father employs three who live with us." I hold out my hand, using the cigarette as a finger. "One is the head maid, Margaret." I put up my ring finger. "Two is Irma, who does all the cooking and cleans the kitchen and dining room." I wiggle my pinkie. "Ethel is the third. She cared for my mother exclusively, and now does the heavy cleaning with Margaret."

"Ethel. Nice woman," Harrison says. "I spoke with her. Is she an honest person?"

"As far as I'm aware, yes, she is. She ministered to my mother with tenderness."

"Think she's a liar?"

"No, Detective, I do not."

"Well, when I was talking to her this morning, I asked about the Underwood."

"And?"

"And she remembers seeing it."

"You look a bit nervous, Noah. Maybe you should have some more water?"

"I'm quite well, Mr. Hawke, thank you." I turn back to Harrison and resist the urge to loosen my tie. "I suppose this is when you tell me where and when she saw it?"

"In ya bedroom. Two weeks ago."

Harrison's long, beaky nose, obsidian eyes, and tufts of black hair sticking up on his head make him resemble a *Harpia harpyja*—a harpy eagle eyeing a sloth.

"Want that drink now?"

Yes, I think but say no to Harrison and take a draw of the cigarette instead.

"I'm going to ask you again, Noah." Hawke pulls my gaze from Harpy Harrison. "Where is the Underwood?"

I blow out smoke rings to give myself time to gather my thoughts. "No idea. Ethel might've mistaken my Hammond for the Underwood." I lean closer to Hawke across the table. "She's taken to nipping here and there ever since Mother died." Reaching over, I flick ash into the receptacle. "Father keeps her on because she took such fine care of Mother, and he's doubtful that anyone else will tolerate her little habit."

"So ya saying this honest woman is wrong?"

"Did you show her an Underwood, Detective? For comparison?"

His beady eyes glare at me. "No, but she knows the difference between a portable and a regular typewriter."

"Are you sure?" I sit back, confident that I've given a reasonable response. Ethel does, in fact, fancy a drink.

"Viola and Julia."

My shoulders twitch before I control them. "Excuse me, Mr. Hawke, but who are they?"

"Don't the names trigger your memory? They're the girls you and your friend picked up the day Bennie Frisch was kidnapped and murdered."

He stares at me, and so do Sever and Harrison.

"We talked to Roman Loewe, and he remembers their names," Hawke says.

I feel the first twinges of an imaginary noose tighten around my neck.

Chapter 12

Friday, 21 July 1922

FRANNIE AND I sat on a blanket spread out in the grass, our necks stretched back, gazing up at millions of stars glittering in the sky.

We were close enough that our thighs touched—mine encased in tweed, hers in a cotton dress—but the proximity of her body did nothing to me. Not a thing. My frequent date whenever I joined Roman at his family's summer house, she and I spent the last twenty minutes discussing Friedrich Nietzsche. She wasn't well read in his philosophies, so I did my best to educate her beyond the requisite reading expected of every philosophy student attending university. Despite being older than me, she was just beginning her junior year in the fall.

"Noah, are you ever going to, well, when will you—"

"What're you trying to say?"

She glanced down, and her thick lashes—her loveliest feature by far, in my opinion—fluttered as she avoided my stare.

I immediately regretted letting my artfully constructed patience slip. "I'm sorry, Frannie. I didn't mean to bark at you or interrupt you. That was rude. Please continue with what you were saying." I put my cigarette on the grass and tried to ignore the disgusting noises and giggling coming from Roman and Lilly on the opposite side of his father's automobile.

She raised her eyes and caught mine. "I...I...I just wondered if you were ever going to kiss me." She lowered her lashes again.

"Oh." Her question took me by surprise, although it shouldn't have. The two of us had been privy to Roman and Lilly's necking all week. I found it repulsive. Frannie seemed to find it stimulating.

She crossed her arms over her chest. "Is that all you have to say on *this* subject?"

I studied her pleasant face. She had brown eyes, like Roman, but unlike Roman's eyes, hers had no shine or sparkle behind them. No mischievous secrets to unlock. Her button nose and high cheekbones gave her face youth beyond her already young age. As far as attractiveness went, she rated high on my chart. Still, I had no burning desire to kiss her. To allow my lips to touch hers when they weren't the ones I craved.

"I didn't know that you wanted me to." I cringed at how dumb my response sounded.

"Well, I do."

"Oh, ah, all right then, shall I do it now?" A sick feeling in my stomach competed with awkwardness.

"Now is fine."

I swallowed and inched my head closer to hers. Afraid to shut my eyes for fear of missing her mouth and humiliating myself, I kept them open.

Silly-Lilly giggled from the other side of the Cadillac. "Oh, Manny, you're awful!"

His face popped into my head, and Frannie's dull eyes transformed into his exciting ones. Her lips, his, as mine touched on them softly. I pulled back from the contact but stayed a mere whisper away.

"Oh, Noah. Again, please."

She spoke, but I heard and saw Roman—who never allowed kissing.

"That's what dames are for, Babe," he claimed. "They're great for the mushy stuff. They love it."

His holding back the act only made me yearn for it more.

"M-M-M, Frannie," I moaned, catching my slip. With no more talk, I puckered my lips and pretended.

Manny's mouth opened with mine, and our tongues met. Warmth rushed throughout my body as I sang his name in my head, the sound more glorious than any songbird recorded to date. My hands ran through his hair as our lips broke for small pecks on his nose, chin, neck, and back to the mouth. When I moved us so that we lay upon our sides, he gave no resistance. The air around us grew hot.

I nibbled his bottom lip, so full, and—

"Nice to see you kiddies getting along."

Every part of my body froze, and I pulled away. Frannie's face replaced Manny's and the throbbing palpitations in my groin dissipated. I looked up at Roman and Lilly.

"Come on, Frannie," she said, snickering as she reached an arm out and helped her friend stand up. "We only have fifteen minutes before curfew, and we don't want to make Daddy upset."

"Yes, Noah, we mustn't let Daddy get mad at these fine fillies." Roman neighed, pulled Lilly close, and smacked his lips loudly against her cheek, never taking his eyes off mine.

The drive to Lilly's house, where Frannie was spending the night, was awkward for everyone but Lilly. She prattled on about some summer dance that she hoped Roman would take her to if his family remained in Michigan for another couple of weeks. Frannie, cloche in her lap, busied herself with smoothing her hair. Flames flickered in Roman's eyes as they darted to glare at me through the rearview mirror.

We drove away in silence after we left the girls at the front door of Lilly's house, a mere sixty seconds to spare. It took a few minutes before I noticed that Roman was drinking from a bottle.

"Where'd you get that, Manny?"

"Had it under the seat."

"Where's your flask?"

"Right here." He patted his chest. "But I wanna finish this whiskey first." Tipping the bottle back, he guzzled, then turned and held it out to me with a devilish smile. "Care for a nip?"

I took it and swigged. "Watch out for that lamppost!" He straightened out the Cadillac. "Where are we going? This isn't the way to your place."

"Thought we'd have some fun first." He grabbed the hooch back while I was taking another drink.

"Ow, careful."

"Wassa matter, Babe, sore from kissing lil' Frannie?"

"Why do you care? You do enough kissing and other things yourself."

"Huh." He suckled from the bottle as if from a teat. When he drained it, he wiped his mouth on his shoulder, and threw the empty out the window. I heard it hit a parked car and shatter. "Popsie's precious auto's a bit swervy tonight."

"You're 'swervy,' Manny." I looked around at the quiet downtown street. All the shops and places of business were closed. "Pull over and let me drive."

"Nah, I got sumthin' in mind."

He continued to drive, turning west and then east, and I wondered if he had any idea where he was going—but the possibilities of what he could be pondering excited me.

We left the businesses behind and entered a residential area. After a few more minutes of erratic driving, he pulled into the parking lot of a grand church.

"Manny, what are you—"

"Gonna park in back."

"Why?"

"Hide the auto, o' course."

His tone carried an undercurrent of something new, which unleashed a multitude of conflicting feelings inside me. Discomfort. Foreboding. Excitement.

He didn't speak when he shut off the engine or when he got out, just walked toward the front of the church and disappeared into the shadows. I left my hat on the seat and followed, guided by starlight. By the time I reached the house celebrating man's greatest blunder, I saw a massive wooden door closing.

What's the damn fool doing?

I squinted into the night, but nothing or no one stirred, so I entered the ornate wood and stone building. Lit votive candles gave the shrine an eerie feel.

Roman stood on the stone steps leading to the altar. As I walked over to him, he ripped off his jacket and newsboy cap and threw them down. He held up his flask.

"Filled it from the bottle while you were busy necking with frumpy Frannie." He took a sip and then rushed to the lectern and attempted to push it over. The solid wood didn't yield easily, and it took him a few tries to topple it. The resulting crash reverberated throughout the large church. His possessive behavior left me shocked, rooted to the spot.

However, I could speak. "I thought you found Frannie delightful enough," I teased.

"And *I* thought you didn't like necking. Least, that's what you always say when I'm doing it."

He stepped over the elaborately carved black walnut that bore not a splinter or a crack that I could discern and approached the matching pulpit. His eyes had the same glow behind the irises they always got when he committed some crime. Vandalism was one of his favorites. Each time we had been *together*, the act was preceded by some form of illegality. Tonight, it seemed, would be no different. However, he had never been jealous before. This was new, and it pleased me.

His hands flew out but stopped short of pushing the pulpit. He smirked and added his shoulder to the task and knocked it over. Exhilaration coursed through me as I watched him.

Out of the corner of my eye, I spotted the missal, which had landed at the bottom of the steps.

Maybe I'll snatch it, and Manny and I can read it to garner a laugh.

I walked over. "Look at this," I said, bending to pick it up.

"Ah!"

Startled by the unexpected voice, I jumped. A man crawled out from under the pew and stood up.

"Who are you?" I cried. "And what're you doing here?"

"N-n-no one, sir. I…I…I'm jus' sleepin' here for the night." He shuffled along the row. "Thas all. I won't tell nobody 'bout what ya done here. I'm jus' gonna move on now."

I took a step back when his stench reached my nose.

He's obviously a bum.

"Oh, no, you're not going anywhere," Roman said, and he rushed down the steps when the guy reached the aisle. "Who else is here?" He pushed him away from the exit and toward the altar. The hobo tripped over his passenger-liner-like feet but didn't fall.

"N-n-nobody, jus' me."

"Check, Babe."

I nodded and walked up and down the aisle, taking time to peer underneath each line of pews on both sides, but I saw no forms or shapes.

"Empty. Now what?" The look in Roman's eyes made me shiver, but from apprehension or desire, I could not differentiate.

"Well, I'll be leavin' now, boys."

Roman sniffed the air. "Hey, did you piss yourself?" He pointed to a wet spot on the fetid man's trousers. "Look at this, Babe, disgusting rummy pissed himself, and it's running down his leg!"

He shoved him hard and fast. The bum stumbled, and his arms flailed about. His large feet helped balance his upper body, and he steadied himself.

Roman shoved again, and this time, the guy fell in slow motion. His look of surprise transformed into a grimace when his head landed on the edge of the stone steps.

The hobo's skull cracked, and the sound echoed in my mind.

"Let's get outta here," Roman said.

I shook my head to clear it and followed him down the aisle.

"Wait! Your hat and coat." I turned back, walked past the body, careful not to step in the copious amount of blood spreading around his head. The sight made me queasy.

"C'mon, Babe, hurry!"

I grabbed Roman's things and joined him in the vestibule.

"I'm gonna open the door and peek out first," he said, taking a swig from the flask before stashing it in his pocket. "Make sure no one's around."

I didn't trust myself to speak.

He poked his head out, then the rest of him. "Okay, clear."

The sky seemed darker than before, the stars duller, so it took forever to make it back to the car.

"I'm driving," I insisted when we reached it.

"Wrong," he said, and he pushed me away. I recognized the voice. My king. I couldn't refuse, so I got in on the other side.

To his credit, he drove slowly, with the headlights off, until we were down the block, but he sped up and began swerving soon after. More than once, I had to grab onto the dashboard and the door to steady myself. I said nothing to him, nor he to me.

I had tried numerous times but failed to identify what it was that connected the two of us to each other. My attraction to him was so strong it rivaled everything else. I examined my thoughts on the guy left behind in the church.

Am I remorseful?

I looked at Roman, and even though the dark prevented me from seeing his face or the expression on it, I saw his smile in my mind.

No. No remorse.

The tiny hairs on my body rose in unison, making me tremble. What would result from this evening?

When the car stopped, I looked out the window. We had entered the Loewe's lavish property while I'd been lost in thought.

"Go to your room. I'll return Popsie's key to Emil, so he knows we're home," Roman said, winking at me. "Emil will cover for me if he notices I've been drinking." He grabbed my hand and placed it in his lap. "Wait for me no matter how long it takes."

I did as he commanded and sat on the bed, in the dark, shirt off, trousers unbuttoned, for thirty minutes and two-and-a-half cigarettes before I heard a light tap on the door.

Guess he didn't pass out or change his mind, I thought, grinding my cig in the ashtray. My booze gone, I tossed the flask on the nightstand and turned on the lamp.

When I let him in, Manny shoved me out of the way, shut the door, and locked it behind him.

Smiling, he backed me up against an armoire and placed one hand on the side of my head. His flask was in his other. He took a sip and smacked his lips.

Leaning in close, he whispered, "So, Babe, how'd you like it?"

His hot whiskey breath made me shudder.

"D-d-do you mean the hobo?"

His smile infected every part of his face, including his eyes. "Nah, I already know how you feel about that." He pushed his knee into my crotch and rubbed it around. "Just like I do." He dragged me by the arm over to the bed and pushed me onto the mattress. "I meant the mushy stuff with Frannie."

"Oh, ah, well, it was pleasurable."

"Leave it to you, Babe, to make necking sound boring." He handed me his whiskey, and I took a nip.

"Well, how do you like it, Manny?"

He didn't undress, just joined me on the bed and lay facing me. "I like it fine, but they always want you to do more."

"Do you do more?"

"Petting mostly."

I found my nerve. "I pretended that she was you," I confessed.

"I don't want that girly, cuddly stuff with us." He grabbed the flask away from me, drained it, and tossed it onto the floor. Climbing on top of me, he smiled. "But tonight was, well, you felt it, right? Imagine their faces when they go in and find the place trashed and a stinky stiff!"

He grabbed my hands and held them over my head.

Leering, he said, "Time for your reward, Babe."

Chapter 13

Whatever does not kill me makes me stronger.

—Friedrich Nietzsche

Friday night, 30 May 1924, through dawn Saturday, 31 May 1924

"Did you hear me, Noah? Roman says the girls' names are Viola and Julia."

"So, Mr. Hawke, you've spoken to him." I sit back and cross my legs, making a concerted effort to control my muscles and keep my face from twitching. The three men stare at me, all with beads of perspiration pooling around their temples. Cigarette smoke fills the hot, stuffy conference room. Detective Harrison takes off his jacket and slings it over his chair. The sweat stains under his armpits account for the musty odor in here. Of the four of us, I'm the driest in the airless room.

"Yes, we invited Mr. Loewe to join us last night, and he's been chatting with us down the hall," Hawke says.

"Ya buddy also spent some time nappin' in a cell on the other side of the jail," Harrison adds.

Sever doesn't speak, just wipes his face with a handkerchief and stuffs it in his pocket.

"Everything Mr. Loewe told us matches what you've said, Noah, except he remembers the names of the girls. He's quite sure about it, in fact."

"And here ya are with your superior intellect and ya couldn't conjure them up."

"Well then, Detective, my level of investment and interest in them should be obvious even to you." I tap my temple, pretending to think. "The name Viola *is* familiar. Julia is not." I shrug. "I dismissed the chippies from my mind once we deposited them back onto their street corner."

"Oh, yeah, right. Ya got rid of 'em when they wouldn't agree to come across."

"Correct."

"So, after you left the girls, Noah," Mr. Hawke says, "you and Roman drove around some more?"

"First, I went into a pharmacy on Garfield Boulevard and called my father to inform him that I would be late." I smirk. "And Roman got a pack of gum to mask the smell of alcohol on his breath. His parents don't approve of drinking and wouldn't appreciate me bringing him home in such condition. I'm sure Roman told you." I take another draw of my cigarette. "But we didn't drive long, maybe thirty or forty minutes."

"What did you do next?" Hawke asks.

"Went to my house, played cards with my father and my aunt and uncle for about an hour, and then brought Roman home."

"Your friend didn't act so calm when the guys questioning him brought up that rumor, the one being spread regarding you two fellas," Sever says. "Detectives talking to him say he got agitated, yelled, banged his fist on the table."

"Roman can be far more dramatic than I at times."

"He also says ya never sent him no letter."

I speak slowly and deliberately as if to a child. "Of course, I never sent it to him, Detective. If I did, you wouldn't have been able to find it in my bedroom. This stands to reason, does it not?"

Harrison glares at me. I finish the cig and grind it out.

"I composed the letter, and as I'm sure you can discern from the scratch-outs, I edited it and read it to him."

"Why didn't ya mail it?"

I shrug and switch my legs, so the right is over the left. It's useless, though; the chair is still uncomfortable. "Because, Detective, I didn't want anyone else to see it as one could misconstrue its meaning as you did. And since I couldn't be certain that Roman would keep the letter secure, I chose to place a phone call asking him to pick me up. I read the letter to him while he drove."

"Did he answer by correspondence?" Hawke asks.

"We spoke about it later in person, but I can't tell you if he ran off his mouth or penned his response prior."

"The guys who searched his room didn't find any letter," Sever says.

"Then I suppose that's your answer."

"Unlike you, Noah, Mr. Loewe recalls the day quite clearly," Hawke says.

"Which day is this now?"

"The day of the boy's disappearance, and ya damn well know it!"

"Well, Detective, perhaps Roman had fewer exams than I did. I assure you my mind was very occupied that week." I turn to Hawke. "Is this when you tell me what he said?"

"At first, he denied being with you on Wednesday, but then he admitted to spending the afternoon with you. He told my men that you two ate lunch at Edgar's. He further corroborates your account by confessing to drinking too much while you chased birds."

"Roman Loewe also agrees," Sever says, "that the two of you drove around in your nice, sporty automobile for hours."

"And, of course, he told us all about pickin' up those fillies and trying to ride 'em." Harrison chuckles. "And them bucking ya off."

"Charming, Detective."

"About the girls, Noah." Hawke picks up the folder and puts it aside, revealing a Chicago rag. He holds it up. The headline screams: VIOLA AND JULIA—WHERE ARE YOU?

I smirk and shake my head.

"The article goes on to request the public's aid in finding two women who might have been picked up by a couple of young guys in a red Willys-Knight sports car." Hawke slams the paper on the table. Pictures of Roman and myself are splayed across the front pages. More ridiculous headlines about the two wealthy boys being held for questioning in the Bennie Frisch murder case: MILLIONAIRES' SONS ON GRILL; SEEKING CLUES IN CHIROGRAPHY.

"I'm quite sure the calls are pouring in," I say, smirking as I readjust my position in the chair.

"Well, kid, ya got calls from three women who want to take ya home for some mothering." The detective laughs. "But ya buddy got calls from fifteen! And the kinda women who fancy getting their shoes fulla dirt, their hems ripped."

Roman will be thrilled by all the attention, I think, but this comment creates a crack in my meticulously cultivated veneer. I ignore Harrison and reach inside my vest, pull on the fob, and check the time. It's after midnight.

"Okay, Mr. Hawke, it's officially Saturday, which means that I've been accommodating you by answering questions for over thirty hours. With all due respect," I choke out the word, "now it's time for a question of my own. Why am I still here?"

Hawke holds up a fist. His pointer finger shoots up. "Your eyeglasses, proved to be yours and yours alone, were found near Bennie's body."

His middle finger joins the other one. "The ransom note sent to Jonah Frisch was typed on the same machine that your dope sheets were typed on."

The ring finger rises. "A maid residing in your home claims she saw a portable Underwood typewriter in your room two weeks ago, and you have no idea how it got there or what happened to it."

His pinkie goes up, and he wiggles it. "And an oddly worded letter from one boy to another that reads like a lover's spat. The very fella you spent time with on the day Bennie was kidnapped and murdered."

I reach for my water. In part, to show how steady my hands and movements are but mostly because the unventilated room is bothering me. I'm about to request that someone fetch more fans when Sever stands up.

"Be right back," he says.

When he opens the door, air rushes in and dissipates some of the smoky haze surrounding us. The cool waft feels blissful in the stifling environment.

"Leave it open," Hawke calls after Sever.

From my vantage point, I have a clear view of the hallway and can watch for sightings of Roman without straining my head in any direction.

I take a drink and place the glass back down.

"As I explained, Mr. Hawke, my reading glasses must've fallen out prior to the murder."

"A coincidence, huh?"

"An unfortunate one at that. I have no explanation for the typewriter. Might I suggest that your expert is incorrect in his assessment of the implement in question?" I go for stretching logic to the extreme. "As for its whereabouts, maybe someone stole the Underwood from my house in the days or weeks before the crime."

"Ya gotta be kiddin'."

I look at Harrison. "No, Detective, I'm not. A lot of people have been in and out ever since my brother announced his engagement."

"Are you implying that a family or future family member is the culprit?" Hawke says.

"I suppose anything is possible, but I thought one of the various service people who milled about. Father hired help for the dinner parties."

"Do service people venture to the third floor of your home? Are they in the habit of entering your bedroom?"

"No, Mr. Hawke."

"Can ya prove that someone did?"

"No, Detective, I can't." I glare at him. "Can you prove that someone didn't?"

Hawke drums his fingers on the table, and I'm about to make another comment when a familiar figure hurries past the doorway, followed by Deputy Melton. Neither man pauses or glances in this direction.

"Something wrong, Noah? You look paler than usual."

I stick a finger under my collar to loosen it. "I'm fine, Mr. Hawke, it's just very hot in here.

"And I already gave testimony on the letter," I say, returning to the conversation. "Overly dramatic reaction to a misunderstanding."

"Then why does Roman say that the two of you avoid being seen in public?"

I stare at the State's attorney, hating his caricature-like features, particularly his chin.

"His brothers never let him forget the nasty falsehood about the two of us." I shrug, trying to convey indifference that I don't feel. "He thought it best to adhere to certain rules. Limitations on our friendship."

"Then why stay pals at all?" Detective Harrison inquires. "Why not call it quits and go ya separate paths?"

This is the one question that I falter on in the many that have been lobbed at me since Thursday afternoon. Why indeed? How to explain?

A smiling Sever pokes his head in the door. "Bert, can I see you for a minute," he says. His animated eyes dart to me, then back to his boss.

"Excuse me, Noah." Hawke rises, walks to the door, and steps outside, closing it behind him.

I lean back against hard wooden slats and close my eyes to block the harsh lighting. Minutes tick by.

"Ah, ahem."

I open one eye and look at the detective. "What?"

"Do ya really believe the superman can create values that apply to him by his actions?"

Hawke and Sever return before I can respond, and the expressions on their faces as they walk over and stand in front of me stirs something in my stomach.

"Well, Noah," Hawke says. "I just came back from talking with your chauffeur." His chin, so prominent, is quivering.

Ah, Erik, loyal but not smart.

"The man did his duty to the Lieberman family and rushed down here to give information to exonerate you." Hawke's smile erases ten years from his face, but it can't pull in his chin and make him less of a cartoon. "After all, 'how could Master Babe have committed this crime when his automobile sat at home in the garage all day and night on the date in question?' Seems the sporty auto needed brake work, so Mr. Lieberman can't have picked up poor, unfortunate Bennie in his car."

"He is either confused as to the day or a liar. Roman and I drove in my car."

"As a matter of convenience, he took his wife to the doctor on the morning of May 21, 1924. He even brought in the prescription with the date displayed. So, this clears up any confusion about the day. Now, your faithful servant might very well be a liar, Noah, but the problem you have is your good friend, Roman." He pauses and places his hands on his hips. "The one who you spent that entire day and evening with. When we confronted him about Erik's insistence that you two did not drive around in your car on that day, that a portable typewriter known to be in your possession typed the ransom note, and that the eyeglasses found at the scene unequivocally belong to you, well, he gave a full confession to the kidnapping and murder of Bennie Frisch. Along with his pal, Noah Lieberman Jr."

I'm unaware of moving until I'm standing. "Rubbish! I've no idea why Roman would—"

"Don't you? Mr. Herbert Bradford?"

Manny sang like a Crithagra flaviventris, the yellow canary.

Chapter 14

Friday, 24 November 1922

I DROVE MY Willys-Knight down the bumpy trunk line at a speed sure to damage the automobile's suspension, but I wanted to reach our destination before dark.

"Hannigan's Service Station is coming up in Paw Paw," Henry said. He sat in the passenger seat with a map spread out on his lap. "I'm almost positive."

"Good." I glanced at the gauge cluster. "We're going to need gas soon."

Tapping the map, he said, "In less than ten minutes, we can fuel up, eat something, stretch our legs."

"Our cabin in Kalamazoo is only about thirty miles away. Do we need to eat and stretch?"

"Well, maybe we can grab deviled eggs for the rest of the drive. Sandwiches for later. Coffee and hooch won't sustain us, Noah."

"You're right. The cabin's rustic, and the nearest restaurant is ten miles away."

I never considered food on this short trip. My focus is the moment when he leaves and Roman arrives.

Some fancy roadster sped by going in the opposite direction. The occupants waved, honked, and blew kisses as they passed us, kicking up dirt and rocks.

Silly girls.

When Henry finished coughing, he asked, "Do you think they liked us, Noah?"

I laughed and shook my head. "Did I thank you for accompanying me with such little notice, Henry?"

"Oh, the pleasure's mine. A chance to bird-watch during a school break, especially somewhere new, is always something I can't refuse. Harvard's tough," he said, and stress crept into his voice. "You'll find out when you get there."

"Two more years for me, and I'm sure it's difficult, but you have the brains to back up the coveted recommendation you received from an alumnus," I lied.

"Let's hope my uncle's efforts prove fruitful. As I told you, in addition to needing the respite, this weekend's perfect since my sister, her husband, and my niece are visiting home for the Thanksgiving holiday and will be passing by here on their way. I can help entertain the little one for the remainder of their trip to Chicago."

"I must say, you've taken quite naturally to the role of uncle."

The map rustled as he folded it. "Yes, well, it's a shame my brother-in-law is picking me up tomorrow afternoon. It would be nice to also spend Sunday morning in the marshes and around the lake hunting down elusive birdies."

I laughed.

"This is it up ahead," Henry said, pointing out the windshield toward the sign for Hannigan's.

Later, after we fueled the car and ate delicious sandwiches purchased from the service station, we sat around the small kitchen table at the cabin. We built a fire in the fireplace and kept the back door ajar to let cool air mix in with our cigarette smoke. We each sipped a small glass of gin. Neither of us wanted to risk sleeping in, nor did we want a headache when we woke. Our plan to study the early morning rituals of whatever species we were lucky enough to find would work only if we arrived at the lake before dawn.

I pulled on my fob and looked at my watch. "It's nearing ten. I think I'll wash up and go to bed."

"I ran into Tony last weekend at a pool hall."

My face burned as I glared at Henry. "Why do I care anything about that son of a bitch?"

"Yeah, well, he regrets what he said. He likes Roman." He smirked. "Says he still thinks you're a strange bird."

"You can inform Tony when you talk to him again that I owe him five knuckles on his chin, and I intend to pay my debt."

Henry laughed, hands up, palms out. "All right, all right, but Tony's leading some to believe that you followed Roman to Ann Arbor like a love-sick puppy dog."

The expression on Henry's face gave credence to his joking manner, but the hairs on my body bristled regardless.

I took a long drag and blew out smoke rings. "Insufferable fool. No, I envied Roman's ability to up and leave. Thought it was time for me to do the same since I'd never lived away from home before." I allowed a sly smile to slip out. "However, enrolling somewhere where I knew no one intimidated me a bit. And Michigan is close enough for trips home."

I winked at him. "The great thing about Roman is his proximity to the fairer sex. I wrangled a few double dates out of our friendship."

Henry drained his glass and stood up. "Time to visit the outhouse," he said and took his leave.

After we went to bed, I tossed about. The lumpy mattress poked into my back and hips. Despite excitement over what we might discover with the light of day—perhaps a pied-billed grebe or, even better, a rare Iceland Gull—thoughts of Roman kept me agitated. I fluffed the pillow, punched it, and flipped it over. Tony's assessment on why I transferred to the University of Michigan had been correct, of course. Roman, fearful others would catch on, decided after weeks of going out on double dates that we couldn't be seen in public together at all. Therefore, we met secretly once a week.

And Herbert Bradford was born.

Claiming to be a traveling salesman, I rented a room for us at the Ann Arbor Suites at least half a dozen times. I always requested a room near the service exit so "Mr. Bradford" didn't disturb people with late arrivals and departures.

The nights in between our encounters were endless, but I spent the days going to classes, debating—winning the debates—studying, and taking exams. Fighting the hollow over and over. My reward came when Roman walked off campus in the thick of night after dropping off his girl du jour and I picked him up. Only when he jumped into the seat and flashed his chase-the-devil smile did I feel energized, filled with life. What excitement would he have in mind?

Roman's thrills came from some sort of adventure or crime. He spoke of his fascination with novels like Frank Packard's *The Beloved Traitor* and *The Adventures of Jimmie Dale*. His obsession with Wyndham Martini's *Anthony Trent, Master Criminal* rivaled my infatuation with Nietzsche.

Each meeting had been precipitated by some act of vandalism in the dead of night: walking down empty streets smashing headlights and bumpers with a bat, throwing bricks through storefront windows, arson. We stopped using the hotel after deciding not to push our good fortune further.

For me, I longed to touch him, press against his skin, and become one with him. Together, our brilliant minds could rule the world.

I flipped over to rest on my back. Henry's snores from the next room resonated through the wall. I placed the pillow over my head. No use.

There's only one way to ensure slumber at this juncture, I thought, unbuttoning my pajamas.

My hand sought release as my thoughts drifted to our last time at the hotel. As I stroked myself, memories flooded my mind: Returning to "Herbert Bradford's" room after setting fire to the gazebo in the park. Roman's conspiratorial laughter in my ear. The drunken noises from the other patrons and the wail of sirens.

As the reward I received from my king for being his loyal slave replayed in my mind, my pleasure grew, intensified. Release in the past triggered an explosive one in the present, and I buried my face in the pillow to muffle the cries that were engaged in a surreal concert with Henry's snores.

* * *

"Shh," I said, my breath fogging in the cool air as I half turned to face Henry. The dim lighting made trudging through the brush in rubber boots challenging, but our tin flashlights kept us from tripping. "We're nearing the edge of the lake. We'll find a log to sit behind and keep watch."

He didn't answer, just followed, his beam sneaking around me every few steps. When we found a suitable place to wait, we each poured a cup of joe from our thermoses and sipped the bitter coffee in silence.

Nature began awakening as I finished my first helping. Familiar songs chirped and twittered from tree to tree, and I closed my eyes to enjoy the symphony. After a few minutes, I reopened them. The sun was poking up over the horizon and orange overpowered the dark sky. A yelp came from the distance.

Dropping the cup and spilling the last few sips onto the cold ground, I brought field glasses to my eyes.

Another yelp, one distinct in its musical parroting. I scanned the area.

"Is it a Golden Eagle?" Henry whispered. "But, how can it be this late in the season?"

"Quiet." I glared at him. He knew better, but since he spoke first, I responded. "Yes, *Aquila chrysaetos*. Recognizable by the fluty—"

A different, more stressed flute tooted, and I motioned for Henry to stay down while I scanned the shoreline.

Two of them, but where?

The answer filled my lenses. A large adult female stood at the edge of the lake, behind a pile of twigs and muck. Next to her was her mate, the obvious reason the pair had not yet migrated south to Kentucky or Tennessee. The male's wing jutted out in an awkward position, likely broken and healing wrong.

An excellent addition to my growing collection, I thought, frustrated that I left my rifle in the car. I'd brought it along despite not being allowed to possess a gun without a license in Michigan. But this fella might be easy to snare.

"Move over, Noah, so I can get a better look."

Henry stood up, tripped, fell over the log, and crashed noisily on the other side. The eagles' angry squawks reverberated as they took flight. Although the male stayed low and struggled, he followed the female across the lake, and they burrowed deep into the trees.

* * *

Later in the afternoon, Henry and I stood outside waiting for his sister and her child to finish using the outhouse. The prude's face had paled when she learned that the rugged cabin offered no indoor facilities, but need had outweighed want. Her impatient husband sat in the driver's seat of a 1920 Nash Touring car, tapping his fingers against the steering wheel after throwing a cursory nod my way at our introductions.

"Again, I'm awfully sorry about scaring off those eagles this morning," Henry said. He scratched the top of his head. "I don't know what happened. I just…well, I fell."

"Don't worry about it," I told him, but I was angry. We had waited, practically immobile, for six hours, and the Goldens never made a reappearance.

"Will you go back tomorrow to look for them?"

"Possibly."

Henry's sister emerged; her face puckered as if she'd eaten a lemon. She pulled her daughter behind her and rushed toward the car.

"Uh, well, thanks, Noah. See you."

"Yes, Henry, safe travels. Goodbye," I said to the couple and nodded to their child.

Dust swirled, dulling the blue paint on their auto as they sped down the road.

I went inside, relieved that the boors finally left. Roman was due to arrive soon. A chill ran through me. I pulled my jacket tighter and went to the small stove in the corner, opened the damper, and threw in a few pieces of wood from the pile on the floor. Satisfied the room would be warm when he got here, I sat down, leaned back in the chair, and put my feet up on the table. What would tonight bring? Arson had, by far, been our worst act of vandalism, but nothing seemed to give Roman the thrill he craved.

Not like with the stowaway on the train or the old hobo in the church. But we agreed not to do anything like that again. Well, I had to convince him of the foolishness of such dangerous endeavors, and after getting angry and not speaking to me for over two weeks, he had acquiesced.

I checked the time.

He was late.

Sighing, I reached for my deck of Luckies and lit a cigarette.

I smoked most of the pack before admitting to myself that he wasn't showing up.

Chapter 15

> If one would have a friend, then must one also be willing to wage war for him: and in order to wage war, one must be capable of being an enemy.
>
> —Friedrich Nietzsche, *Thus Spoke Zarathustra*

Just before dawn, Saturday, 31 May 1924

FIRST REACTIONS CAN make or break a case. If a suspect of a crime dares to allow any emotion to escape his bear-trap mind and play out on his face, the enemy will pounce with teeth bared, claws extended. Stoicism is tantamount to survival.

Although I keep my face under control, my legs tremble, so I grip the edge of the table for support.

"Sit down, Noah," Hawke nearly sings.

"I don't believe you," I say, taking his suggestion. "Who's Herbert Bradford?"

"Ah, c'mon, ya practically fainted. Ya must know who Mr. Hawke's talking about."

I glare at the detective. "I did not almost faint, and I never heard the name Herbert Bradford before."

"Mr. Bradford rented a car at the U-Drive on South Side Street," Hawke continues. "A nice green Willys touring auto. The good fella keeps an account at Union State Bank over on Ninety-Second Street and likes to stay at the Grande Hotel on Sixty-Seventh when visiting town. A traveling salesman, Mr. Bradford is. Any of this triggering your memory, Noah?"

"I'm afraid not."

"Well, how about a Plumb hammer with the Hickory handle cut down to seven inches and taped off to prevent splinters?"

Without conscious thought, my hand reaches for the fresh deck of Luckies on the table. I tap out a cigarette and gaze past them, thinking.

It's true, Roman confessed.

"Want to hear more?" Sever asks as I'm framing my next statement.

I shrug, light the cig, and toss the lighter on the table.

"Two red hots and a can of pop apiece at Paul's Hot Dog Stand while Bennie's body lay wrapped in an auto blanket in the back seat of the touring car. Any of this familiar?"

The room goes quiet, but I'm roaring inside.

"A stenographer is typing Mr. Loewe's account now," Hawke says. "Would you care for me to bring a stenographer in here? I took the liberty of rousing a fella out of his bed just for you, Noah. But don't answer right away. We'll give you a few minutes of privacy to make sure of your decision." He nods to Harrison and Sever. "Marv, Jim."

They exit, but it isn't necessary. I am aware, though, that this will be the last time I'll be alone. From now on, someone will always be keeping some sort of controlled watch over me. Until I'm hanged.

Hawke, Sever, and Harrison return as I'm blowing out my first set of smoke rings. A man comes in behind them, carrying a bulky case. Curly red hair spills out from under his derby, and the hem of his dark shirt is untucked. He sets the case on the table, opens it, and pulls out a Stenotype machine.

"Noah," Hawke says. "This gentleman will take your confession now if you're ready."

I nod. "I suppose, since Roman confessed, I shall do the same."

The man sets up his machine and sits down.

Everyone else takes a seat, Hawke to my right.

"Okay, Noah," Hawke begins, picking up his fountain pen and scratching on a notepad. "State your full name, date of birth, and address."

"Noah Freudenthal Lieberman Jr., November 19, 1904. I reside at 1137 Greenwick Avenue."

"Who resides in the house with you?"

"My father, Noah F. Lieberman Sr., and my older brothers Saul and Levi. And my cousin, Manfred Felder, who came to live with us when his parents died. I consider him to be another brother."

"You're a student, correct?"

"Yes."

"Please list your schooling history."

"Starting when, sir?"

Hawke rubs his prominent chin and says, "At the beginning."

"Very well. At age five, I attended the Spade Institution of Learning for two years."

"Isn't that a school for girls? Ya went to a school for girls?"

"Strike that from the record," Hawke says to the stenographer. He throws down his writing implement and snaps at Harrison, "This is an official confession, Marv! I ask the questions, and if you can't keep your trap shut, then leave."

I delight in the detective's discomfort as he hangs his head.

"Afterward, I went to the Douglas School for four years. After that, five years at the Dravah School." I glare at Harrison. "For *boys*. I skipped my senior year of high school and went to the University of Chicago. I transferred to Michigan for one year, and then went back to Chicago. The last nine months, I've been attending the University of Chicago Law School." I smirk. "Harvard Law is supposed to be next in September, provided I passed the entrance exams I took last week, and I'm positive I did."

No one comments, but Harrison's lip curls into a nasty smile.

"You stated earlier that your father employs three full-time maids who also reside in your home."

"Yes, Mr. Hawke. Margaret, Irma, and Ethel. I assumed you meant family when you asked me this question."

"What is your father's business?"

"He owns Morrison Lumber Mills."

"All right. Now, Noah, please tell me about the events in your own words. When did you begin planning?"

"Oh, sometime in late November. We struggled with the kidnapping aspect, although I'm sure Roman left this part out. He fancies himself quite the crime afficionado due to his voracious appetite for detective novels and such."

"Who came up with the idea of kidnapping a child for ransom?"

"Roman."

"What about killing the boy?"

"Also, Roman, but I agreed since we couldn't risk the boy turning us in to the authorities."

"All right, the money."

"What about it, Mr. Hawke?"

"How did you decide on what amount to ask for?"

I shrug. "Ten thousand is a nice, even sum. I think I brought it up, and Roman agreed. How to notify the father and how to get the money led to discussions on methods, however. We came up with a few plots between us but settled on using City Railroad for him to toss the money from. We picked an obscure area near the end of the line by a factory."

"Which one?"

"The Chesterfield Plant."

"And the, ah, notification system, Noah?"

"This proved trickier since it needed to be convoluted enough to keep the father moving and not afford him time to fill the police in on what he was doing. Our initial contact with the family would be a phone call telling them to wait for further instructions in the morning. Then we put a ransom note into a mailbox using overnight delivery postage that we purchased earlier."

"Who typed it?" Hawke asks.

"Roman dictated, and I did the typing."

"Tell me what it said."

"Well, as you know, for the safe return of his son, we demanded ten thousand in small denominations. Seven thousand in fifty-dollar bills and three thousand in twenty-dollar bills. Old bills only, and none of them marked. We told him to place the money in a large cigar box, tied and wrapped in white paper, and await our call at twelve forty-five in the afternoon. During that conversation, we would send him to the Save our City sanitation receptacle on Lexington Avenue. There, taped under the lid, he'd find a note sending him to a phone booth in a specific pharmacy on Thirty-Second Street for his final instructions.

"We wanted him to arrive at the train with only enough time to purchase a ticket and board. Once onboard, he was to proceed to the rear where he would find, adhered to the bottom of the last seat, another directive, this one telling him when to throw out the package."

My throat's dry, so I stop speaking and take a sip of water. "After we established the how, we needed to figure out the who."

"Are you saying, Noah, that you didn't have a victim in mind at this juncture?"

"No, Mr. Hawke, we didn't. Our only requirement was that the boy's father be wealthy enough to pay the ransom."

"And you had no particular child in mind when you began planning this back in late November?"

"No, sir, but I believe, at the very beginning, we did throw around a few names."

"Such as?"

"Daniel Fishman, son of David, who owns a few vaudeville places downtown. Also, Walter Coleman, whose father owns multiple restaurants in Chicago. But we dismissed them for one reason or another and left it to chance on the day."

"So, you typed the ransom note beforehand but left the envelope blank?"

"Yes. Roman and I drafted the letter two nights prior and addressed it as 'Dear Sir,' intending to fill in the envelope on the day."

"For the record, Roman who?"

"Roman Loewe. He and I drove around—"

"What day is this?"

"Wednesday the twenty-first of May 1924. We shadowed a couple possibilities, but they didn't work out. I was heading north down Essex Avenue when I spotted a boy by himself, walking south. Kid turned out to be Bennie Frisch, a friend of Roman's brother. He got in the back while I turned around, and we pulled up behind the boy. I didn't see anyone else nearby, so I reached across the seat and opened the door. Roman leaned forward and asked him if he wanted a ride."

"Excuse me, Noah, where was this?"

"Close to Forty-Nineth Street. Bennie refused our offer, said he was almost home anyway. Roman claimed that he wanted to talk about some racket the kid used when he played tennis with Roman's youngest brother at their house."

"When?"

"I believe he said a week or so prior. Likely on the weekend. In any event, the boy got into the car. Roman introduced me and asked him if he minded a spin around the block to discuss the racket. Bennie said no."

"What occurred next?"

"I turned down Fiftieth, and as I did so, Roman pulled the boy into the back, placed a hand over his mouth, and hit him several times with a hammer we fashioned for the occasion."

"Where did you get the hammer?"

"He purchased it at a hardware store at the corner of Cove Avenue and Twenty-Third Street. Granger's, I believe."

"What kind of tape did you use on the handle, Noah, and where did you buy it?"

"Zinc oxide, and I found it in my brother's bathroom at home.

"The boy struggled and moaned more than we anticipated," I continue, "so Roman stuffed a rag in his mouth to quiet him. When the boy stilled, Roman covered him with an automobile robe I brought along and got back into the front seat. I drove out into the country, near the Indiana border to a remote, swampy area that's a nice place to spot a double-crested cormorant or a blue-winged warbler. There, we stopped, removed the boy's shoes, stockings, and trousers."

"Why did you remove these articles of clothing?"

"To save time later when we disposed of the body."

A disgusted snort comes from Detective Harrison, but he doesn't speak. Sever, an unlit stogie hanging from the corner of his mouth, says nothing as well. Both wear the same expressions on their faces that Hawke is wearing, horror mixed with excitement.

"What did you do with them?"

"Buried them under grass and bushes. I took the shoes and belt about fifty feet into the woods off a spur road near the Indiana border, and Roman hid the trousers on the other side of the road."

"Then what, Noah?"

"Drove around waiting for dark. We were hungry, so I stopped at a small roadside joint. Grabbed a couple red hots and two bottles of root beer."

"And can you confirm where Bennie was while ya ate hot dogs?"

Hawke glares at Harrison but says nothing to him. The detective jumps up and starts pacing the room.

"In the back seat of the Willys."

"When did you boys decide where to dispose of the body?" Hawke asks.

"Oh, I knew at the outset." I look down at the forgotten cigarette in my hand. The ash is an inch long, so I flick it into the receptacle on the table and take a draw. "I bring my bird-watching students out to Fox Lake often and am familiar with the area. The wetlands in the forest preserve are an ornithologist's utopia, wading migratory birds and exotica like the snowy egret in the spring. The variety of tree and flora species makes it a magical spot." I rub my thumb over the filter and stare into Bertram Hawke's magnified eyes. "The area's distance from the city and lack of public transportation struck me as a good hiding place. Seems I was mistaken."

"Ain't that an understatement," Harrison grumbles.

"Please continue, Noah."

"When we reached the disposal area, I parked off the road and changed into hip boots that were in the car."

"Whose boots, yours or Roman's?"

"Mine, Mr. Hawke. I grabbed a flashlight, which I also brought with me, and the two of us carried the body to the culvert."

"Still in the robe, which is the auto blanket, correct?"

"Yes. We used the robe as a stretcher. I believe Roman carried the head while I carried the feet. We placed the body on the ground near the culvert and finished undressing it."

"Is this when you poured acid on Bennie's face and genitals?"

"Yes, sir."

"Who did the pouring?"

"Me. I bought hydrochloric acid at a pharmacy down the street from the hardware store where Roman purchased the hammer. Actually," I correct myself, "they didn't have any at the first drug store, so I went to another one farther down on Cove."

"What was the purpose of the acid?"

"To make identification difficult were the boy to be found before we received the ransom money."

"The genitals?"

"Again, identification purposes. I hoped to make it impossible to tell if he was circumcised."

"Then what, Noah?"

"We picked up the body again, and this time, I took the head and Roman the feet. When we got to the culvert, I climbed down and stuffed it inside."

"Did you have any trouble?"

"Yes, Mr. Hawke, I did have difficulty, but I managed. We went to the opposite end of the culvert where the water comes out and cleaned our hands."

"They were bloody? So, Bennie bled profusely?"

"There was quite a bit of blood, and the auto blanket was saturated."

"What did you do with the clothes and the robe?"

"I gathered the boy's remaining clothing inside the robe, and Roman picked up my jacket from the ground where I'd left it."

"When did you take it off?"

"Before I poured the acid."

"This is probably when the glasses fell from your pocket."

"I assume so, Mr. Hawke. We put the robe in the car and started toward home. I stopped at a drug store in the area to ring my father and tell him that I would be detained."

"What time?"

"Around ten o'clock. Roman came in with me and looked up Jonah Frisch in the telephone directory. I wrote down the number on a slip of paper and copied the address on an envelope, which I posted to Frisch. We then went to Roman's house and burned the clothes in his furnace."

"What about the auto robe, Noah?"

"No, it would've smelled too much, so we hid the blanket outside by the greenhouse shed to contend with later. Roman fetched up a pail, soap, and a brush, and we cleaned stains off the seat and carpet as best as we could in the dark."

"When did you phone the Frisch house?"

"After we gave up washing the car. I made the call since I can make my voice deeper and less distinctive than Roman can. We then parked the rental down the street from my house, went inside, drank, and played cards with my father, aunt, and uncle."

"The time?"

"Oh, about eleven-thirty I would say. I drove my aunt and uncle home soon after, and Roman came with me."

"Did you take the rental?"

"No. Erik had fixed my brakes, so we took my car. But earlier, we threw the hammer out the window."

"You can show me where?"

"Yes, Mr. Hawke. The next day, Roman came over and drove my car while I drove the rented touring car."

"Both vehicles are a Willys?"

"Correct. We returned the automobile, and I took him home and went to school. I had class in the morning, so we met afterward, had lunch, and proceeded with our plans. However, when we arrived at the Save our City sanitation box on Lexington, where we had added a stop into the ransom note, the box was full. We didn't want to risk taping the letter to the lid only to have the city take it away, so we decided to omit this part of the plan and tell Mr. Frisch to go directly to the phone booth at the drugstore on Thirty-Second Street and wait for our next call at one forty-five."

"He didn't catch the address," Hawke says.

"Pardon?"

"The numbers. When you called, Mr. Frisch either didn't hear them or couldn't recall them. He didn't know which pharmacy to go to. Remember, he was quite flustered."

"Really? He sounded perfectly calm." I shake my head. "Well, then I drove us to the train station where we purchased tickets, boarded, and installed the note under the last seat. But things went wrong soon after. Roman, out of cigarettes, wanted to stop at a newsstand, and that's when we saw the headlines about an unidentified nude body, a boy, found near the tracks."

"So much for ya cabbage, huh?"

"Shut up and sit back down, Marv," Hawke says. "Continue, Noah."

"We still tried to collect, called the pharmacy twice, but Frisch never showed. This is when we knew the boy had been identified."

"Did you dispose of the auto blanket and typewriter then?" Hawke asks.

"No, not until Friday evening. We pried the keys off the Underwood with pliers, put the keys in a bag, and tossed them into the lagoon off the north bridge near the Palace of Fine Arts. The typewriter went into the outer harbor on the east side. I soaked the blanket with gasoline out in a little clearing in Washington Park and burned it. Damn thing wouldn't turn to ash, so I hid the blackened remains under some leaves."

"Can you find the places where you disposed of the shoes, belt, and trousers?"

"Yes. The boy's school pin is with the trousers."

"So, Noah, what time would you say you put Bennie in the drainage pipe?"

"About nine thirty in the evening."

"And when did you pick him up on the street?"

"That would have been approximately five fifteen, Mr. Hawke."

"Can you estimate when you believe young Bennie died?"

"Five seventeen." I sit back and cross my legs.

Hawke stares at me from behind his round spectacles. "Well, Noah, as far as the planning of and the events leading up to and after the murder of Bennie Frisch goes, you and Mr. Loewe tell corroborating stories." He leans closer, extending his comical chin forward. "Only difference is Mr. Loewe claims that *he* was driving the rented auto and *you* struck the blow that killed the boy."

Chapter 16

Early Sunday morning, 26 November 1922

SOMETHING STARTLED ME awake. My feet slipped from the chair I had them propped on, and they fell to the floor.

"What the...," I mumbled and looked around. *Where am I?* A full ashtray sat on the table, a nearly empty deck of Luckies and lighter positioned next to it. I rubbed my eyes and pulled out my watch: four nineteen in the morning.

How can I see in the dark?

Headlights. The realization hit me just as the light shining through the window went out.

Damn, rifle's still in my car.

A door slammed, and I heard cursing before, "Open up, Babe!"

Roman's voice, slurred and forceful, sent shivers of relief and exhilaration throughout me. He did show up. Tardy and inebriated it would seem, but he showed up. I turned on the lamp, went to the door, and opened it.

"You cocksucker!"

The word slapped me as he bunched my shirt in his fist and pushed me back into the room. Kicking the door shut behind him, he screamed, "You followed me to Michigan like a damn girl, and now you're ruining everything!"

I flinched, not only from his sour alcohol and deviled egg breath, but from the "girl" comment. I'd confided in him about attending a school for the opposite sex when I was five. Mother had enrolled me hoping to instill a more feminine side to her third son, perchance? Or perhaps she wished for a daughter like Saul implicated on numerous occasions. No matter, Roman's remark stung.

"Remove your hand, Manny. You're wrinkling my shirt."

"Ha," he spat, spraying me with spittle before shoving me again. "Should slug you. Don' think I won't." He advanced but stumbled and grabbed the edge of the table to balance himself.

"Why are you so aggrieved now? We've been through this already and worked things out. We're careful."

"I'm not talkin' about being careful. I'm talkin' about why you came to Michigan in the first place."

"I already explained that I needed a break from Chicago and—"

"Bull! You don't fool me, Babe. Tony either. He knows why you came, and guess what? Now, the fellas in my fraternity are warning me, telling me they hear rumors about you being a Nance. Stay away from me or else."

"What are you scared of, Manny? That the guys might kick you out of your coveted fraternity? Afraid they won't believe their own eyes when you neck with every filly who prances your way? Chase every looker who crosses your path?" All the hurt and frustration at witnessing him parade around with silly girl after silly girl erupted inside me. "Catching a dose at a cat house isn't enough evidence of your manhood?"

"Jeez, juss go back to Chicago!"

Another verbal slap. I shook my head. "Why? We don't go out on double dates anymore and aren't seen together. Besides, you need me, Manny. Who will keep your secrets?"

His eyes darkened, and the smile he turned on and off hardened into a menacing grimace. "Keep your mouth shut 'bout everything if you know what's good for you. And go home, superman," he screamed, and he kicked the table leg.

That's Übermensch, I thought but said nothing as he tottered out the door and disappeared into the dark. His car started, and I heard tires crush dirt and stone before a thud. I walked over to the window. My heart felt pierced by the beak of an *Ardeidae* as I watched him drive away from the tree he'd hit. The heron released me, leaving puncture wounds, and a throbbing chest in its wake.

It wasn't that Manny left, blotto, when he shouldn't be operating an automobile that caused me to reach for my own bottle. No, I finished the gin mourning the loss of love. Or, at least, what had been love for me.

* * *

Saturday, 10 February 1923

"Do you regret transferring back to good ole U of C, Noah?"

I paused in my search. Henry and I stood in my study before a floor-to-ceiling bookshelf. The change of topic took me off guard, because we'd been discussing the possibility of returning to the Au Sable River to retrace Norman Wood's 1903 expedition in search of the Kirtland's warbler. The two of us, along with another birding chap, went on a five-day trip last year, and although we heard the Kirtland's excited, low chirp, thick vegetation prevented us from spying the elusive songbird. Henry wanted to study up on the warbler and came over to borrow a book.

"Gee, Henry, I thought you might ask if my father will sponsor another expedition to Oscoda County this summer. We can find the Kirtland's this time, I'm certain. What brought about this subject change?"

He fingered the label on a *Buteo jamaicensis*, the red-tailed hawk, that sat on my desk. My growing specimen displays were everywhere: inside and atop multiple glass-fronted china cabinets, on shelves, windowsills, a dropleaf table.

"Oh, I don't know, Noah. Guess I'm rethinking Harvard, so I wonder if you ever have regrets too."

"No, running from Mother's death, and my home, wasn't the right decision for me, so I came back to Chicago."

"Roman sure seems to be having fun in Ann Arbor," Henry said. "Turning into a boozehound."

"According to Levi, he's enjoying his second year at Michigan."

"How does Levi know?"

"He's friends with Emil Loewe. The two frequent some of the same speakeasies. From the reports my brother shared, I gather that Zeta Beta Tau agrees with Roman's lifestyle. I never did go for the fraternity nonsense. Too infantile and cultish." I kept the proper muscles busy, keeping an impassive look on my face, and maintained the nonchalant attitude I had adopted for dealing with the topic of Roman. An attitude that cost me every time, even though I grew better at pretending with each passing day. But the lash of pain in my stomach remained a lingering presence.

"Tony says he and Jim saw Roman at some frat party when they were visiting Jim's cousin who goes to the University of Michigan. Said Roman is wilder than ever and boozing a lot. He's dizzy with one dame or another but always winds up passing out on them." Henry winked. "Of course, Tony says plenty of fillies are lined up to take their place. Sly chap does well with the fairer sex." He shook his head. "Wish I had some of his luck."

"Don't talk to me about Tony, that scallywag," I said, but Henry's casual remark about how Roman's dates ended stirred feelings I fought hard every day to suppress. "Anyway, Roman's flagrant cocksmanship behavior caused me a good deal of embarrassment with our double dates. My lady friend inevitably took it out on me when his date ended up with hurt feelings. This behavior is why I don't regret coming back to Chicago." I returned to searching for the volume I thought would be the most useful to Henry. "Nor do I regret my decision to leave in the first place."

"Understandable. So, you don't speak to him?"

"Not in some time. I've been busy. I told you that I'm translating works for one of my literary clubs. They asked me to do it because I speak and write in both Latin and Greek."

"Geez, Noah, when do you find time? How many courses are you taking this quarter?"

"Four, plus I'm in an undergraduate society devoted to Italian culture and other clubs."

"Well, I don't know how you're doing it. I can barely keep up at Harvard."

"Is that why you took a hiatus and hopped on trains to come home midsemester?"

"Yes," Henry answered, but he wouldn't meet my eyes.

I found the correct book and slipped it from its slot. "Here, this should be helpful. Don't worry about returning it right away. I won't need it until the summer when I begin working on a couple of scientific papers I intend to submit for publication to *The Aux*." I winked. "I hope to go on another expedition to find the Kirtland's warbler, and I can write about that as well."

"Wow," he said, shaking his head as he accepted the book. "Well, thanks again, Noah. See you soon." He waved the heavy volume at me and left.

I stood at the door long enough for him to go downstairs and exit, catching sight of him out the window as he walked through the gate toward his roadster at the curb. Instead of going out for a short while with my field glasses as I planned for the late afternoon, I went to my mahogany rolltop desk and sat in the tallback chair. I lit a cigarette and gazed around the room in which I felt the most comfortable.

"Henry and his infernal gossip, stirring up reflections best left locked away." The *Limnodromus griseus hendersoni* I addressed did not respond. The short-billed dowitcher just stared blankly ahead, its pale orange chest puffed out, beady black eyes devoid of opinion on the subject.

I had not seen Roman since that fateful night at the cabin. Unable to deal with my emotions after he left, I drank gin until I passed out. The next morning, I began the long drive home. Although I knew he meant what he said, I couldn't help hoping that he might change his mind and contact me.

No such communication came.

The loneliness has been unbearable.

Ash dropped in my lap, and I looked at the cigarette, having forgotten that I lit one. Taking a long drag, I held it in, rubbed my thumb against the sticky butt, and let out a few smoke rings.

"However, I got over it and didn't let his behavior affect mine," I assured the medium-sized shorebird, who still showed no interest in my wallowing.

Is this true though?

After I returned to the University of Chicago last autumn, I attacked all my classes with determination and excelled in everything, including Classical Greek, Latin, Russian, Romance Languages, and Sanskrit. This term, I enrolled in more than the normal course load. Instead of dulling, the lure of ornithology grew stronger with time.

Every moment of my life since Roman rejected me can't be spent thinking about him if I keep myself so busy. A necessary evil for living one's life without the ingredient that makes life itself worth living.

I glanced out the window. Snow was falling—flurries—but the sky promised that they would get heavier and continue throughout the evening. I took another draw of my cigarette before grinding the butt in the ashtray.

Rising, I shook my head at the colorful male dowitcher that I bagged and stuffed myself. "No more self-pity. If I were merely of acceptable intellect and standing, then perhaps I could enjoy the luxury of the common man's emotion." I checked my watch and was surprised to see how much time had passed since Henry left. "I can make it to the dance at the university. An evening away from studying will prove beneficial, I'm sure."

Levi opened the door and came inside as I descended the staircase. He wiped his feet on the entrance rug, removed his wet hat and overcoat, and placed them on the coat tree.

"Oh, hello, Babe," he said when I fetched my fedora. "Are you going out?"

"Yes, I decided to attend a dance at the university."

His eyebrows rose, but he erased the surprised look from his face and said, "Well, that's great. The roads are fine for now, but the *Tribune's* reporting a few inches by morning. You shouldn't have trouble driving such a short distance."

I sat on the bench to attach spats to my boots and then donned my wool overcoat. "I remember your driving instructions, which happened to be in the winter months."

He laughed. "Father gave up trying to teach you after you slid into a lamppost. You went to your rooms, and he fixed himself a cocktail. 'Levi,' he said. 'I taught you and Saul to drive. Your cousin, as well. As the oldest child, I am now bestowing the task of instructing Babe to you.' Then he took his drink into the library and shut the door."

My face burned. "Yes, well, Father was a horrible instructor. You didn't hold onto your derby while gripping the door handle, making me nervous like he did."

Levi clapped me on the shoulder. "You mastered the skill like a natural, and I have confidence in your ability to make the ten-block journey safely. Have fun." He patted his flat stomach and headed in the direction of the kitchen. "Now, I'm going to find Margaret and have her fix me a plate of that delicious roast chicken from the other night."

I didn't have the heart to tell him that I had eaten the last of the leftovers earlier. "Good night, Levi."

The short drive took no longer than usual despite the slushy road, and I saw as I neared that no snow stuck to the red-tiled dormitory roofs on the impressive Gothic-inspired, limestone structures.

I entered the building hosting the dance, followed blaring music down the hall to the gymnasium, and opened the door. A swing band played. Girls wearing colorful dresses with low waists and short hemlines gyrated with boys in cuffed trousers and vivid argyle socks. Oxfords, suspenders, and ties competed with fancy jeweled headbands, feather boas, and scandalously high heels. I took off my spats, overcoat, and hat and found an available hook in the coat room.

Looking around, I spied a few people I knew. My good friend, Dick Renford, stood by the punch bowl, speaking to someone unfamiliar. I spotted a table full of girls from *Il Circolo Italiano*, the society devoted to studying Italian culture that I told Henry about. I sidestepped dancers to walk over, intending to say hello to the group.

Before I reached their table, I noticed a girl standing alone at one of the interior doorways. Her blue and cream-colored dress hung well below her knees, and she wore white gloves and dainty pearls around her neck. None of those things caught my attention. She had smiled at something or someone I didn't see, and that brought about a tightness in my chest.

She has Manny's carefree grin!

Rerouting, I nodded to the table I'd intended to stop at and clapped Dick on the shoulder when I passed by him, still engrossed in conversation.

I studied her as I neared. Her dark hair, parted on the left, was set in waves that hugged the side of her head and reached just below her ears.

"Hello," I said when the song ended. "My name's Noah Lieberman. I wonder if you'll allow me to get you a drink?"

She turned away from the dancers, faced me, and smiled, revealing substantial dimples in her cheeks. "Thanks, that would be nice. I'm Sally Lord."

Up close, her quick, infectious grin hit me in the gut. Sally looked nothing like him, and yet, when she smiled...

The band started another song.

"Would you care to dance instead, Noah?"

I, a philologist and linguist, could not form words. So overcome by emotion, all I managed was a nod.

Chapter 17

You have your way. I have my way. As for the right way, the correct way, and the only way, it does not exist.

—Friedrich Wilhelm Nietzsche

Saturday, 31 May 1924

I CLAMP MY teeth together so I don't shout out, but my face burns. For the first time since I began the habit, I grind my cigarette in the ashtray before smoking it all the way down.

"Got nothing to say now, smart guy?"

"Yes, Detective Harrison. I didn't kill the boy. Roman is lying. The rotter!" I sneer. "Not that it matters anyway because two will hang from the gallows as easily as one, right?" Harrison doesn't answer, so I continue, "Roman must be angry with me."

"Why would he be mad at you, Noah?"

"The only reason I can conclude, Mr. Hawke, is timing."

The State's attorney's protruding chin quivers, and his beady eyes shine behind his thick, round lenses. He looks as if he can barely contain his excitement.

"Explain what you mean, Noah."

"You see, we planned the thing and came up with an alibi. We agreed, though, that if either one was picked up within seven days of the crime, we would claim to not remember what we did on that day and use the alibi only if pressured. However, if we were questioned a week or more after the crime, we were to ditch the alibi and claim that too much time passed to remember a specific day in our busy lives. The problem is we neglected to come to terms about what constituted the crime. Our reconnaissance in the afternoon? The moment the boy died? At the time the body entered the culvert, or when it was found?"

"So, because more than a week passed since ya killed the boy, Loewe's angry ya used the alibi?"

"Yes, Detective. As I said, timing."

I'm tempted to light another cigarette but don't. Damn Saul for forcing that first cig on me. "Stop being such a girl," he had yelled when I said I didn't care to try it. I drum my fingers on the table to distract myself.

"Well, Noah, I'm going to give you boys an opportunity to correct the record." Hawke nods to Sever and Harrison. "We're heading to the press room." Turning to me, he says, "Let's go."

I stand up and tug on my vest to straighten it. "Can't this wait? It must be six in the morning and—"

"This won't take long, then ya can rest," Detective Harrison says, grabbing my arm and leading me out the door.

Our footsteps echo on shabby wooden floors as we march down the hallway to our destination.

Men in various suits and uniforms are in the room. Sitting at a long conference table identical to the one I just left is Roman. The familiar tightening of my chest and momentary loss of breath at the sight of him is not dulled by my annoyance with him. He's slumped forward in the chair. Seeing his face form into such a hostile expression when he looks up at me is jarring.

Detective Harrison prods me over to the table. "Sit," he says, kicking out a chair a couple away from Roman. Sneering at Harrison, I don't look at my cohort in this legal journey. The one who is a liar.

Harrison takes the seat between Roman and me. Mr. Hawke sits on my left. Fresh air filters in through the open door, and the smoky cloud in the room undulates with the help of a fan. But overheated body odor sparked on by adrenaline, mixed in with cigars and cigarettes, permeates the air along with excited chattering, nervous coughing, and pencils scratching notes on pads. I recognize the stenographer who recorded my statement; Mr. Hawke; Assistant State's Attorney Jim Sever; and Deputies Barney and Melton. The remaining five men are strangers, but this pushes the total to thirteen in the cramped room, including Roman and myself.

Thirteen. Indicative?

Dispelling the bad-luck theory, another deputy walks inside, both rows of five buttons fastened on his khaki double-breasted jacket, his six-pointed star positioned over his heart. Max Ester follows, trailed by a uniformed officer. Three more policemen walk in next. All carry hats in their hands.

"Do you have the confessions typed?" Mr. Hawke asks the stenographer.

"Yes."

"Fine. Begin with Mr. Loewe's statement since his came first." He turns to everyone else. "I want complete silence in here, or I'll clear this room. Understand?"

Murmurs fill the air before they cut off.

Roman straightens up, and the expression on his face leaves no doubt that he's bothered by Hawke's "first" comment. I lean over and smirk his way. His brown eyes blacken, and his easy-going features twist into a grimace.

"Sit back, Noah."

"Yes, sir, Mr. Hawke," I say, amused but also wary about what secrets a cornered, scared, and infuriated Roman might divulge. He may diverge from the script.

"Uh, ahem." The stenographer clears his throat. "The beginning question is 'State your full name.'

"'Roman Alfred Loewe.'

"'Where do you live, Mr. Loewe?'"

The reading continues with Roman nodding at his own answers, sometimes emphatically, while making scratches on a sheet of paper. I'm taking notes myself: mental notes.

"'Yeah, well, in conclusion, I just want to state,'" the stenographer says, seeming to wrap up Roman's confession, "'that I would never have committed this act were it not for the authoritative influence of Noah Lieberman. The idea or desire to do such a thing, indeed something that fulfills one of his fantasies of being some sort of superman, would never occur to me. Killing young Mr. Frisch, or otherwise, is not in my nature, and my family will agree, that it's not possible for me to have dealt the blow to the lad. I make this statement under no duress.'"

"Is your statement, Mr. Loewe, dated Saturday, 31 May 1924, at four o'clock in the morning, correct?"

"Yes, Mr. Hawke, sir, it is."

"And everything contained in said confession is true?"

"Yes," Roman reiterates.

"All right then—"

"I wish to rectify some points in Mr. Loewe's account," I say, interrupting Hawke in my haughty, lawyer tone, unable to resist annoying Roman despite fearing how much further off script he might venture.

Reaching for the Lucky Strikes I brought along with me, I tap one out and light it. Roman snickers. I take a drag, lean forward, and poke a finger at the table. Every eye in the stuffy, smoky room is on me.

"What he says about the planning of the matter, composing the ransom note, the scavenger-hunt route we mapped out for the father to take, is true. However, he's the one who came up with the idea of collecting payment when he had every intention of killing the boy."

"Rubbish!" Roman smacks his hand on the table and jumps up, causing Harrison and Sever to grab his arms. "I was driving the car!"

"Sit down," Hawke says. "Continue, Noah."

"Thank you. I rented the car as he says, using the name Herbert Bradford, a traveling salesman. Yes, I created this identity by opening a bank account in this name using letters we addressed to Mr. Bradford at the Grande Hotel for identification purposes. Mr. Loewe is correct in his assertion that I deposited a hundred dollars into the account. *He* is the one who drove us to the rental place in his mother's Milburn because the brakes on my Willys needed attention.

"And Roman came up with the idea of using the Underwood we stole from his old dorm, as was burglarizing the frat house in the first place."

He's sitting with his arms crossed over his chest, which is rising and falling rapidly. I can almost see steam emitting from his ears, but I'm sure it's all the smoke. Someone coughs in the quiet room.

"Mr. Loewe purchased Dentyne gum and not Wrigley's at the pharmacy. The auto blanket used to cover the body came from me and did not come furnished with the rental car. Roman was in the passenger seat when we spotted the boy. He climbed into the back, leaned forward, and called out to him. And I phoned my father after we ate. Not before."

"No! I said you *wanted* to call before we ate. I didn't say you did."

I wave my hand, dismissing him. "As far as who was driving, *I* was. Mr. Loewe masterminded the kidnapping scheme, and he is the one who struck the blows to kill the boy."

"Other than these issues, his statement is correct?"

"Yes, Mr. Hawke." I shift around, so the slats don't aggravate my spine.

"Very well. Please begin reading Mr. Lieberman's statement," he says to the stenographer.

Roman neither speaks nor makes a sound when my testimony is read, but his pencil moves furiously.

"Okay, now," Mr. Hawke says after the reading is over. "Any remarks about this account? Any corrections?" He's looking at Roman.

"Most of Lieberman's amendments to my statement are rubbish and don't mean a damn either way." Roman's knee is bouncing up and down. "Who cares what gum I got? I nicked it anyway. The dumb auto robe? Makes no difference to the case. None. If he wants to throw around inconsequential details, then the ransom money was to be wrapped in brown paper and not white. We drafted the note the night prior to the abduction and not two. So there. And I never carried the head of the body. Never. I took the feet.

"Now, let me tell ya, he says I came up with the ransom plot. Nope. My memory is that we came to this idea together." His face reddens. "And I didn't kill the boy, he did." He points to me. "I remember because you were behind the wheel when we pulled up to the curb. Ah, I mean, *I* was behind the wheel! You were in the back. I'm getting confused, it's early, and I've not slept.

"Anyway, you reached into the front, opened the door, and I called out to him. Remember, Noah?"

I shake my head. "False. I drove, and you spoke to the boy."

"Makes no sense. I knew the kid, not you. Why would he get in the car with a stranger? I introduced him when he got in. Said, 'This is Babe. Mind if I drive around the block so you can tell me about your tennis racket? I might want to buy Thad one for his birthday.' So, I was driving, and I didn't hit the kid, you did.

"I feel like a patsy 'cause you told a story at a time when you shouldn't have. A week's a week, and a deal's a deal. When the coppers brought me to their clubhouse here, I think, 'Well, they figured out the glasses are Babe's, and we're known to hang out sometimes. Babe will stick to the story, a week's past.' So, I deny being drunk and having lunch with you and hanging out, but I realize them knowing these things means you told the story and shouldn't have because a week had passed. Me, I tried helping you out by sticking to the plan. A damn sight more than you would do. I thought, at worst, you'd admit what you did and keep me out of it. Instead, you left me smelling like rotting fish on a dock. That's all I have to say."

"Anything else?" Hawke turns to me.

"Yes. Roman's lying to protect himself. I drove the car. I reached across and opened the door. He leaned up from the back and spoke to the boy. He struck the blows and stuffed the rag down the kid's throat. Of this, I'm certain. Now," I direct to Roman, "I'm sorry if you feel the fool. I used the alibi because we never clarified when the seven-day limit would begin. I'm sorry if you came out stinking in this, but it's not my fault you broke down."

I turn to Hawke on my right. "This is all I have to say on the matter of the confessions."

"Okay. Now boys, my officers and I have treated you with decency and respect, haven't we?"

"Yes," we both reply.

"No physical harm has come to either of you while in my custody?"

"No, sir," I say, and Roman repeats the sentiment.

"Let's gather around for a photo. Marv"—Hawke turns to Detective Harrison—"go grab one of the papers' photographers. Just one. Doesn't matter which."

The room fills with hushed conversations when the detective leaves.

"Quiet," Hawke says, holding up a hand. "Mr. Loewe, Mr. Lieberman," he continues. "After the picture, we'll bring you back to your cells for some rest. Later, we'll discuss the whereabouts of Bennie Frisch's clothing and the Underwood. Do you think you can take us to their locations?"

Roman and I exchange glances. "Yes," I answer. "On one condition."

Hawke's chin trembles, and he grips his pen so tightly his hand turns white. Clearly, he's lost patience with me. I wait until his mouth opens to speak before cutting him off.

"But we can discuss the condition later, Mr. Hawke. You're right—we can use some rest."

"Well, then, gentlemen," Hawke says, "if you want a bargaining chip, I think we'll leave within the hour."

Roman glares at me, looking more tired than ever.

Guess I played this one wrong.

Chapter 18

Tuesday evening, 20 March 1923

"To Babe," Father said, holding up a crystal flute. "Congratulations, son."

"Cheers" followed as everyone raised their glasses and sipped champagne. I did the same, looking around the dining table at my family. My father's moustache twitched, and he wore the slight smile that always adorned his face whether he was happy, proud, or aggrieved. His eyes were bright, likely from the two gin Rickey's he drank when we returned home from the University of Chicago's spring convocation ceremony. Levi grinned and sipped, as did Saul. My aunt and uncle didn't imbibe, so their glasses held sparkling water. My cousin, Manfred, finished his champagne in one gulp.

Levi stood up and tapped his fork against his flute. The ting resonated in the room. "I want to make a toast," he said, holding the glass in my direction. "Excellent work achieving your bachelor's degree with honors, Babe. Because of your unmitigated drive and dedication, you accomplished every tremendous goal you set for yourself. You've made our mother proud, brother."

"Thanks, Levi."

Saul rolled his eyes, but his genuine smile doused my anger. He couldn't help being envious since he had never been able to learn another language, and therefore, my mastering five languages proved a sore subject for him. Added to the fact that our mother developed chronic nephritis during her pregnancy with me and became frail and eventually bedridden before her death, it didn't surprise me that he harbored ambiguous feelings toward me.

Margaret came into the room and began collecting dinner plates. "I'm so proud of you, Master Babe."

"Thank you."

"After this is cleaned up, Margaret, please gather Irma and Ethel and join us for dessert," Father suggested. "I have an announcement to make while we feast on sweets."

The maids joined us when everyone was served coffee and a slice of either my favorite, chocolate cream cake, or the alternative, upside-down pineapple cake.

My father rose a bit unsteadily, tottered, and sat back down. He took a sip of joe and remained seated. "Son, your outstanding performance this year at school and your matriculation to the University of Chicago Law School in the fall have earned you another trip to Oscoda County. I know how disappointed you were last year when the Kirtland's warbler eluded you, so I'll fund another adventure for you and a few of your birding pals. I don't know anything about these things, so you'll have to make arrangements yourself," he said, and then he took another bite of chocolate cake.

"Wow, thank you!"

"When will you go, Babe?" my aunt asked.

"In June, but I think a week earlier than last year because—"

"Why do you spend so much time hanging around birds?" Saul said around a mouthful of pineapple cake. "And keeping all those stuffed ones upstairs is creepy."

"Saul!" Levi scolded, although Saul hadn't offended me.

I'm already phoning Heinzie in my head.

"Sorry, Babe, but you have a lot of dead birds."

I raised my hand. "No offense taken," I said. "I have plenty more study skins as well that aren't on display. Analyzing birds and their breeding colonies, their habitats and migration needs, is essential for conservation." Anxious to plan the trip, I stood up and grabbed my cake and coffee. "I'm going to call Henry and then finish this upstairs. Thank you all for a wonderful celebration, and Father for what I'm certain will be a fruitful expedition."

A little later, a knock at my door startled me. I looked up from my desk. I'd only just finished my dessert after speaking with Henry. We were meeting in the morning to discuss details.

"Yes?"

"It's me. May I come in?"

"Of course, Levi."

He entered my study, looking around as he did. It always took me a little aback to see my favorite sibling. Other than height— he was a couple of inches taller—we resembled each other down to matching bulging eyes, but Levi sported two separate eyebrows that stopped where they were supposed to.

"Saul doesn't know what he's talking about, Noah, don't pay attention to him."

"This is why you wanted to talk to me?" I teased. I knew he had more to say. "Our middle sibling has never understood nor cared to understand my passion for ornithology."

"Yes, well, Saul deals with his own problems stemming from...well, our former governess's actions caused him to be a bit cynical about things."

I averted my eyes away from his, being only too familiar with what he was speaking of. I understood; however, Saul didn't always have to be such an ass.

"I appreciate your words, but is this why you traveled all the way up here, Levi? Two flights of stairs?"

He laughed, but it sounded disingenuous. "No, I wanted to tell you that I spoke with Emil Loewe the other day."

The chocolate cake threatened to come up, so I rose from my chair to try and stop it, walked to my bookshelf, and pretended to scan the spines. My fingers fell on a random volume, and I carried it back to the desk. Levi remained just inside the entrance.

"How is Roman? I trust you have news?" I heard no tremors or cracks in my voice.

"Carousing and getting into trouble."

"What kind of trouble?" I forced myself to ask.

"The usual, cheating at gambling and picking fights, but he recently got nabbed trying to steal someone's Milburn. The owner found Roman when he was going to work in the morning." Levi shook his head. "Fool had a duplicate key in the ignition but passed out before starting the car."

"Sounds like he's becoming out of control." *What if he talks while he's drunk?*

"Yes, well, I mention it, Babe, because Emil says his father is bringing Roman directly to the house in Michigan after graduation where he's to remain all summer. Instead of continuing his education in Michigan as Roman planned, he'll be taking an American history course at the University of Chicago in the fall." Levi met my eyes, and I stared at ones so like my own it gave me chills. "I wanted to tell you that he'll be hanging around campus and didn't want you to be surprised. Despite the ugly rumor Roman's friend tried to smear you both with, Emil thinks that Roman was better off when you two were friends. At least he didn't drink as much and get into trouble. But as your brother, I feel it necessary to warn you against reestablishing a friendship with him."

"I understand, Levi, and it won't be an issue. I'm taking law classes in the fall, and Roman has never shown an interest in the law. I doubt that we'll see each other on campus, but we'll likely run into each other since we share mutual friends.

"Now, I don't wish to be rude, Levi, but I'm excited to plan my trip. Henry and I discussed bringing Dewey James and Sid Straub. They're both avid birders. We'll have to leave early and pack food for the drive and—"

"All right, Babe." Levi laughed, held up his hands, and backed away. "You have lots to do. I'm glad you're looking forward to this trip. Father asked if I thought it would be an appropriate gift, and it appears we were correct. Enjoy your evening. I'm going out. I have a date." Winking, he shut the door behind him.

My legs wobbled the second he left, and I grasped the edge of my desk for support. Fury with the indecent way Roman had treated me warred with concern. Would he do something reckless?

* * *

Saturday, 16 June 1923—Michigan

"Let's find a hotel, Noah. I'm tired, and my legs and bum are sore from the long drive," Dewey grumbled from the back seat.

Sid, who sat next to him, said, "Yeah, gotta agree with Dew. We should stop before dark. Find a decent place, chow down some grub."

I glanced at Henry in the passenger seat. "And you?"

"Vote number three."

"All right, let's go a bit farther, though. We're almost to Bay City. We'll find plenty of acceptable places to stay along the Lake Huron shore, and it's only a hundred miles from our destination. Do we all agree?"

"Sounds good," Dewey said. "Think there'll be any speakeasies around?"

"I thought you were tired."

"I am, Noah, but some hooch and flappers might regenerate me."

"Well, my vote would be with you, Dewey," Henry said, "but Straub here is a teetotaler, and we're getting up early in the morning."

"Dancing with pretty fillies isn't on the agenda this trip, fellas." I glanced at Henry, then into the back, before returning my eyes to the bumpy road. "This adventure is dedicated to the Kirtland's warbler. And we didn't have room to bring more than one change of clothing each, so I don't think our appearance will be enticing to the fairer sex. We can ride fillies at home. Deal?"

The guys hooted and whistled in the back.

"What about you, Heinzie?"

"I agree." He winked. "But it would be fun to behave raucously here without fear of reprisals from girls we want to date back home."

More hoots from Dewey and Sid.

* * *

Sunday, 17 June 1923

By the time we four adventurers finally made it to Oscoda, it was close to noon. After finding an appropriate hotel, we dropped off our stuff, refreshed ourselves, and started driving north down the state trunk line toward the Au Sable River. I turned my Willys west onto a sandy road and headed toward the dam. After a few miles, Heinzie stuck his head out the open window.

"Stop, Noah," he said, and jumped out before the auto came to a complete halt. "Listen. Hear it?"

The rest of us got out, and I stretched my legs and back. As I did so, I heard a warbler singing.

Can it be? Can we be on the path of the Kirtland's already? What a difference from last year!

"Follow me." I led the way as we slogged through dense jack pines in various stages of life. Branches slapped my face, and one knocked off my tweed cap. I caught it and kept moving. The bird's call, so forceful and dynamic, filled me with excitement.

"Over there!" Heinzie and I said at the same time, pointing to a large pine tree where the songster sat, perched high on a limb.

I reached for the field binocs around my neck. The amazing bluish-gray bird bore a bright yellow belly and dark stripes on his back, sides, and flanks. The male had white crescents above and below beady black eyes and a mask reminiscent of a raccoon. But his stunning looks weren't what kept me mesmerized; it was the way he moved when he sang. I could watch him sing all day. Small but sharp, dark gray claws gripped the branch of a young jack pine as he lifted his head, exposed his throat, and released a Wren-like song that bubbled from his open beak. His throat muscles rippled, and his tail wagged behind him in symphony.

"Should we continue, Noah?" Henry asked sometime later. "We've been here for over an hour. He doesn't seem to be feeding nestlings."

"Oh yes." I lowered the glasses and smiled at the guys. "I got lost in his music."

We returned to the car and continued toward the river, and although we heard more males in the distance, we saw no others and headed back to the hotel to eat and sleep so we could start out again early in the morning.

* * *

Monday, 18 June 1923

"C'mon, Sid, Dewey, hurry," Henry said, as he knocked on their hotel door. They shared a room, and Henry and I shared another.

One of them grumbled behind the door before it opened.

"Geez, guys, it's four thirty in the morning, have pity," Dewey said, rubbing his eyes when he came out. His hat sat skewed on his head.

Honestly, why did I invite such a boob?

"Well, Dewey, I shouldn't have to tell you that birds are hungry and active in the early hours."

"Yeah, yeah, I know, Noah."

Although dark, I managed to find the same place that we stopped yesterday, and we heard the male Kirtland's warbler right away. The four of us used flashlights and followed his voice. We watched him for hours, hoping to find his nest, and even though the fella sang his bubbling, enthusiastic chirp, none of us observed him with food.

I checked the time. "It's nearing nine thirty. I say we head east, look for another warbler."

The fellas agreed. Dewey and Sid paired together, as did Henry and I, to try and locate a nest.

I moved in the direction of singing. "Look, Henry," I said when I spotted a male with my binocs. "Notice how he sits on a dead branch in a tree taller than the surrounding ones? He sings, food in his mouth, before dropping to the ground. When he returns to his perch, the food is gone."

"Yeah, the nest must be below him."

"Correct, Henry. And did you see how he whets his bill when he goes back to the branch after feeding? Like he's cleaning off before grabbing more food. This behavior is distinctly sparrow-like in nature." I shook my head and looked around at the crowd of trees growing in abundance. "I'm afraid trudging through this to find the nest will be difficult."

"It's time for lunch anyway. Maybe we should gather up Dewey and Sid and go back to the hotel?"

"Good idea, Henry. The male sang with regularity about every eight seconds, with each song lasting about a second and three-quarters. He's now down to a song every thirty-six seconds."

"What are you saying, Noah? You think the bird needs a nap?"

I laughed, removed my cap, wiped sweat from my brow, and placed the moist cap back on my head. "This is as good an explanation as any. Let's go eat."

Although the sun shone brighter and hotter upon our return in the afternoon, when we reached the sandy road that led to the Au Sable River, we all felt better. Refreshed.

"I think we should go back to the sight of the first male warbler," I said to the fellas as I pulled the car off the dirt road onto the brush. "We heard others, even though we didn't spot them. Perhaps we'll locate a nest in an area that will be easier to access."

"Good idea," Henry agreed.

The chaps in the back whooped.

When we reached the site where we watched the first bird, we headed west toward the river. We walked about a quarter of a mile when I heard a male singing.

"This way," I said, pivoting in the direction of the chirping.

"Whoa, look," Dewey said.

I turned right back around.

He pointed to the ground where he'd startled a female bird not a foot away from him. She hopped-flew about before ducking into bushes, dragging a wing behind her.

"Can it be? No." I moved closer and leaned down.

"What?" Sid and Dewey asked at once.

"Broken-wing ruse? A common trick among other birds, but not something observed in the Kirtland's. Not to my knowledge. Fascinating. The nest is here somewhere. Everyone, stay still, and let's wait."

I looked around. We were in an open area, surrounded by a clump of young jack pines. The male chirped, fast and clipped, from a branch on a six-foot-tall tree, wagging his tail with each beat. The female sang from her hiding place in the shrubs.

A good half an hour passed before the male flew off. I knew he would return, likely with food, so I didn't bother to follow his path and kept my sight trained on the female who hopped out of the bush. The male touched down on a twig, a caterpillar in its beak. Both parents flitted about before the male dropped to the ground. When he returned, the food was gone.

"There," I said, pointing to the area where he landed. "Follow my lead, but be careful because the thick vegetation will make discovering the nest difficult for us and dangerous for them."

I got on my knees and crawled over the heavy mat of evergreen and ferns growing over sandy earth. After a few minutes, the female's chirps grew frantic, and she jumped along the ground.

"No one move," I warned the guys. My shirt stuck to my back, and my armpits dampened as the sun glowed.

Finally, the female settled down a bit, and I spotted the nest, which was almost completely covered in vegetation. Four nestlings, approximately three days old, twittered around inside.

Mother and father bird flew, diving at our heads to show their displeasure, while the young waited for food, beaks open to the air, their infantile chirps barely discernable through the thick plant life. After a while, I crawled backward, causing the fellas to do the same.

"The parents are agitated, so what do you say we mark the area and come back tomorrow? We can spend the entire day observing and studying the habits at the nest. I plan to write an article, so I want to note everything."

"All right, Noah," Dewey said, and he got up and stretched his long legs. "But I brought a lot of gin, and we're drinking tonight, fellas. Sid can make sure we don't oversleep, right Sid?"

"Sure, Dew, but only if we can play auction bridge, five cents a point."

The rest of us stood up, and I wiped my trousers and my arms of dirt and bits of greenery. "This isn't the trip for boozing and gambling."

"Come on, Noah," Dewey argued as we walked back to the road and the Willys. He slapped a bug that landed on his face. "We're hot. We discovered a nest like we hoped to. Let's celebrate."

The impact of his words hit me. We found a Kirtland's warbler nest! "A celebration dinner sounds about right. Steaks, potatoes, gin, and cards. A fitting commemoration."

* * *

Wednesday, 20 June 1923

If I found the abundant overgrowth of jack pine, bearberry, and juniper difficult to maneuver in the daylight, four o'clock in the morning proved nearly impossible. Despite ample moonlight, I carried a bulky flashlight in one hand, my birding rifle in the other, and a knapsack filled with rags slung over my shoulders.

I tripped for the fourth time and fell to the soft ground.

"Blasted!" I set aside the light and got to my feet again. I brushed myself off with one hand, gripping the rifle in my other. *A shame I can't confide in Heinzie*, I thought, but as a Harvard Law student, he wouldn't agree to an illegal collection of the protected Kirtland's warbler.

The guys getting drunk again last night proved beneficial as they lay snoring in their beds at the hotel. I shone the light around. "Has to be here somewhere," I hissed. The beam landed on the marker, and I trudged forward, being conscious of where my feet landed.

Upon reaching the nest, I looked over the little family. Mother and father, awake, regarded me warily. The four young were quiet, beaks closed, including the cowbird. I shook my head. A cowbird. The fellas and I discovered this avian parasitism phenomenon of a bird laying its egg in another bird's nest while observing yesterday. We'd spent all morning taking notes and photographs at the nest. I recorded every movement the parents made. It didn't take them long to adjust to our presence, and they fed their nestlings worms and centipedes while singing and wagging their tails. But it would only be a matter of days before the cowbird would crowd out the smaller birds, causing them to starve.

I shot the father, then the mother, and placed both in the knapsack, each wrapped in a rag. The nestlings I swaddled in a rag apiece, opting to let them all suffocate. I decided to take the cowbird as well.

The trip back to the road and my auto took some time, but the sun was rising when I returned from retrieving the nest, a three-foot section of the surrounding habitat, and a small jack pine. However, I didn't return from taking the specimens to the train station and shipping them to my taxidermist in Chicago to create a lifelike display until a little after nine in the morning.

I found the fellas having coffee in the hotel restaurant. They looked terrible.

"Oh, Noah, I got your note," Henry said, rubbing his temples. "How was early bird-watching? Spot any Kirtland's?"

"No, I'll wait for you sorry sots for the warbler. I did see a variety of other species which were just as delightful."

I turned to Sid. "Are you regretting following the direction of these boozers?" I pointed to the culprits who talked him into drinking last night for the first time—to my advantage.

He lifted his head from the table, opened one eye, and said, "Can't believe they got me boiled as an owl," and plopped his head back down.

"Well, if you haven't eaten yet, fellas, let's order some grub. I hear chatter about James McGillivray of the State Conservation Commission being in town today." I raised my arm to signal the waitress. "I hope to convince him to film us at a nest tomorrow. We'll have to find another nest, of course, but I'm positive we will."

"Why can't we use the one we already discovered?" Dewey asked.

"The lighting in that area is unfavorable for photography. We'll go east where the conditions will be better. And we heard plenty of males singing out in that direction."

The waitress appeared. "What can I get for you boys?"

I smiled at the fellas. "Eat up. This is proving to be a magnificent trip!"

Chapter 19

> Truths are illusions which we have forgotten are illusions.
>
> —Friedrich Nietzsche

Saturday, 31 May 1924

"'Their confidence, their astounding aplomb deserted them at dawn today,'" I say, reading from the early edition of the *Chicago Daily News*, "'when daylight began creeping through the dusty windows of the Criminal Court Building revealing the climax of their terrible drama.'"

I drop the ridiculous paper on the mattress and slap it.

"Hogwash!" I light another cigarette, having lost count of how many I've smoked since being in the custody of State's Attorney Bertram Hawke.

At least two decks of Luckies. By the time the bastard hangs me, I'll resemble a craggy old man.

The thought darkens my mood as I sit in a cell waiting to go on a scavenger hunt. Typewriter, shoes, belt...but probably the last time I'll see the outside world again. Other than before a corded rope slips over my neck and snaps it, or if I'm fortunate, or unfortunate enough depending on one's perspective, to spend time in the yard at Joliet Prison.

I sip burnt, too-strong coffee to coat my queasy stomach from the stale buttered roll Detective Harrison gave me.

It'll take a while for my palate to adjust to jailhouse slop, I suppose.

I check my watch: one quarter after nine. Hawke and his minions should be coming around soon to take me on a road trip with Roman, who, according to the newspaper, "lost his cocksure attitude and slumped in the chair while gasping out his confession." I smirk, before remembering that I had been depicted as "ashen" and "haggard" when I made my confession in another room. My eyes go to my picture in the paper. I suppose I should be grateful they used the adjectives they did. *Sullen* and *buggy-eyed* are ones I've heard my entire life. The image they chose is a rare one of me smiling into the camera. However, my smile is stilted, awkward. I'm leaning forward, one hand grasping the other in my lap, suit jacket unbuttoned. My globular eyes, protruding ears, but, worse still, the eyebrows that connect and dip at my nose highlight the contrast between my photo and the one of Roman. His mesmeric energy jumps from the print, although he's only shown in profile. His light hair is slicked back, and his smirk is boyish and not morose and glum as Saul likes to tease me that mine is.

"Let's go, Lieberman."

I look up, surprised to see Detective Harrison and a sheriff's deputy I don't recognize. The deputy takes his keys and unlocks the cell. The sound of bars opening strangely affects me more than when they closed, but I have no idea why. I take a moment to collect myself before rising from the lower bunk, careful not to bump my head on the empty one above.

"A change of clothes would be nice," I say, pulling on my vest and grabbing my hat and jacket from the end of the bed.

"Soon. Ya father's working on a writ of habeas corpus, but court's only open half a day on Saturday, and tomorrow's Sunday."

I nod at the detective. What difference does a writ make now? We aren't being unlawfully held, not when the police have the facts, our confessions, and, after today, all the physical evidence they'll need.

It's a relief to trade the stuffy Criminal Court Building for the hot, blinding sun when I step outside. I blink at the glare, lowering my hat to shield my eyes. When they clear, I regret the action. Newshawks fill the street, most of them holding cameras with large flashing bulbs. I count nine sedans idling, all with various officers, detectives, and deputies waiting outside them, and many other automobiles. Everyone is shouting over the traffic noise, but I can't make out what they're saying.

"This way, Noah." Mr. Hawke is at my side, pointing to the first Marmon in line at the curb. Then I spot Roman, smiling at something one of the men is saying as he ducks his head to get into the auto behind ours. When he sees me, he straightens up and moves closer.

"Whoa, there now," says one of the officers.

I step toward Roman, aware of various lawmen surrounding us. He glares at me, his full lips parted. My heart does what it always does when I see him. No matter if he's angry, happy, or indifferent, my palpitations speed up, skipping and tripping over each other in their rush, and I feel a twinge in my lower stomach. Only this time it's warring with growing anger.

Look at him, standing here like he's going to a dance. He's in his glory, the master criminal aiding the pathetic police.

He cleaned up since we were in the press room together. His light brown hair is slicked back, no part, and his eyes, although weary, are a curious mixture of mischievousness and fury. He's also wearing the same clothes, but his jacket looks sharp, not wrinkly like mine. His perfectly positioned bowtie screams, "I drove the car and bluenose Noah and his straight tie killed the kid! Plus, he screwed up the alibi timing."

I'm about to unfreeze my smirk and speak when Detective Harrison grabs my arm.

"Come on, Lieberman," he says, leading me to the car. Hawke, Harrison, and Sever get into the automobile, and the two prosecutors ride in the back with me. I don't know who the driver is, but he turns around after we're seated and asks, "Where to, boss?"

"U-Drive on South Side Street." Hawke addresses me, "This is where you rented the car, right, Noah?"

"Yes, sir."

Our vehicle pulls into traffic, and I watch out the rear window as the remaining police cars follow us. The reporters all run to their autos and join the caravan, but I can't see how many there are because we make a right turn.

When we arrive at U-Drive, the lot is woefully inadequate for the number of vehicles, so most of them park in the road. Only Roman and I, along with our guards, are brought into the rental office.

Hawke marches up to the man behind the desk. "Are you the manager? I'm State's Attorney Bertram Hawke." He turns around and points to Roman and me. "Did either of these young men lease a car from you on Wednesday, the twenty-first of May?"

The man studies us and then points to me. "Yes, this one. He's the one who paid for and signed out a dark green Willys-Knight touring car in the late morning of that day."

"Under what name?"

The man rifles through an open file on his desk. The police or the press must have pre-warned him of our arrival.

"Uh, yeah, here it is, Mr. Hawke." He pulls out a sheet of paper. "Rental agreement is with a Mr. Herbert Bradford."

"May I inspect the vehicle?"

"I'm sorry, sir," the man says, looking anything but sorry that his single moment of relevancy will be extended. "The automobile went out again yesterday before you called and hasn't come back yet."

Hawke's face turns purple, but to his credit, he doesn't flinch. "Notify my office the minute the car is returned. And nobody is to touch it!"

"Y-y-yes, sir, Mr. Hawke," the manager stammers, no longer looking happy to be involved in this mess.

I catch Roman's eye as we leave and go back to our cars. His almost imperceptible smirk gives me reason to believe that he might be getting over his temper tantrum. But his pallor causes me concern. His eyes are glassy, the lids drooping, and he keeps blinking. My determination to spend a few minutes alone with him ratchets up.

We pile back into our respective automobiles, and the cavalcade moves to our next stop: Granger's Hardware on Cove and Twenty-Third. The clerk working is the same man who was on duty when Roman purchased the hammer. Reporters cram in behind us, and the small store is stifling.

"Yeah, this is the guy who got the hammer," the clerk says.

Roman pales further, and without warning, his legs buckle, and he falls to the floor.

"Give him room," Hawke says, waving for reporters and detectives to back out of the store.

The clerk produces water, which revives Roman, but he still looks exhausted.

After driving down Cove to the drugstore, the man behind the counter identifies me as the purchaser of the hydrochloric acid.

"I remember because of the large quantity," he says.

We then proceed to my house where Hawke sends one of the men inside to retrieve the hip boots from my bedroom.

Next, we go to the harbor. Cars line both sides of the street as our motorcade halts and passengers spill out. Our sideshow spectacle causes onlookers to stop their vehicles on the road to gawk at us.

"All right, boys," Hawke says when we reach the bridge in Washington Park. "Where did you throw the Underwood and the bag of keys?"

"The typewriter," Roman says, "we threw, intact in its case, from the bridge leading to the outer harbor." He points at the Golden Lady statue. "Tossed the bag of keys into shallower water over there."

Men with rakes climb down the embankment. Despite the heat, everyone is wearing gray or black overcoats with fedoras or derbies on their heads. Roman is the only one sporting a light-colored coat and boater hat. He's kicking at the curb with brown, calf-finished leather oxfords. Dozens of men, including reporters, are walking around.

Someone whistles from below and yells, "Got 'em!"

"All right," Hawke says. "Sounds like we have the keys, but we'll have to come back tomorrow with a dive team for the Underwood. Harrison, Sever, and the rest of you"—he nods his comical chin toward the three men surrounding Roman—"stay here. Everyone else go back to your cars. Now."

I hear the distinct whinnying call of *Picoides pubescens* while Hawke's conferring with Sever and the reporters and the remaining policemen are leaving. The downy woodpecker's excited string of high-pitched notes descends in the last millisecond of the two-second cry.

Hawke turns to me. "Show me where Bennie's stockings, shoes, and belt are buried, Noah. How close to the Indiana border did you hide them?"

I glance at Roman, so pale and weak looking. Hungry and exhausted myself, I reach into my pocket, pull out my cigarettes, and light one. I turn to Hawke, take a draw, and blow out smoke rings.

"No."

"Excuse me?"

"With all due respect, sir, now is the time for my condition."

No one speaks as I stare down Hawke; his eyeglasses are steaming from the heat coming off his rapidly reddening face.

The grin Roman flashes me is worth the State's attorney's wrath.

"Now, listen here," Hawke begins, but I put my hand up to stop him.

"May we speak in private?"

He glares at me. "Jim, Marv," he says to Sever and Harrison, never taking his eyes off mine, "and the rest of you step back to the road. Take Loewe with you."

Roman looks like he's going to protest, but one of the detectives grabs him and pulls him away.

"Before you say anything," I tell Hawke, whose face is puffing and turning more into a caricature than ever, "I'd like to thank you."

His eyes widen, and his hat slips when he takes a step backward. I hold in a smirk as he trips over something or his own feet.

"For what?"

"For the decent way in which I've been treated by you and your men. I'm aware that under different, ah, circumstances, a confession might be obtained in a more unpleasant manner."

Hawke says nothing.

What can he say, since his department is infamous for its brutality?

"Second, I feel like Roman and I, after our initial denials, have been courteous and cooperative in our confessions. We haven't asked for lawyers, nor have we been given the opportunity to request one."

"Are you saying you want a lawyer, Noah?"

"What I want is a favor in return for such assistance in helping you frame your case. Or for future assistance. I'll accept whichever reason you choose."

"What favor?"

The afternoon sun is beating down on me, so I take off my jacket and place it over my arm. Loosening my tie, I say, "How about you send one of these guys out for sandwiches for Roman and me." I point to the sedans on the dirt road. "A couple bottles of root beer too. Let two fellas talking their way to the gallows have a few minutes alone in a Marmon to eat and act normal for the last time."

And because we've handed you a hanging case, you ungrateful fool.

The thin-lipped State's attorney stares at me, jaw set, hands on his hips. "All right, Noah." He takes off his Panama hat and wipes his forehead before replacing the hat back on his head. "But we'll look for the shoes and belt first, then stop at Paul's Hot Dog Stand and get you something there."

"Thank you. You've proven yourself decent in this matter, so I trust that you'll keep your word."

"Don't get excited, Noah. It's hot dogs and five minutes alone."

"It will feel like any other Saturday afternoon, which makes it priceless."

"Let's go." Hawke takes my elbow and leads me to our car. Everyone is standing around their vehicles, smoking and talking. I try to convey a message with my eyes to Roman as I pass by him, but his demeanor is hostile again, so I sneer instead.

"After you, Noah," Hawke says, holding the car door open.

Detective Harrison is already sitting next to the driver. "Where ya taking us, Lieberman?"

"Drive southeast out of the city on the main highway, then head toward the Indiana border," I say, leaning my head over the front seat. "We'll travel north before turning onto a little spur road. I'll direct you further from there."

The trip takes about forty minutes, and we search both sides of the road. Roman and I are not only allowed but encouraged to help search. It had been dark that night when we hid the items, so we mistakenly begin our hunt a half mile in the wrong direction. My error. I thought Roman and I had stopped where I once acquired a *Bubo virginianus*. I drove past this area after birding with Henry Heinz one weekend, and we stopped to relieve ourselves. I had my rifle with me, so when I heard the distinctive whoot, whoot, whoot…whoo, whoo call of the great horned owl, I acquired him. The yellow-eyed predator with earlike tufts and a deep hooting call now graces the top of a china cabinet in my study.

I admit my mistake to Hawke, and we travel down the road to the correct location. Police officers, Roman and I, and even reporters poke through grass and brush. Fat Jim Sever finds Bennie's shoes and belt buckle, and one of the guys from the *Tribune* locates his school pin. The belt eludes us.

Perspiring, I take off my hat and roll up my sleeves. My shirt is damp in the armpits. The afternoon sun is shining through the trees. I don't check the time, but it must be nearing three o'clock. My stomach is rumbling, and I'm ready to faint.

The damned belt must be here!

"I think that's good," Hawke says. He puts his fingers to his lips and whistles for attention. Everyone around us looks up from digging. "Enough for today. We'll come back tomorrow after the divers find the typewriter in the lagoon. Go back to the Criminal Court Building." He turns to me. "Lieberman, wait in the car with Sever and Harrison."

Fifteen minutes later, the Marmon is parked at the small roadside stand, and I'm sitting in the back, alone, with a red hot and a double order of greasy hand-cut fries wrapped in paper in my lap. The car door opens suddenly, and Hawke's cartoonish face glares at me.

"Eat fast, Noah, because you have five minutes." He slams the door shut as the other one opens.

"Boy, that's some big smeller on that dick, Harrison, huh?" Manny says, grinning and holding a hot dog. "And Sever? What a baby grand!" He gets in beside me and closes the door. "Gonna be honest, Babe. I didn't think you'd be able to pull this off. Good job."

"Simply a matter of knowing your opponent. Hawke fancies himself quite the intelligent man, and on some level he is."

"Ah, but not on your level, Babe." He's still grinning, and his eyes are sparkling. "Now, let's eat like we did the night we did the brat." Taking a bite of his red hot, he uses his other hand to unbutton his trousers. Grabbing my hand, he places it in his lap. "Be quick about it, though, 'cause we're down to four minutes, and we have fries too."

Chapter 20

Thursday, 27 September 1923

T*HERE'S A CRISP bite in the air*, I thought as I wrapped my jacket tighter, took a draw on my cigarette, and hurried toward my car. Colorful leaves rustled and swirled around my feet along the way, and a brisk breeze caused me to hold down my hat to keep it from flying off.

"Hey, Noah, nice debate with Professor Thomas."

I adjusted the book strap slung over my shoulder and turned to acknowledge someone from one of the four law classes I was taking this year. The chap's name escaped me, but regardless of whether I remembered his name or not, I didn't wish to speak with him. Or anyone. I had a long, taxing day, and I wanted to go home and rest away a headache.

"Boy, I thought ole Tubby Thomas was going to blow his…" An attractive girl walked by and caught his eye. "Yeah, well, see you Monday, Noah," he said, waving as he followed the dumb Dora.

Tipping my hat at his back, I continued, miffed by the long trek to my auto.

My own damn fault for going bird-watching early this morning and hunting migratory songbirds, losing track of time.

I tossed the butt onto the sidewalk, ground it out with my shoe, and continued walking. When my Willys came into view, I stopped. My sporty car, distinctive by its tan top, nickel bumpers, and disc wheels, was parked where I left it; however, someone was sitting on the passenger side. Although too far away to confirm who the gentleman wearing the newsboy cap was, my heart seized in my chest. When the pounding beats resumed, I moved closer as emotions, questions, hurt, rage—a million feelings warred inside me.

And I knew it was him despite only seeing the back of his head, his shoulders.

"Gee, Babe, hurry up and start driving. I have a few things to say to you."

Until he spoke, I hadn't realized that I'd reached my auto. "Oh, you do, do you now?" I said, opening the door and tossing my books in the tonneau. Heat burned from my neck to the tips of my ears.

How dare he order me around? Especially after all this time.

Furious, I got in, slammed the door shut, and started the engine. Before engaging the gear, I turned to face Roman.

"And where, oh, King, am I going?" My intended delivery failed miserably. Instead of a haughty tone, neediness crept in.

He smiled, and in a flash, it disappeared. "Just drive outta town, Babe."

That feeling in my stomach I got whenever I was near him— like tiny beaks pecking at my insides—began regardless of my ire.

"You assume I have no other plans?" I said, although I steered the car in the direction he ordered.

"Do you, Babe? You're not seeing Sally Lord."

"How do you know?"

"Our fellow bluenose chap, Dick Renford, filled me in on the details. Boy meets girl. Academically overloaded boy talks to girl on telephone for months. Girl boards ocean liner for a summer trip before the two shy lovebirds can go on a date. Boy sad, but soldiers on. Boy and girl haven't spoken since."

The sonofabitch sounded so damn smug!

"Yes, well, Roman, while you boozed in Ann Arbor, I maintained a full course load. I didn't have time to meet with Sally before she set sail, and she only just returned from Europe weeks ago. I'm letting her settle in before I call on her."

"Ah, don't bother. I got us a couple of tomatoes, real lookers, and we can double up tonight. We can even meet up with Dickie and the girl he's stuck on and make it a real party." His hand touched my knee. Then it was gone. "What say you, Babe? You in?"

* * *

3:00 a.m., Sunday, 11 November 1923

"Park under this tree," Roman demanded.

I pulled the Willys over, and he jumped out.

"Damn, what a long trip!" he said, stretching his back.

I turned off the ignition and joined him on the sidewalk.

"Yes, six hours driving to Ann Arbor over bumpy roads at night is tiring." I reached into my jacket for my flask and took a nip. Roman did the same.

"Okay, now, you ready?" he asked. His eyes glowed in the dark as he patted his coat pocket. "Loaded bean shooter, just in case."

"I have my gun as well, but we won't need them."

"You never know, Babe. Geez, wouldn't that be the ultimate revenge on the dirty, rotten blokes who censured me? What a way to treat an upperclassman just because he fancies getting blotto sometimes."

"I should think you became quite an embarrassment to the fraternity for the executive committee to suspend your privileges in your senior year."

"Ah, baloney. A fella oughta be able to relieve the stress of his educational pursuits here and there."

"Yes, Manny, but getting soused in the morning and urinating on the frat house lawn is frowned upon."

He laughed, tipped his flask back, and winked. "Come on, let's go. They always forget to lock the door, but I know where they leave the key. If we run into anyone, we tell them we came here for the football game earlier and stayed for the parties." He tapped his pocket again. "Any real trouble, and we handle it." His eyes shone.

With our flashlights pointed downward, we walked along the path to the three-story mansion set back from the street that housed Zeta Beta Tau, Roman's old fraternity. The front door, situated under a rounded arch, swung open when he turned the knob. We went inside the quiet frat house and walked into the large meeting room. Glasses and mugs littered every table and flat surface available—including the floor. Cigarette butts overfilled multiple ashtrays. The ghostly apparition of smoke lingered, attaching itself to my hat, jacket, and trousers. A deflated football floated in a punchbowl filled with clear liquid. I dipped a finger in, tasted it, and gagged. Gin. Homemade brew.

Roman stood at the foot of the stairs and gestured for me to come over.

I strained my ears but heard no sounds of anyone awake upstairs. We ascended the steps, my excitement, fear, and anticipation rising with each tread. I followed him into the coat room.

Jackets and overcoats were hanging on hooks and slung over benches. I took his lead and began searching pockets. One handsome tweed coat held a fancy fountain pen, which I availed myself of, another some change. Roman elbowed me and held up a wallet he'd found. He pulled out a ten-dollar bill. The money went into his pocket, the wallet back in the coat.

Halfway through our riffling, a loud snort and then a dull thump made me freeze. I looked at Roman, and when his eyes locked on mine, I recognized exhilaration in them.

He wants to be caught. He wants to use the revolver.

Minutes passed. When enough silence followed that one fraternity brother's likely fall from his bed, I tugged on Roman's sleeve and gestured toward the stairs. We left the room and headed back down.

"What, Babe?" he hissed under his breath when we reached the landing. "We could've taken care of him if he woke up and saw us."

"Don't be a stupe. The guns are last resort only. What good's making a racket and getting nailed?"

"We wouldn't get pinched for it, and nobody would even know we did it."

"Baloney. The noise would wake everyone, Manny."

"Aww, you're nuts."

Another thump came from above.

"Let's just forget this and scram," he said.

Something caught my eye on our way through the living room to the front door. I took a closer look.

Finally, something I may be able to use, I thought as I walked over. My hopes were confirmed. *A portable Underwood typewriter! One of the newest models.* I picked it up, thrilled by its size and weight. *Why, this can be carried around easily, so unlike my bulky Hammond at home.*

"Pssst," Roman said from the doorway.

I nodded and followed him, pausing on the way out to grab one more thing and slipping it inside my jacket. We didn't speak until we reached my car.

"Damn!" he cried when I was putting the Underwood in the tonneau. "What a bust. Such a long trip and for what?" He pulled his spoils from his pocket and counted. "Twelve bucks. What kinda dough is that? The louses won't miss it, won't even know they were looted."

I took out the change from my trousers and added it up. "And forty-three cents." I pointed behind me. "Plus, a nifty portable typewriter and a fountain pen."

He yanked open the passenger door and plopped into the seat, immediately reaching for his flask that he'd left on the floor. "Good for you, but a bust for me." Tipping back the flask, he drained it, then threw it down. "Long ride home, and I'm outta hooch too!"

After I started the car and steered onto the road—not a soul or another auto to be seen in the early morning hour—Roman's leg bounced up and down in the seat next to me. His frustration about not getting even with his old fraternity brothers for kicking him out was palpable.

"Let's go back, Babe, before we get to the trunk line and head home. Come on, quick, before anyone wakes up!"

"Why?" I glanced over at him. "Did you drop something? So what? You lived there and came back to visit for the big game. Perfect alibi."

"Nah, I just remembered that I have matches. We can light the place up."

Flames rippled in his eyes when he spoke. I squirmed around to make it easier to remove the bottle that I swiped.

"Here," I said, giving it to him. "I lifted this on the way out. Instead of burning them down, we can get blotto on them."

His mood flipped, and he grabbed the bottle. "Well, the brothers do like their bathtub gin. Gimme your flask, and I'll fill her up."

* * *

An hour out of Ann Arbor, I tossed my empty flask in the back and wound up swerving to avoid a tree.

"Where'd that come from?" I muttered. Roman burst out laughing.

"You're zozzled, Babe," he cried, slapping his thigh. With no warning, he stuck his head and shoulders out the window and howled into the wind, which promptly took his hat and sent it sailing behind us. "Stop! I gotta get my cap. It's my favorite."

"Forget it, Manny, it's gone. Probably landed in the woods. You'll never find it."

"Ahh," he said and sat back down. "I gotta go visit a tree anyway."

The urge hit me too, and it wouldn't hurt to stretch my legs, but we were about to go through a small downtown area.

"Can you wait a few minutes?" I looked at Roman, and his knee bounced in a furious rhythm. "There's a spur road about five miles outside this next town. We can stop there. This way, I can fill up the tank from the gas cans."

"Sure, sure," he said, putting the almost-empty bottle to his lips.

The air, still but chilly, had a sharp, clean smell as I drove through the town, going under twenty miles an hour. We didn't speak. Everything had an eerie black-and-white haunting quality in the dead of night. Men, women, and children asleep, tucked in their warm beds. Deserted streets, with only a dull glow from street lanterns, gave glimpses of closed barber shops, five-and-ten cent stores, and shoe-repair businesses.

One gets a sense of superiority from being alone in—

The sound of shattering glass cut off my thought, and I whipped my head toward Roman.

"Stop, Babe, now!"

My foot hit the brake when he yelled, and the auto jerked to an abrupt halt and stalled. My nose grazed the steering wheel.

He jumped out of the car and ran down the street before I could utter a word.

Where's he going? Then I saw the jewelry store with a shattered window. *Did the reckless fool throw the bottle?* No lights turned on in any of the buildings, but I had to rein him before he got us caught. Leaving the car, I raced after him.

I needn't have rushed.

"Ready, Babe?" he asked, stepping away from broken glass and holding up his loot. "Mumsie's birthday's next week, and now I have a pretty necklace for her." He winked and grinned while I stood rooted to the sidewalk. "This swell watch for me too."

My head spun, and I felt both inebriated and sober. "Let's go, Manny."

"Sure, sure, least this trip wasn't a complete waste of—"

"Say…waz goin on here, boys?"

Icy chills ran down my back. I turned to the voice and saw a man, drunker than us judging by the strong smell of alcohol that barely mixed in with the repulsive body odor clinging to him like a shadow. His overcoat, tattered at the hem and frayed at the elbows, hung from frail bones. Dirty hair stuck out from under his skewed hat. We had encountered another hobo.

I grabbed Roman's arm to pull him out of there—the drunken bum wouldn't remember what we looked like and who would believe him—but Roman jerked out of my grasp. He ran straight at the tramp, who spun around and fled down the alleyway between two buildings, surprisingly fast for someone who looked to be older than my father.

Roman chased the bum, and I chased Roman. The short passageway ended behind Main Street, and before I went a hundred yards, I found myself running down a grassy incline led only by moonlight and the sounds of huffing, puffing, and rushing through the brush. I glimpsed one figure, then another, enter the line of woods before I tripped. Drunk when I began the roll down, I felt sobered by the time my back hit a tree, stopping me.

Clearheaded but sore, I remembered the flashlight in my overcoat, so I pulled it out and shone it around. I didn't see Roman anywhere. I continued in the direction I hoped I'd been heading prior to my tumble.

"Now what, old man?" I heard Roman say. His voice came from my left.

I found him and the bum in a small clearing a few yards away, the hobo's home judging by the tent, clothesline strung tree to tree, and a blackened firepit. The guy stood, breathing hard and panting, hands on his knees. His hat lay on the ground. The early morning air was calm, but soon, the birds would awaken, the sun would rise.

Roman turned to me with that look in his eyes, but I left my car in the street at the scene of a vandalism and burglary. We needed to leave.

"Manny," I said through gritted teeth, "we're going. Now."

"Sorry, Babe." He nodded at the vagabond, who was still bent over. "Can't leave this skid rogue as a witness."

"No, we're leaving," I said, but then the old man started gasping. I shone the light on him.

His face, red with a sheen of sweat, seemed to swell. His eyes bulged, and his mouth opened and closed. Both hands clawed at his throat. He made choking, gurgling noises, then fell to the ground and landed on his face.

Neither of us moved. In fact, the woods grew quieter than before.

"Is he sleeping the big sleep?"

I used my foot to turn the man over, a burdensome task. The hobo's eyes, wide open, stared at nothing. Although loathed to do it, I checked his crusty neck for a pulse. Nothing.

"Yes, Manny, he's dead," I said, wiping my hand on my trousers.

When I looked at Roman, his eyes shone, his grin a demand. My king calling his servant. However, someone needed to be responsible.

"It's imperative that we go back to the car," I said. His eyes narrowed as they grew colder, and he opened his mouth to speak.

I nodded in response to his silent command. "Okay, then we'll go to the spur road."

Chapter 21

> Every deep thinker is more afraid of being understood than of being misunderstood.
>
> —Friedrich Nietzsche

Sunday morning, 1 June 1924

"How about another jelly donut, sugar?"

I look up at the waitress and smile over the rim of my coffee cup. "Only if you'll sit and eat it with me," I tell her.

She giggles, but Detective Harrison says, "No, he's had enough."

Roman snorts from across the small table as the homely woman sashays away. Our moods are switched for a change, and he's the one who is sulking. But today is shaping up to be pleasant, much nicer than yesterday. Less hot and humid. After Roman and I spent time alone in the Marmon, albeit too brief, we stopped to retrieve the partially burned automobile blanket from its burial spot. Next, we headed back to the jail located behind the Criminal Court Building, wherein I discovered that my father, Levi, Roman's brother, and his uncle had come to see us. Father, disappointed that he missed me, had our chauffeur bring my nightclothes to the jail.

It feels good to be not only the smartest man to sleep in a cell, but also likely the only one who ever wore silk pajamas.

"Guess you don't want anything else, Loewe, since you didn't finish your scrambled eggs," says Captain Zachary, one of Roman's escorts.

"Aww, my stomach's upset." He glares at me from across the table, but I feel his foot touch my leg. "Must be from yesterday's hot dog."

Harrison takes another sip of coffee before standing up and saying, "I'm gonna go pay the check now."

Zachary nods, and Harrison walks over to the register by the exit.

I look around as I finish my coffee. Decorative plates sit atop shelves spanning all four walls about three-quarters of the way up. Large coat hooks, with no coats hanging from them, line one wall. Darren's Restaurant has been here on Sixty-Third Street for over thirty years.

Some of those desserts in the showcase by the register look that old too, I think, pulling my oxford off sticky, worn linoleum.

"All right, let's go," Harrison says when he returns. "Mr. Hawke wants us back by noon, and we have ground to cover."

I raise an eyebrow and tilt my head before standing up and grabbing my jacket from the back of the chair. "Is he planning a surprise party?"

Another snicker from Roman.

"Well, wise guy, he does have something special for ya." Harrison grabs my arm and leads me to the door.

When we step outside, people are loitering in the street under the El, in groups of threes and fours, huddling, whispering, and pointing, but the sound of a passing train drowns them out.

The news spread that Lieberman and Loewe are dining here.

We take two autos—Roman goes with Captain Zachary in one, Harrison and I are in the other. The ride is short to the yacht harbor, built to accommodate big racing and pleasure yachts. This is where I disposed of the Underwood.

At least a hundred spectators are waiting at the outer edge of the harbor. Seeing them all here because of us makes me nauseous, and I will my stomach not to expel breakfast. Both cheers and jeers rise from the crowd as Roman emerges from his Marmon, and more as I climb out of mine. People are pointing and shouting. The only word I make out is "murderers."

Harrison leads me to the bridge; Zachary escorts Roman, whose mood has flipped again because he's grinning and practically prancing at the attention.

"Now, just where did ya toss the typewriter, Noah?" Harrison asks.

Men in diving suits are sitting on a large boat rocking gently in the lagoon below. Smaller rowboats are sprinkled along the inlet.

"I leaned over the parapet," I say, miming the motion, "and threw the Underwood in this direction. I estimate it landed about fifteen feet over there." I point to where I'm sure the mangled machine is lying in muck.

Captain Zachary yells directions to the divers below.

"All right Lieberman, Loewe," Harrison says. "We have to search for the belt again." As we're walking back to the cars, he gestures to a group of newshounds. "Hey, Snyder, Krumley, come here."

The men rush over with hopeful looks on their faces.

"How about ya ride with us, get yourselves an exclusive?" He turns to Zachary. "Whaddaya think, Captain?"

"Sure, they're two decent fellas who've always reported about my men fairly. Why not?"

"Really?" one of the reporters says. "That'd be great."

I glance at Roman, unable to stop from smirking.

Well played. How can it hurt a hanging case to have the guilty parties speak unfettered with reporters? Why, the public will want to supply the rope themselves.

One gets into my car while the other rides with Roman.

I settle into the back seat. Detective Harrison sits in the front with the driver, and the newshound comes into the back with me.

"I'm Wally Snyder with the *Tribune*. So, why'd you do it, Noah?"

I sneer at the hound dog. So much for seducing me with questions designed to impress. He goes for direct. I don't respond.

"Okay, well, is Roman Loewe telling the truth? Are you the one who came up with the plan? You struck the blows that killed Bennie Frisch?"

"He's lying," I snap. "Kidnapping a child for ransom was his idea. And further"—I flick ash out the window—"it's inconceivable for me to cause an injury that would bleed. Why, my aversion to blood is well established, well documented. Loewe knows this too. He's the one who planned the thing, and he is the one who used the hammer on Bennie and stuffed the rag down his throat."

"Why do you think he's saying it's you who did it?"

What an insufferable idiot. "He thinks he'll go free eventually if I'm proved to be the one who did the actual killing."

"But, despite who done it, you two boys murdered that kid. Best Roman could hope for would be spending the rest of his life in prison."

I shrug.

Wally Snyder writes copious notes.

"All right, so even if he is the slayer, if he's the one who did the killin', then what do you think, Noah?"

"About what?"

Snyder stops scribbling, and he uses the pencil to scratch his temple.

"Well, about the killin', of course. A boy's dead. His momma and his family's missing him. How do you feel about that?"

A fair question. One I know how to answer, but how to make this lesser man understand? While not a simpleton, he doesn't have the mental acuity to comprehend the complexities involved in such a response.

"I don't believe in your God," I say, "or any other Supreme Being, which releases me from moral and ethical restraints. Man is the Supreme Being; however, not all men are equal. There are men who farm, men who coalmine, and men who are railroad workers. All necessary professions, but what of the men who cure the farmer's ailments, design the mines coalmen mine, and the train others drive and ride? Intelligence is at the core, Wally."

"And?"

"And I treated the act as one would a science experiment."

"But for what purpose?"

I look at him and not at the front seat where Harrison is conversing with the driver, seemingly ignoring us.

I doubt it.

"Education, of course. I liken it to dissecting frogs in school. Distasteful, but essential to garner knowledge." I shrug before turning to stare out the window, tired of talking. "I desired to know what the experience would be like."

* * *

Sunday afternoon, 1 June 1924

Again, a convoy of autos follows our motorcade back to the Criminal Court Building, wherein Roman is shuffled off in one direction, and I toward Mr. Hawke's office.

When we get there, Hawke is standing outside in the hallway with his hands on his hips. He's scowling, and his face is in dire need of a shave. "You're late! I wanted the boys returned by noon, Marv."

I smirk when Detective Harrison bows his head.

"Sorry, sir, but finding the belt took time."

"You got it then?"

"Yes," I say, although Hawke isn't speaking to me. "Roman found it." I shake my head remembering his enthusiasm in "lending you fellas" a hand as he'd said to the officers and reporters who searched the thicket and adjacent meadow, and the excited, smug look on his face when he held up the blue belt striped with yellow and red.

"And the typewriter?"

"Divers pulled it outta the lagoon sir," Harrison says.

"All right." Hawke nods and turns to me. "Your father's here, and I'm going to graciously let you speak with him for a minute."

I wonder if this is the surprise spoken of earlier.

Hawke opens his office door and steps aside. "After you, Noah. Marv, come back here in five minutes."

"Would you mind bringing me something to drink, Detective Harrison? Maybe water?"

He looks at Mr. Hawke.

"That's fine, Marv."

"More cigarettes too, please," I add.

"Sure," Harrison says, but his face, neck, and ears darken. "Back in five."

I walk into Hawke's office for the first time and am impressed by the size. It's as big as the conference room and holds a massive desk with papers and files littering the surface, three oak barrister bookcases, a watercooler in one corner, and a scattering of eclectic chairs made from wood and metal. My father is sitting in one, and he rises when I enter.

"Hello, son." He's gripping his hat in both hands.

"Hello, Dad." I walk over on shaky legs, struck by his watery eyes.

"Mr. Hawke, I want to speak with my son in private please."

"I'm afraid I can't allow this, Mr. Lieberman."

"Are you telling me, sir," my father says, and his voice wavers like it does when he becomes upset, "that a father is not permitted to be alone with his child during such a time?" He grips his hat tighter. "After I trusted you by letting you keep him in your custody for days in the hopes that you would catch the real killer?"

"And we have," Hawke responds, his chin jutting. "Now, I've given you this opportunity to see for yourself that the boy is unharmed." He points to me. "No physical injury has come to him."

I keep my expression impassive.

"Yes, Mr. Hawke, but as is every parent's duty, I stand by my child. There might be things he wishes to tell his father that he cannot say around anyone else. Would you begrudge me from being a confidante?"

Hawke's jaw twitches. "I'm sorry, Mr. Lieberman, but no legal provisions support your request at this time."

"Well, he has certain rights, constitutional and such, and I am advising him not to speak further without benefit of counsel." He grabs his overcoat from the chair and places his hat on his head. "Counsel, which I shall be hiring forthwith."

With this, he squeezes my shoulder and marches out of Mr. Hawke's office. The door barely shuts before Detective Harrison comes back with my drink and cigarettes.

"Sit down, Noah," Hawke says, and then he leaves me with Harrison.

When Hawke returns, it's with two more detectives and a handful of men. The man who typed my confession walks inside after them, carrying his stenography machine. I try to catch Hawke's eye as a table is brought in from another room, but he's busy addressing a tall, meticulously attired man who looks to be somewhere in his fifties. The gentleman's fleshy face and jowly neck jiggle, and he keeps leaning back on his heels while conversing with Hawke.

Another surprise? No, more likely my father's visit came as a surprise to Hawke, and this is what Harrison alluded to earlier.

Roman walks into the room, followed by Captain Zachary, and yet another elegantly garbed man carrying a black leather briefcase with two straps.

The alienists have arrived.

Hawke glances up and gestures for the man to come over to him, and Captain Zachary and Roman join me at the table. Roman is smirking.

A third gentleman walks inside the room and joins his peers at Hawke's desk.

I pull out a cigarette from the fresh deck.

"Captain Zachary, would you mind?" I say, holding up the stick. "I'm allowed cigarettes but not a lighter anymore. Quite an inconvenience."

He obliges me.

I inhale smoke and look over at Roman. He's grinning back at me. I try to convey my self-congratulatory thoughts to him.

I knew that they would call in head doctors to ensure that we can't plead insanity.

Chapter 22

6:00 a.m., Sunday, 11 November 1923

I SAT BEHIND the wheel, quiet, as we left the spur road. Echoes of gin pounded my temples. Roman rocked in the passenger seat, still high from either alcohol, the old guy dying, or from us afterward.

"That was something, hey, Babe?" he said. I didn't respond. A realization hit me earlier, one that burned my stomach and my heart.

Although perception, awareness, had been pecking around in my brain for a while.

"I was talking about us mostly, you know."

I nodded, too overcome with emotion to speak. Hearing him say words reflecting how *I* felt about *him* was bittersweet.

Our commitment to each other would likely make or break tonight.

After I drove a few miles, I pointed toward the tonneau. "Get me some joe, will you?"

"Sure, sure." He reached into the back and grabbed the thermos.

I kept my eyes on the road, but my mind traveled to a million different places.

Roman tapped my shoulder. "Here," he said and handed the cup to me.

I took a sip, then said, "You won't stop, will you Manny? *We* won't stop."

"What're you yapping about?"

"Earlier. The hobo."

"Ah, that's bunk. We didn't do anything to the bum. Fella's pump quit on him or something." He squeezed my knee. "We just took advantage of the situation, huh?"

"Yes, and the stowaway on the train didn't die by our hands either, but what about the rummy at the church? Bricks through windows, arson, thefts, cheating. Will these things stop?"

I slowed my speed, hoping to keep the tires where they belonged, and looked at him. His happy expression flipped.

"Whaddaya mean, Babe?"

The sky was brightening. Soon, other vehicles would be on the road.

"We're going to get caught, Manny."

"Ah, you're nuts! We're a couple of smart fellas. No one's nailing us."

"Everyone, even the Übermensch, can be snared in the inferior man's trap. And getting blotto and committing vandalism, burglary, is dangerous. And our holy sacrifice at the church in Michigan? How long before it's repeated? Tonight, if the derelict's own heart hadn't attacked him first."

"So, then we plan what we do." Excitement raced through his words. "I have this fantasy about kidnapping someone for ransom, a kid's easiest, I think. Send pops on a scavenger hunt searching for clues on how to get his snot back. Course, we'll have to bump off the brat so he can't turn us in."

His voice rose with each sentence.

The cool morning breeze coming in the windows did nothing to temper the heat flowing through my veins at his passion, which confirmed my initial fears: he could not—or would not—stop, and I couldn't refuse him. I took another sip. Lukewarm coffee burned down my throat like acid. Nausea roiled in my stomach either from the motion of tires over bumpy roads or from the truth if we continued in this trajectory—our one hope to live as far as I saw it.

"Yes, Manny, I'm confident our brains can come up with a foolproof method to concoct, carry out, and get away with such a scenario. But then what?" Again, I turned to study him. He wore a sour puss, but he could be dangerous when sullen.

"Why don't you say what you need to say? Spill it."

"I'm simply asking a question. Will it end with the child? Do we split the money and go our separate ways? Stay together and hide from the world as we do now?"

"Ah, geez, shut your kisser, Babe."

"You left before," I whispered, despite willing myself to hold it in. "What assurance do I have that you won't leave again?"

He pounded his fist on the dashboard. "Horseshit! I told you why I left and why I came back. Things can go on like they are. I mean, we'll probably both hitch up with a couple a dames. That's what people do, right? And the rest…"

He gestured wildly with his hands. "This and us, well, it can stay the same."

"You must be joking, Manny."

"Why? Stepping out on wives is more dangerous and exciting than on dates, and for the occasional extra thrill…well, we can find some trouble that works for us." He squeezed my thigh.

I shook my head. "This is what I mean. You won't quit, which means I won't, which equates to us getting caught one day. And likely sooner than later."

"We won't get nailed, Babe."

My retort stuck in my throat when I spied something on the side of the road up ahead.

As I drove closer, I saw that it was a blue Model T coupe. A man in a rumpled, threadbare suit stood by the open driver's door, bent over, as he looked inside.

Roman pulled the revolver from his pocket.

"What say you, Babe? How about we bump off this jobbie before we start making plans for snatching a kid?"

"Who said anything about going through with your kidnapping idea, Manny?"

He didn't answer. The Willys inched closer.

"We don't even have to stop, just fill him full of lead and keep moving."

The man straightened up and turned in our direction when we were right behind him. As our auto reached him, I saw that his vehicle was full and counted three children and a woman.

Roman raised the barrel of the gun higher, nearer to the open window.

"Put it away," I hissed.

He flashed that grin of his again, returned the revolver to his pocket, and waved to them as we passed by.

"You've made my point, Manny. The slaughter of an entire family deserves a few minutes to develop a plan."

"Ah, rubbish, I was kidding."

I wanted to believe him, but I recognized the tone in his voice and didn't need to see his eyes to know that he'd been serious. Something inside of him, and me too, hidden from the world, was unleashed when we met. By ourselves, left to our own devices, neither of us would ever act on those urges; but together...well, our destinies were entwined.

He slapped his hand on his knee. "Come on, Babe, you have more yapping to do, so get on with it."

"I propose that we enact your fantasy."

Silence weighted the air. His leg began bouncing up and down in a furious manner. Miles passed before he made a sound.

"But you believe," he finally said, "that we'll get pinched, at least one day?"

"Yes."

"Well, I say let's take our chances and start planning."

"The two of us will dance for sure if we're caught, Manny."

"We're jumping off the gallows whether we're nabbed today or tomorrow."

"Perhaps not."

"You've gone screwy, Babe. I think the brothers put something in their bathtub gin recipe that's messing with you."

Sweat leaked from my forehead, and I gripped the steering wheel.

Can I do this? Tell him my outrageous idea?

I took the coffee, wedged between my legs, and tossed it out the window, cup and all. "We plan the thing, Manny, like you said, kidnapping a kid for ransom whom we kill anyway." I kept my eyes on the road and didn't so much as glance his way. "But we make sure that we're caught."

His revolver was out, cold barrel pressed against my temple, before I could even look at him. I resolved not to flinch.

"What good in damnation does this accomplish? We'll still be hanged. Why, I oughta shoot you right now and be done with it!"

"Then do it, Manny. Shoot me."

The gun shook, along with his hand, and I imagined his finger incrementally pressing the trigger. I slowed the Willys, pulled it to the side of the road, parked, and faced the person on whom I could not turn my back. The person I loved, although the words never left, and would never leave, my lips.

"There. I've made it easy," I said, with the weapon now pointed at my forehead. "You don't have to worry about getting into an accident when you kill me."

"Don't think I won't! 'Make sure that we're caught.' Are you nuts?"

"No, Manny, I'm not. Put that away, and I'll explain."

He kept it leveled. A car with its headlights on was coming from behind. We stared at each other while time slowed. He lowered the gun and stashed it in his jacket right before the Model T pulled alongside us and stopped.

"Fellas need some help?" It was the man we passed earlier. One of the children sat in the wife's lap in the passenger seat, and her arm went protectively around it.

"Just watering the weeds," Roman said. Grinning, he added, "Sorry for my language ma'am, young'uns."

The woman looked relieved as the man drove off.

Does she realize that I saved her life today? No, she has no idea.

"So?" Manny demanded, but he left the gun in his pocket. "Explain."

"Our age."

He shook his head. "What rot does—"

"Our one chance of escaping the gallows is our age."

* * *

Saturday evening, 24 November 1923 through Sunday, 25 November 1923

The open books strewn across my desk mocked my futile attempts to concentrate. Frustrated, I whipped off my new eyeglasses and threw them down on a volume about Illinois criminal statutes. Leaning back in the wooden chair, I pinched the bridge of my nose and closed my eyes.

I had not seen or spoken to Roman in two weeks. Not one word. He didn't speak the rest of the way home on that fateful early morning drive, nor would he let me talk. Every time I tried, he pulled out his gun.

A knock broke into the quietude, startling me. I opened my eyes.

"May I come in?"

"Yes, Margaret."

She pushed the door with her expansive hip, bringing with her the pungent aroma of sauerbraten. "I took the liberty of fixing you a plate since you didn't come down for supper, Master Babe."

"Thank you," I said. I jumped up, took the tray from her, and waited impatiently for her to leave.

She smiled and backed out of the doorway. "Oh, I almost forgot! Mr. Loewe phoned and said to tell you he'll be outside in front of the house at ten."

I stood there holding the tray, with my mouth open, as she closed the door.

Forty-six minutes later, I paced the sidewalk, smoking a Lucky, wondering if Roman would show up. The food I had devoured was a sodden lump in my stomach.

"Hey, Babe," I heard, just as I felt a sharp tap on my shoulder.

I whirled around. "Where's your car?"

He shrugged. "Revoked again."

I didn't ask why. "We can take the Willys," I said and pulled out my flask. "Got anything to fill this?"

He grinned that grin of his again. "Of course."

We went to our clearing in Washington Park, and for the first time ever, all we did was drink, talk, and argue while owls hooted and the occasional coyote howled in the distance. To his credit, he listened to my argument about the political climate seeing a shift in attitude regarding executions by hangings, especially when it came to juveniles, and agreed that we would at least have a chance at a life sentence—and parole one day—if we got caught committing only one capital crime at our age. He even admitted that the prison scene was another fantasy of his. However, nothing I said convinced him that we *would* get caught. He believed that we could go on doing whatever we wanted without repercussions. Although I agreed that men of our high intelligence should be able to, I knew there would be consequences from the common men in charge. Never once did Roman suggest altering our behavior.

"Ah, come on, let's scram," he said after a few hours. "I snuck out when Popsie went to bed, and I don't want to push my luck." He got to his feet and reached out a hand to help me up. "Drop me home."

"Okay, but consider yourself lucky because, this time, *I* could've killed *you*." I patted my jacket pocket. "I brought my bean shooter tonight."

He laughed.

It was almost two in the morning by the time we drove past the University of Chicago campus. All looked quiet at the school and for the next few blocks.

"Pull over, Babe, and don't turn the engine off."

I glanced at him. "Why?"

His face wore the expression I knew so well. The king commanding his slave. A chill went down my spine.

He took my hand and placed it in his lap. "I thought of your punishment."

"For what, Manny?"

"For suggesting the coppers could ever nail us, of course." He grinned and winked.

"Here? So close to the university?"

"More thrilling. Besides, no one's around." He unbuttoned his trousers.

I scanned the tranquil, residential street and lowered my head.

Sometime later, I heard, "Hey, that you Lieberman? Oh!"

Roman pushed me off him, and I straightened up. The guy staring in the passenger window with a horrified look on his face was a former student who I barely knew and whose name I couldn't place. But he, apparently, recognized my automobile. Before I could form a response or make up a plausible excuse for what he witnessed, Roman reached into my jacket, grabbed my revolver, and shot him in the head.

The bang rocked the peaceful night. Sulfur burned my nostrils as the nameless guy dropped to the sidewalk.

Lights turned on in one house. Then another.

"Move, Babe, get us outta here!"

But I couldn't make my hands and feet work. Not until I heard the siren.

Chapter 23

What is the truth, but a lie agreed upon.

—Friedrich Nietzsche

Sunday afternoon, 1 June 1924

"Now, Mr. Loewe, we'll start with you," says the spiffy alienist that Mr. Hawke introduced as Alexander Chapel. "Tell us again about plotting the crime and the execution thereof."

"Well, like I already said, I don't remember when we started planning the thing, but if Babe says November, then I guess it was in November."

I study the three head doctors while Roman talks. Chapel is the tallest by far, likely six foot four or five, and scrupulously dressed. Jacket, vest, bowtie—everything buttoned, fastened, and pressed. His gold monocle, with like chain, fits between his cheekbone and brow bone.

The second doctor, whose flabby face reddened and jiggled when Chapel initiated the conversation, is the opposite. Short in stature, thick, and square, his clothes are tailored poorly, making him look like a child in his father's suit. He's taking notes.

If not for his glowing green eyes, the third man would blend into the walls. He, too, is recording everything, judging by how fast his pen is moving. The air is hot despite multiple fans that succeed only in swirling the cigarette and cigar smoke so that an eerie haze surrounds us.

Bertram Hawke is indeed a formidable adversary. In the two-and-a-half days that he held us without benefit of counsel, he wasted no time in not only obtaining the confessions he craved but most of the physical evidence as well. Now, he's using alienists to acquire assurance of our moral turpitude while proving that we're not insane.

Well played, Mr. Hawke, I think, as Roman retells his confession.

I sneer when he states that he drove the Willys, and I'm the one who bludgeoned Bennie Frisch.

"Can you tell us if you believe that doing this, kidnapping a child for ransom and killing him, is a right or wrong thing to do?" Dr. Chapel asks.

Roman, scrunching his forehead, smiles his quick, infectious grin. "Why, it's wrong of course."

"And did you, at any time, consider backing out of this, ah, situation?"

"You mean quitting? Being a quitter? No, never. I'm no coward."

"All right, then, can you explain why you did this?"

Roman doesn't answer right away, and I can tell by his eyes that he's processing Chapel's question and trying to come up with an honest response. At least, as honest as he can be in our situation.

"Beats me, Doc. I guess for the adventure of it."

The men turn to me as one.

"All right, Mr. Lieberman," Dr. Chapel says. "Can you tell us, in your words, how this came about?"

And so, it goes.

* * *

Monday, 2 June 1924

The lawyer's cage is hot. Even without a jacket and my top button undone, sleeves rolled up, the oppressive air makes breathing a chore. This tiny room for Cook County prisoners and their attorneys has no fan. I sit back in the hard seat, damp, uncomfortable, and for the first time, I'm having doubts.

I glance across the table at the man, the legend, before me: Maurice Milton. Jurist extraordinaire.

In his illustrious career, Mr. Milton has defended many criminals—murderers—and won the lives of all but one. Although I've followed his legal career in the newspapers here and there, more so in the last five months, I never saw a picture of him. Vivid imagination notwithstanding, I couldn't have predicted the person before me.

Close to six feet tall when standing straight, Milton looks as if he stumbled out of bed and put on clothes from the floor, pushed each plump foot through the wrinkled pant legs of faded gray trousers, donned a coffee-stained white shirt before hastily knotting a rumpled tie, now lying crooked on his chest, and attaching colorful galluses over a substantial gut. His craggy face fallen, he appears to be around sixty-five, sixty-seven, with eyebrows that form upside-down vees over light blue eyes. A clump of graying brown hair keeps breaking free from its greasy compatriots, causing him to shove it back in place.

What if Manny's right, and we're doomed to hang no matter what?

"The State's attorney is already linking you both to other crimes in the area," Mr. Milton says, tapping his fingers on the tabletop.

"Hogwash!"

Walter Rachben, the barrister assisting Milton, nods at Roman's outburst.

Curious, I ask, "What other crimes?"

"A taxi driver was drugged and maimed while unconscious," Milton answers. "Castrated. The man identified you and Roman as his attacker."

I catch Roman's eye and take note of his delight. He's loving the attention.

"Back in November," Rachben says, "someone shot a young man in the head near the University of Chicago. No robbery as evidenced by his untouched wallet, but the bullet matches the type used in the same kind of revolver found in your bedroom, Noah."

Roman doesn't look at me. We had barely turned the dark street corner that fateful night when the police arrived at the scene.

"And then there's the case of the forty-five-year-old woman who swears that you two abduct—"

"Enough," Milton says, and he brushes hair from his eyes again. "There will always be speculation to drive the herd wild with conspiratorial theories on every crime in the vicinity when a confession occurs." He waves a hand dismissively and stands up. "We're concentrating on this matter, and your constitutional rights as human beings and citizens." Banging on the door to be let out, he says, "I petitioned the court for a writ of habeas corpus, and the State's attorney filed his objections and his own motion, of course. Hearing is in twenty minutes. See you then."

* * *

"This motion is, by far, the most outrageous one I've heard in all my years gracing a courtroom!" Maurice Milton is rocking on his heels, pulling his galluses out with his hands, and letting the suspenders snap back as he stands before Chief Justice Jack Castaner.

I lean forward for a better look at Mr. Milton, aware of Father's eyes on me. He's sitting with Levi, a row behind Roman and me, along with Roman's uncle and brother.

"Surely," Hawke shouts, "keeping two murdering miscreants in my custody until the inquest into the poor Frisch boy's death is complete cannot be the most outrageous petition my adversary has come across. Why—"

"My clients are minors. Juveniles!" Milton points in Roman's and my direction. "They have rights, basic human civil liberties, and even more so because of their ages. The law demands certain procedural steps, and one of them is for these boys to be in the custody of the sheriff and not the State's attorney, regardless of a pending indictment."

"What difference does their age matter?" Hawke's nose is red, along with the rest of his face and his ears. "They willingly, under no brutality or coercion from my men—"

"Ha! The State's attorney brags about not beating the boys. Well, good job, sir."

"They gave their confessions, told of their callous and merciless plot to kidnap Bennie Frisch, murder him, and steal ten thousand dollars of his father's hard-earned income!"

"Enough." Justice Castaner slams down his gavel. "This courtroom will come to order."

Roman chuckles and nudges me with his foot. I don't dare look at him, but I'm enjoying the show as well. Despite his slothful appearance, Maurice Milton has won back some of my respect.

"Motion for the People is denied," the judge says. "The defendants will be placed in the immediate custody of the sheriff but will be available for questioning by both the prosecution and defense before trial begins. So, ordered!"

Another bang of the gavel, and the hearing is over.

* * *

Wednesday, 11 June 1924

"Five minutes, Lieberman, then we're moving," a guard calls from down the hallway. I sit up in the cot, adjust my vest, and debate the advisability of taking another sip of black coffee. *Might as well get used to it sooner rather than later,* I think, picking up the cup.

Today is our arraignment, wherein Roman and I will plead not guilty, despite our admissions of guilt. A predictable legal move, but the illustrious Mr. Hawke is more formidable an opponent than I first believed. Not only did he parade seventy-two witnesses before the grand jury, unheard of in a case where the facts are not in dispute—hell, we confessed and gave them all the physical evidence—but Hawke also secured two indictments. The first indictment, containing eleven counts, is for murder, and the second one, kidnapping for ransom, charges us with sixteen counts. Each.

Bertram Hawke is covering every conceivable base as I knew he would.

I take a deep breath, let it out, and decide against another sip of mud. I'm placing the cup back on the floor by my feet when a sheriff's deputy appears at the bars, keys in hand.

"Time to go," he says, unlocking the door.

I rise and stretch my spine before holding out my right arm. He slaps handcuffs on me and then himself, and we walk through corridor after corridor, pausing only for him to unlock a gate and slide it securely behind us.

The Cook County Jail is located behind the Criminal Court Building, connected by a bridge. We walk through and head for the sixth-floor courthouse.

Spectators and newshounds are everywhere.

I slow my steps, and the deputy turns to me and chuckles.

"Oh, this is nothing, kid, only hundreds compared to a thousand outside. A door got broke when a crowd tried rushing inside. Had to call in extra patrols to keep things under control in the streets."

"Why?" I ask, although I can assume why, and my adrenaline soars. Manny must be enjoying this immensely.

"Everybody wants to catch a look at the millionaire boys that committed the 'crime of the century,' as the rags are saying."

A lightshow begins when I enter the crowded, stuffy courtroom. I put my hand over my face to block the cameras. Most of the occupants are men, but a few women join them in the aisles, lean against the walls, and sit on windowsills. All crane their necks to get a better look at me. Roman is already here, tethered to his own deputy on his left side. To my delight, I'm directed to the seat next to him, and my guard sits on my right. Misters Milton and Rachben are in front of us, and Bertram Hawke is at the prosecutor's table flanked by Jim Sever and two other assistants.

Roman looks at me, holds up his cuffed hand, and mutters, "Swell bracelets, eh, Babe?"

Mr. Milton turns to face us, and we lean forward.

"Justice Castaner announced yesterday that he'll be the trial judge, boys. This is good because he's much more liberal than his colleague."

Roman grins, but only half his mouth rises. I know this sneer; he's enjoying our dual roles of puppeteer and puppet. I gaze around. A large pillar to my right blocks some of the prosecutor's table from my view, but the room is crammed with spectators. Multiple fans do nothing to afford relief from the stifling heat. I wish I could remove my jacket.

"All rise," the bailiff says.

Everyone stands up. Judge Castaner enters from his chamber behind the bench, sits down, and bangs his gavel. Murmurings take a minute to quiet, and when they do, he calls the court to order.

"The defendants will stand before the bench as the indictments are read."

Roman and I shuffle forward, dragging our leashed guard dogs with us.

"Regarding the first indictment for murder, handed down by the grand jury on the sixth day of June 1924, how do you, Roman Alfred Loewe, and you, Noah Freudenthal Lieberman Jr., plead? Guilty or not guilty?"

"Not guilty, your Honor," Roman says first. I repeat the same.

Flashbulbs go off from different angles as newshounds push through spectators and vie for photographs. The random bursts of light give me an instant headache and fill the air with the acrid smell of burning bulbs.

"As to the second indictment of kidnapping for ransom, handed down by the grand jury on the sixth day of June 1924, how do you, Roman Alfred Loewe, and you, Noah Freudenthal Lieberman Jr., plead? Guilty or not guilty?"

We both repeat in kind with "not guilty."

"The defendants will return to their seats," Judge Castaner says. "Mr. Hawke, Mr. Sever, Mr. Rachben, and Mr. Milton, approach the bench so we can set a trial date."

Roman and I sit, and the room fills with chatter again as the prosecution and defense step up to the bench. Deciding to test the limits of our escorts, I lean into Roman.

"What do you think?" I whisper.

He grins and looks over at the deputy next to me, who either isn't paying attention to us or doesn't care. Roman's guard appears unconcerned as well.

"All good calls so far, Babe." His eyes shine with a look embedded in my soul. He points toward Milton. "But I have my doubts about our country-cousin mouthpiece here keeping us off the scaffolding. Letting this guy lip for us might be a big mistake." He shakes his head. "Should've just gone on a spree and let the coppers take us out in some good ole Chicago lightning."

I'm not sure I disagree with him.

Our legal counselors return.

"The next appearance is set for the twenty-first of July," Judge Castaner says, "at which time I'll hear any motions brought before the court and dispose of them. Trial will commence on the fourth of August. Court is adjourned."

Another rap of the gavel resonates throughout the room.

"Get ready, boys," Mr. Milton says as he stuffs papers into his briefcase. "Our scientists are coming."

With a wink, he's gone, and I'm yanked to my feet and led back to my cell.

Chapter 24

Saturday evening, 22 March 1924

"Oh, come on, Noah, let's dance again!"

I did my best to smile at my date, another blind one set up by Dick Renford and whose name I couldn't recall, and said, "We just sat down. I'll go get us some punch, and we can talk for a while, all right?"

The insufferable girl's face screwed up, but she nodded. I took my leave and weaved through dancers. I barely avoided an arm to the head and a kick from enthusiastic students having fun at the university's First Weekend of Spring Dance. Streamers hung from the ceiling, confetti littered the floor, and a live band blared swing music. Laughter and smoke filled the enormous hall.

By the time I returned with a drink in each hand, the song had ended, and the seats at the round table were full again. Most of them, anyway. Roman's date, a girl he recently began spending time with before meeting up with me afterward, sat on his lap cooing and giggling.

"Oooh, you're such a hoofer, Roman. I love your moves." She played with his bowtie, clipped only to the left side to accommodate his unbuttoned shirt. His sleeves were rolled up, and a sheen of perspiration coated his forearms.

As jealous as I became whenever forced to witness Roman's tasteless interactions with the fairer sex, I couldn't help but fantasize about later. The two of us together, after our dates were tucked in their beds, his girl reliving every word he uttered, and more so, how each syllable flowed from his full lips while mine wondered how she got stuck with me.

The band began another song.

"Let's dance some more!" his date squealed.

Roman glanced around, pulled his flask from inside his vest, took a quick nip, and snuck it back.

Keeping the flask hidden, he offered, "Want some, doll?"

She shook her head. "Oh no! Daddy grounded me the last time I came home with giggle juice on my breath."

"More for me later," he said, and he jumped up, taking her with him and twirling her around before putting her back down. "Come on, toots, shake those tootsies," he sang, and they disappeared into the crowd.

Dick Renford rose, pulling his silly girl with him, and hands and feet flapping, they too became swallowed up in the mass of swinging arms and legs.

I expected Henry, home on spring break, and his steady filly to take flight as well, but she was leaning over the table shout-talking to my mismatched partner for the night. Something to do with hairstyles.

"Have you decided on Europe yet, Noah?"

"Yes, Henry, I'll join you abroad for the summer. I'll fill out the passport application next week. That'll give me enough time for our June eleventh departure."

"Great! I'm excited. I've never been birding in another country before. I hear the Mauretania's a lovely ship, and…"

Two guys walking over diverted my attention. When I recognized them, my stomach hardened, and I clenched my fists. With a calmness I didn't feel, I pulled out my deck of Luckies and lit one.

"Hey, Henry, how are you, chap?" Tony said when he reached us. His friend, Jim, accompanied him, but I saw no one else with them. Although Tony addressed Heinzie, he smirked my way. I took a draw and blew smoke rings at him but didn't speak. His eyes moved to my date next to me and my arm draped over the back of her chair.

"You sonofabitch!" I heard, and then Roman charged at Tony, fists flying. Tony dropped to the floor. It happened so fast no one reacted until Jim was helping up a bleeding Tony.

"Get the drunkard outta here before the chaperone sees," someone yelled. The girls' mouths hung open, and their eyes widened as we gathered our belongings and left. Tony and Jim followed behind us.

Outside, Henry said, "I think Dick and I should make sure that the ladies get home."

"Good idea." I turned to my date. "I'm sorry things ended up this way. Perhaps we can have dinner next week?"

She nodded, appearing stunned by the sudden turn in our evening.

"Give us a kiss, baby," Roman said, pulling his girl against his body and planting a wet-sounding smooch on her cheek. She giggled and waved goodbye.

The second they left with Henry and Dick, Roman ran up to Tony and shoved him. "I got your peeper, now how about some chin music!"

"Hey, hey," Jim said, grabbing Roman's arm before it connected with Tony's face again. "Enough. He apologized a long time ago."

"Yeah, well, tell me why I shouldn't knock hell outta you every time I see you," Roman said, and he spat on the ground next to Tony's feet.

"I don't remember ever receiving an apology," I said.

"Look, I'm sorry, okay?" Tony held a hand over his eye and winced. "I only mentioned to Roman's brother that it was strange how you two spent so much time together. What do you want me to say, Noah? You're an odd bird, and, well, you bothered me, and damn, I was drunk, okay? I made a dumb remark, and I'm sorry."

Roman's eyes blazed, and his hands trembled at his sides. His anger fueled mine, and I decided to return the favor and add some excitement for him.

"Well, Tony, the curious thing is that Roman and I don't spend half as much time together, at least not alone, as you and Jim do. You managed to deprive us of our dates this evening, but where are yours?" I looked left and right. "Where are the girls?"

"W-w-we, ah, we were hoping to meet some here," Jim said. Tony remained quiet, but his face reddened at my implication.

"Yeah, Noah." Roman punched my shoulder and glared at his old friends. "My pal here makes a good point for debate."

"You're bonkers, both of you. Bonkers," Tony said, still holding his eye. "I told you I was sorry. Let's go, Jim. I'm gonna clean this up and ice it, then maybe we'll head downtown to find some real lookers." He jerked his head toward the building. "None of these bug-eyed Bettys will do."

They left, and Roman and I went to our private spot in Washington Park.

* * *

Sunday, 23 March 1924

Warm sun filtered through faded curtains at the diner, reflected glare off the silver napkin holder, and landed on scruffy linoleum. I resisted the urge to take out my watch and check the time and instead grabbed my coffee cup and sipped. Roman told me on the telephone earlier that Dick could only meet with us for a quick lunch, and I already knew that Henry wanted to go home and spend time with his sister and his niece, who were visiting. This was a perfect way to get time alone with Roman to talk.

A shiver went through me at the duplicity of our friendship.

"Well, last night was interesting," Dick Renford finally said. "And it sure made for good conversation, but I gotta blow." He rose and slapped a few bills on the table to cover his share. "Coming, Roman?"

"Oh, you're leaving, Dick?"

"Geez, Noah, how'd you figure it out?" Roman teased.

Henry snorted. "I better go too. I promised my sister I'd be home early to take the little one 'birdy watching.'" He stood up and knocked into our waitress. "Sorry," he muttered, his face coloring.

"You can make it up in my tip," the woman said. "Now, can I getcha boys anything else? Slice of apple pie, maybe?"

"Pie!" Roman slapped his hands on the table like an excited toddler. "With a big ole glob of blond ice cream. Thanks for the ride, Dick, but Noah here can drop me home, right?" He pointed to my satchel. "When's your bird tutoring thing?"

"I'll have the same," I told the waitress, who waited with her pencil poised, her lips pursed. "Yes, Roman, my class is at three, so I have time. I already drove you and your date to the dance last night, might as well continue the chauffeur service."

He grinned at me from across the table. "Ah, thanks!"

"When will your driving privileges be restored, Roman?" Henry asked, as he reached into his billfold, counted out money, and threw it down.

"Ah, Popsie's just mad because I dented his car a little."

"A dent? You tore off the passenger fender." Henry grabbed his hat and jacket from the hook next to our table and put them on.

Dick laughed. "And you were doing so good ever since returning from Ann Arbor. See you later, fellas."

"Goodbye," I said. Roman saluted them.

Henry and Dick zigzagged through a group of men who walked in, and then they left. I waited until the door shut behind them before speaking.

"Let's go over the route for the ransom again." I kept my voice low despite our table being secluded in the corner and the chatter of diners, clinking utensils, and vocal kitchen staff, which made most conversation challenging.

"Oh, sure," he said, and I felt a slight breeze as his leg pumped up and down. His eyes lit with that special look, powerful enough to intoxicate and terrify me at the same time. "Gimme paper, I want to doodle."

I reached into my bag, bypassing ornithology books, and pulled out a composition notebook. He scribbled feverishly after I handed it over.

"Good ole Pops will have to toss the spinach from the train at a remote clearing fourteen seconds after passing the Chesterfield

Plant." He licked the tip of the pencil, held it up, and pointed it at me. "That's counting to fourteen, quickly, in his head."

I scanned the area as he spoke. No one was near enough to overhear, but the waitress was approaching with our desserts in one hand and a pot of coffee in the other. I kicked Roman to make sure he kept his mouth shut.

"Here you go, boys," she said, placing a plate in front of each of us. She pulled out two forks from a dirty apron, put them down, and hovered the pot over my cup. "Another shot of belly warmer, luv?"

I nodded.

"Me too," Roman said.

She refilled us and then left us alone.

He dove into the pie. "Course, we'll call him that night, after we snatch the kid, tell him we got his brat, and to wait for further instructions," he said around a mouthful before swallowing and taking a sip of joe. "Meanwhile, we send Pops an overnight post which outlines the ransom demands, eventually sending him to the Save our City trash box on Lexington, where he'll find a little love note sending him to the pharmacy by the tracks. The dupe waits at the phone booth for us to call and tell him to board the two seventeen."

"He should have enough time to purchase a ticket and entrain," I said, enjoying my own slice of pie, although not as voraciously as Roman.

"Pops will have to hurry, so it'll be hard for him to give instructions to any coppers or private dicks he might have hanging around." He stuffed a massive forkful in his mouth.

I shook my head.

Manny has sure come a long way from believing that we would never be caught to planning our inevitable capture.

But our close call with that guy in November had been the turning point for him. He figured out that he, and by extension, I, would be hanged one day. My way, a gamble for sure, at least gave us a chance for freedom again. Because a life sentence didn't always mean life. I was betting, and he agreed, that with laudable records in prison, we could earn a commutation of our sentence and make us eligible for parole after a couple of decades. And we wouldn't be typical prisoners either. Our intelligence and education would make us useful, and our family status and wealth should buy us at least some privileges.

After that, he treated the plan like the world's greatest caper. For him, it didn't matter that we would be caught, tried, and convicted because he would know how we outsmarted them all. And that one day, before we died, we would write about the truth.

Provided my idea worked, and we weren't sentenced to death.

Roman picked up his coffee cup and sipped.

"All right, Manny, what next?"

He put his drink down. "We send Pops to the rear of the last car, where we'll have a letter of instruction taped to the bottom of the seat telling him where, when, and how to toss the dough." Without warning, he slammed his hand on the table and sent a butter knife clattering to the floor. "Damn shame we won't get to spend it."

I laughed. "I'm pretending that I wanted to gamble away my half on the ocean liner. But what would you do with five thousand, Manny? You already have more than that in your bank account." I took another bite and savored the cinnamon, sugary treat. There would be no warm apple pie in prison. Meals were sure to be revolting except during visits from family. "Speaking of the bank, Thursday I'm going to Union State on Ninety-Second Street to open an account in Herbert Bradford's name."

Roman, still drawing, nodded. "I'll go to the Grande Hotel and rent a room for Bradford."

"The esteemed Mr. Bradford is traveling to Chicago," I added.

He slapped his knee and howled, causing the nearest diners to scowl at us. "A right successful chap he is!" He shoved the last piece of pie into his mouth, and I wondered if he was savoring, or even tasting, it.

I patted my satchel. "Letters to Mr. Bradford addressed to the Grande will post from Michigan on the first Tuesday in April when I take a short birding expedition with Heinzie. These measures will establish Bradford's identity, enabling me to rent a car from—"

"U-Drive on South Side Street." Roman pushed his empty plate to the end of the table. "Willys-Knight touring auto's our best choice." He winked. "Plenty of room in the back and curtains to hide everything."

"We'll dump the body out at Fox Lake near the Indiana border. Stuff it half in, half out of a culvert by the tracks. It's a popular bird-watching area, one I frequent often alone or with peers or my classes. It's a trip out there, so we can stop and bury some of the kid's clothes along the way, but we'll wait and pour the acid on him at the disposal site."

"Sure, sure, but why are we bothering with acid at all?"

Our waitress passed by, and I placed my hand over my cup and shook my head at the unasked question I read on her face.

"Because, Manny, we want it to appear like we're attempting to disguise the victim's identity."

"Yeah, yeah, I know, make them think we're trying to outsmart them, when we're really setting ourselves up. 'Our arrogance will reflect our youth and help us in the end,'" he said, mimicking me.

"Precisely. Now, it's time to work on what to say when we telephone the father and how to word the ransom letter and the instruction letters—"

"Ah, we'll do that stuff soon, Babe. Let's talk about the kid. Who're we gonna do? I think—"

"It doesn't matter who."

"Order up!" came from the kitchen, followed by a dinging bell. As the waitress rushed by, she slapped our check down onto the table.

Roman picked up the bill, looked at it, and counted the money the guys had left. "I got the rest of this, but what do you mean?"

"The who is irrelevant. The only important thing is that the father can pay the ransom."

"That's crazy, Babe."

"Is it? You chose the date. The twenty-first of May. I propose that we type the letter, Dear Sir, and fill in the appropriate name on the envelope after we snatch the kid."

"Where're we going to find this kid?"

I thought about it. "We'll hang around the Dravah School and pick one."

Roman nodded. "Sure, sure, I like it. And what snot in that school doesn't have loaded parents?"

Chapter 25

> I know of no better life purpose than to perish in attempting the great and the impossible.
>
> —Friedrich Wilhelm Nietzsche

Saturday, 14 June 1924

"I BELIEVE THAT the key to mental health," Mr. Babcock says, "lies within endocrinology."

I'm sitting on the edge of a mattress in a small room located in the bowels of the jail. Other than the metal-framed bed there's a table with chairs, along with a sink in the corner, and a couple of strange-looking apparatuses.

Babcock is staring at me, so I stare back at the middle-aged man. He's only an inch or so taller than I am, but he gives off a powerful aura. His bald head and thick neck make him resemble a turtle wearing eyeglasses. According to Misters Milton and Rachben, Keith Babcock is the Chief Medical Examiner at Boston Psychopathic Hospital and is an expert in ductless glands, which include the thyroid and parathyroid glands in the neck, the thymus in the chest, pituitary and pineal glands in the head, as well as the gonads—or sex glands. Maurice Milton prewarned me of the man's visit along with Hank Hudson, a tall, thirtyish, Chicago neuropsychiatrist with experience in psychiatric disorders that Milton hired to assist Mr. Babcock.

"It's my conviction that a correlation between dysfunction of a glandular nature and mental illness or instability could pinpoint a specific gland to be the cause of a particular psychological affliction."

The younger Hudson's head bobs enthusiastically. Dressed in a stiff, white hospital gown, I say nothing.

"Now, this is a Jones metabolimeter," Babcock continues, pushing the glasses back up on his nose when they slip. "It's used to calculate metabolic rate. We tested Mr. Loewe earlier, and his results, minus seventeen percent, are low. I'm curious and excited about your outcome, so please lie on the bed and let us begin."

Well, I never anticipated this, I think, lying supine while Hudson places a cumbersome mouthpiece over my face. A lesser man might experience claustrophobia, but I'm just annoyed by the hard, uncomfortable mattress. *Wonder what Manny thought?*

When the testing is over, I wait for two hours to find out that my results, minus five percent, are only a tad lower than the average boy of my age and physical structure. I've no idea what this means.

Mr. Babcock and Mr. Hudson take Sunday off and return at nine Monday morning. This time Roman and I are in the small "examination" room together sitting next to each other at the table.

"This," Babcock says, pointing to another contraption, "is what's called a plethysmograph and is used to calculate fluctuations in blood volume during emotional stimulation."

I can hold my tongue no longer. "And what, gentlemen, is the purpose of this experiment?"

Roman chuckles.

"Please, allow me," Hank Hudson says, holding up his hand when Mr. Babcock attempts to answer. The two men are standing over us, but Hudson sits down to address my question. He rests his elbows on the table and his head on his clasped hands. "Obviously, we are aware that you two are exceptionally intelligent and superior to your peers."

The man gets my attention.

"But what of emotional development? Is it possible your vast intellect allows no room for emotional growth? It could be that this area is withering like an untended flower."

Roman's foot nudges mine, and it takes great effort not to smirk.

"There may be a link," Babcock adds, "between lack of emotional development and the desire to commit such an offense."

"And if a link exists and can be verified," Hudson says, jumping back in to reclaim the narrative. "A cure to prevent such events from occurring in the future might be the outcome." He looks at Babcock. "Do you agree, Keith?"

Mr. Babcock nods. "Yes. Now, tomorrow, a Victor X-ray machine is being delivered with the hopes of determining if physical pathology exists in either or both of you, which can be scientific evidence hard to disregard."

The testing continues.

* * *

Wednesday, 2 July 1924

Dr. Henderson, one of three alienists Maurice Milton hired to examine myself and Roman, is still talking.

He's been blabbering for over ten minutes straight, I think as the cigarette I'm holding burns, building up ash. Since Mr. Hawke already procured the top psychiatrists in Illinois, Milton flew Walter Rachben to Atlantic City, New Jersey, to attend the annual meeting of the American Psychiatric Association. It took convincing to persuade some of the best men in the field to acquiesce, because no one wanted to be involved in such a sensational case. But Rachben used their own arguments against their objections and turned those arguments around. The men, who Hawke has dubbed "The Three Wise Men from the East," capitulated one by one.

"It means 'I am small, my heart is pure,' in case you didn't know," I say, interrupting Dr. Henderson.

"Excuse me?" he asks. He's sitting at a table across from me in a room at the Cook County Jail, one crisp linen-trouser leg crossed over the other. His beady eyes, almost lost in a doughy face, stare over the tops of gold-rimmed spectacles, and his pencil stops its checking motion as he reads information gleaned during the past few days.

"The German prayer I recited at three years old. '*Ich bin klein, Mein herz is rein.*' I assume either my father, Levi, or Saul told you this information. You did say you spoke with my family members."

The alienist smiles, softening his stern face a bit. "Yes, this came from a proud father." His serious expression returns. "Well, then, as I was saying, your birth was unremarkable. However, you were a precocious child who, according to the baby book your father presented, stood up at three months old and wobbled a few steps to reach your mother, whom you adored. At a mere four-and-a-half months, you spoke, saying, '*Nein, nein, Mama.*' You developed measles at age five and suffered from gastro-intestinal occurrences until age nine."

I tap ash into the receptacle and take a puff of my Lucky. "A condition of which I fear a recurrence, what with the abysmal cuisine jail offers."

Henderson doesn't speak, just writes something.

Patient's smug arrogance is, perhaps, a cover for feelings of inferiority? I smoke the cig down, grind it out, and light another.

"I talked to your brother, Saul," the doctor continues. "He spoke of the last governess employed by your family."

"Ah, 'Honey' as she insisted that we call her. Vile woman, as I'm sure Saul advised you."

"Yes, she took many liberties with him. Bathing with him, wrestling, and sleeping in the same bed with him when your parents were away. He told of her playing with his penis and of his getting an erection, although he never inserted it anywhere."

I shift in the uncomfortable chair.

"Did she take such liberties with you, Noah?"

Henderson stares at me, pencil hovering over his notebook, while I contemplate my answer. An alarm sounds somewhere outside the room. I take a big draw and hold smoke in before blowing it out in his direction.

"She did. However, we never bathed together. With me, she enjoyed kissing inappropriate places."

"Where?"

"My neck and lower stomach. Mother fired her one afternoon when she walked into Saul's bedroom and found a naked Honey napping in bed with Saul."

There's a knock.

"Come in," Dr. Henderson says, and I glimpse a deputy standing outside the door when another of the doctors from the East Coast walks inside. "Noah, you remember Dr. Garson?"

I nod in lieu of responding.

"Hello again, Noah," Dr. Garson says to me and to Henderson, "William is in with Mr. Loewe. That's Dr. William Black, Noah, and he'll be in to speak with you later." He turns back to Henderson. "I'm sorry. Please continue."

"I was just going to ask Noah if he was close to his mother."

My body heats up. It's still difficult for me to talk about Mother after almost two-and-a-half years. "Yes, she was above average. A model for others."

"Saul suggests that she wanted more children."

"She might have, Dr. Henderson, but her last pregnancy—mine—resulted in complications, which made this impossible and, in fact, led to her ultimate death." I grind out my cigarette in the full ashtray. "A verifiable truth Saul feeds on."

"Let's talk about your education for a while."

"Well, I'm not certain where you want me to begin, but I'm a proficient philologist, linguist, and have an aptitude for ornithology."

"So, you speak different languages?"

"Yes."

"How many?" Dr. Garson asks.

"German, of course, along with French, Italian, and Spanish, and some Greek and Latin, although I've studied at least fifteen languages. I'm a student of law and was heading to Harvard before this derailment."

"What about sex?"

My muscles tense. "What about it, Dr. Garson?"

"Have you had sexual intercourse with a woman?"

I smirk. "I've had no complaints from the fillies," I say, avoiding the question. I pick up my deck and tap out another—my sixth since this examination began. "However, my fantasy sex life involves engaging in more"—I search for the words—"perhaps rough encounters."

Garson follows my lead and asks, "Who do these fantasies involve?" while Henderson scribbles notes.

I don't answer.

"Explain a fantasy."

"Well, if someone is passed out drunk, I find it enjoyable to take advantage of the situation."

Henderson's head pops up from his notes. "Noah, was Bennie Frisch's murder a sexual crime?"

Of course, I expected this to come up, and here it is.

Time to reveal more.

"No. At least, not in the way you mean."

"Can you expound on this?"

"Yes, Dr. Henderson, I can." I take a draw and blow out smoke rings before saying, "Manny and I made a pact a long time ago. Every act of vandalism, burglary, or any crime in which I accompanied him came with a reward for me." I lean back in my seat and give the doctors what they want to hear. "Sex with Manny. And Bennie's murder was the ultimate."

* * *

Friday, 18 July 1924

The lawyer's cage has never been so hot, I think as I wait for Maurice Milton to be let into the room by the guard. I had requested a meeting with him sans Roman.

I drum my fingers on the table, anxious for this part to be over. With the next hearing looming on Monday morning, time is running out.

Can I trust Milton to come to the correct determination on his own? Does he need a nudge?

The door opens, and he walks inside, again looking as if he slept in his clothes, the disobedient shock of unruly strands breaking free from the rest of his hair.

"What's wrong, Noah?" he says, not bothering to sit down.

"I'm concerned, Mr. Milton."

"About?"

"Our chances of life in prison and not stepping off the gallows." I run my hands over my face. "I fear they're too slim."

He's staring at me with hooded eyes, the deep lines in his face unable to completely camouflage the strong features of his past youth. He doesn't speak.

"We talked our way into a hanging case, the fools we are. We pleaded not guilty and now we're at the mercy of a trial." I give him a sly smile. "Manny and I even made it impossible for you to use an insanity defense. And according to the newspaper accounts, this story is prevalent all over the country. We couldn't find an impartial jury if we paid for one."

"I agree," he says. He rests his fists on the table and leans across it, and his eyes bore into mine. "This is along the lines of how I've been thinking. You're going to have to trust me, Babe. I'll see you Monday morning." He straightens up, whirls around, and knocks on the door. "I'm finished."

I sit back in the chair and wait for the guard to escort me to my cell.

The old hayseed doesn't need a push after all. I'm correct in my original assessment of him. Maurice Milton is a brilliant attorney.

* * *

Monday, 21 July 1924

I find myself in the lawyer's cage again, only this time, Roman is with me. He's pumping his leg up and down while we wait for Misters Milton and Rachben, who we've been informed want to speak to us before the hearing.

"No way you're right about this, Babe," Roman says. "He'll tell us he's going to bug us out."

I shake my head. "We can't bug out now. No insanity defenses."

He waves a hand at me. "Ah, he'll figure it out, brainy guy that he is."

The door opens, and our attorneys walk inside, solemn expressions on their faces. I'm continually struck by the dissimilarities in the men's appearances. Rachben is impeccably attired. His spiffy, dark-gray suit is crisply pressed. A white shirt, sporting a colorful silk tie, lies below a lighter-gray vest.

Milton looks like he's going to a barn dance; however, he left his crumpled tie at home and opted for an off-kilter bowtie.

"Boys," he begins, while Rachben remains quiet. "I'm going to do something this morning that will terrify you."

Roman straightens out of his slouch.

Damn, I wish I had a cig to calm my stomach.

"This is a strategy, a legal maneuver that I've concluded is the only way. I apologize for not discussing it when the idea came to me, but it was imperative that the motion I'm making in"—he pulls out his pocket watch and studies it—"sixty-nine minutes, well, this motion must remain a total surprise to the prosecution. I couldn't chance you discussing something out in the yard or in the mess hall and being overheard."

My gastric issue disappears as Roman kicks my foot. I don't dare look at him because I won't be able to keep the smug expression off my face.

"Now, Babe, Manny, you're both intelligent enough to understand that you can't walk away from this matter. The only thing we can hope for is to save your lives. This motion I'm going to make, well, you trust me, don't you boys?"

I read genuine pain in Mr. Milton's eyes, the set of his mouth, the creases lining his face.

"Yes," I respond, as does Roman.

"All right then, this is what we're going to do." He leans forward and whispers his legal strategy to us.

An hour later, Roman and I are sitting outside the courtroom on a wooden bench. We're spruced up; him in a dark tweed suit, white shirt, polka-dot bowtie; me also in a dark suit, a vest, and tie. Both of us slicked back our hair, and his is parted on the side. I tried cleaning the brown stains off my fingers, but the ghost of nicotine remains. He's on his third cigarette now as we wait; I'm on my second. He hasn't said much since the lawyers left.

"All right, put 'em out," a deputy says, pointing to the tall metal ashtray stand next to our bench.

We oblige and he leads us into the courtroom; our guards come along, but we're no longer cuffed. Every head in the packed room turns toward us as we enter and walk past the octagon-shaped pillar to our seats on the defense side.

"All rise," the bailiff says. After the judge enters from chambers and sits down at the bench, we sit again.

"No photographs are allowed once the proceedings begin," Judge Castaner instructs the newshounds as flashbulbs go off in a frenzy of flashing lights. The smell of sulfur adds weight to the hot air in the room. The jury box is filled with photographers and spectators. Hats hang from every available hook.

When the picture-taking ceases and the commotion dies down, Mr. Milton stands up.

"I would like to address the court," he says, gripping with both hands the red galluses holding up his thin trousers. "My esteemed colleague and I"—he nods at Walter Rachben—"wish to present a motion."

Not a pin dropping can be heard, I think, gazing at the rapt faces around me. Hawke's expression at the prosecution table is one of cautious curiosity as he puts down his writing implement and leans forward. I turn and spy my father and brothers a few rows behind me; Roman's uncle and brother are next to them. Jonah Frisch is sitting on the other side of the room. I see no sign of the child's mother.

Milton points to us. "These boys must not be released back into society."

A collective gasp fills the room, and murmurings begin.

"Order!" the judge demands, banging his gavel.

I wait, along with everyone else, for Milton to continue. I don't look at Roman but can feel heat radiating from his body, sense the vibration of his leg bouncing.

"Their families don't wish for them to be free," Maurice Milton says. "No one does, including the boys themselves." He straightens to his full height and pulls the suspenders away from his ample stomach. "Mr. Rachben and I have considered our options and have determined the only way to save them while giving the people their due."

Roman leans forward, arms on his knees, an awed look on his profile.

"Your honor, if it pleases the court, I would like to make a motion at this time for permission to withdraw our not-guilty pleas on *both indictments* and enter pleas of guilty."

It takes about ten seconds for the words, and the impact, of Maurice Milton's statement to sink in before the courtroom erupts.

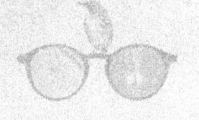

Chapter 26

Sunday morning, 27 April 1924

"Geez, Babe, you drive slower than Mumsie," Roman said.

I looked at him, dressed in a light suit, jacket but no vest, newsboy cap perched on his head, his arm draped out the window.

"There's no need to drive recklessly and draw attention to ourselves, Manny."

"Rubbish! No one's on the road this early."

"Six isn't early, not in the bird-watching world."

"Well, it is in the I-drank-too-much-rotgut-last-night world." He unscrewed the cap on his thermos and took a swig of coffee. "Besides, I didn't think we were actually going to chase birds."

I jerked my head toward the tonneau. "I brought my hip boots, binocs, and a notebook, so of course, we're going to do some birding. It's the ideal cover for being in the area during our reconnaissance. It's important to do a run-through so things go smoothly next month."

"Ah, what difference does it make if we're planning on getting nabbed?"

I didn't answer, just turned onto the spur road, drove until we weren't visible from the trunk line, and parked.

I kept the motor running and looked at him. "Because, Manny, we're orchestrating this entire thing."

"But no one will know!"

"You're right."

"Then why the hell are we doing it?"

"To save your, our, lives!" I pinched the bridge of my nose and took a deep breath. "We've gone over this a thousand times. Unless you intend to stop your criminalistic behavior, it will continue to escalate. Are you willing to stop? Will you make a vow, a declaration right here and now, to never engage in another illicit activity to enhance your sexual fantasies? Or for any other reason?" My eyelids twitched as I stared at him, daring him to speak honestly.

His knee bounced furiously, and he smacked the dashboard and glared at me.

He hates me. In this moment, at least. Can I blame him when I brought truth to his door?

But then he leaned against the seat, stretched out his legs, and ran his hands over his face. When he turned back to me, he flashed his quick grin my way.

"Ah, I'm just miffed because if it works, this plan of yours, Babe, and we don't hang, well, folks should know we plotted the entire thing."

I put the car in gear and continued down the road. "If we receive life, I predict that we'll be eligible for parole in twenty years, twenty-five at the most. A long time, yes, but after we're out, we can write books about the truth, everything, and arrange to have them published after our deaths. Don't you see? Our brilliance will outlive us, and people will speak of our superiority for a hundred years." I glanced at him and saw the way his lips curled into his devilish smile. "This is where we can undress the kid and bury some of the clothes," I said and pointed to a clearing on the side of the road.

"I'm not happy with people thinking that we're a couple of pervs," Roman griped and not for the first time. He hated the letter I wrote and planted in my room, one hinting of our "abhorrent" association. He was uncomfortable with our relationship being revealed despite my assurances that such "perversions," as would be ascribed to us, would help when it came time to adjudicate our sentences. That didn't appease him. The only thing that worked was me promising to tell the alienists sure to be called in that he was always blotto when we were together.

"Should be fodder for some entertaining court moments, though," I said. "Watching the prosecution fight to hang a couple of deviants."

He laughed, and his knee performed a solo from the rest of his body, bouncing to its own rhythm.

"What about our mouthpiece, Babe?"

"I manipulated the conversation at dinner last week, and Saul, Levi, Father, and I enjoyed a lengthy discussion on the esteemed Maurice Milton and his reputation for saving his clients from hanging. The barrister's name should automatically occur to them when the time comes."

We were quiet for the remainder of the ride. When we arrived, I parked where I always did when bird-watching there.

"No one else appears to be here, but I'm taking my gear to be safe." I got out, reached into the tonneau, and grabbed rubber hip boots and field glasses. Roman stood outside and smoked a cigarette while I changed into the boots and put the binoculars over my neck. "This way," I said.

We walked about eight hundred yards before he complained, "We have to lug the stiff this far?"

"No, we can drive farther provided the ground isn't too soft. No sense attracting attention now if we run into someone."

When we arrived at the culvert, I jumped down into the water.

"We'll leave him in here with his legs sticking out," I said. "If no one comes by and spots the body after a week, I'll happen upon it with Heinzie."

I held up my arm. Roman grabbed it and pulled me out of the ditch.

"Man, it's going to be something, Babe! Do you think Henry will recognize the spectacles as yours?"

I shook my head and raised the binocs—I'd heard the call of *Rallus elegans*, the marsh bird king rail. I scanned the swamp. Nothing. All was still.

"No, Henry's never seen them. I only filled the prescription in the fall after getting too many headaches from studying. Eyestrain. However, the migraines ceased, so I stopped wearing them."

"What a lucky break that those glasses are special," Roman said as we started back toward the Willys.

"Indeed. The second I remembered overhearing the clerk gossiping about the new hinge on the earpiece, only a few pairs being sold in Chicago, I knew they would be perfect incriminating evidence."

"Ah, Babe, but how much fun it'll be playing cat-and-mouse with the coppers when they come calling. You have the best excuse for those readers to be out here."

"Yes, which means they'll come for me first. I'll hold them off for a while before giving up your name."

"I want to toy with them too."

"You will. You'll act furious with me for 'telling the alibi too soon.' Even though we're both accusing the other of doing the actual killing, you get to do the deed, but blame me."

"Yeah, sure, sure, and I get to be the one to confess."

We reached the Willys, and I sat in the driver's seat, legs hanging out of the auto, and changed back into my oxfords. "Let's try to keep their heads rolling, Manny. If they believe we're mad at each other, at least most of the time, our chances of winding up serving our sentences together without requiring our families to bribe anyone will be better. It also refutes the notion that we're pulling strings in this matter. If they become aware of the extent of our calculation, the lesser man will retaliate and—"

"And we'll hang."

* * *

Tuesday, 20 May 1924

"Sorry, we don't have hydrochloric acid," the clerk behind the counter said. He pointed north. "Check Adler's Pharmacy down the block."

"Thank you," I responded through gritted teeth. *What rotten luck*, I thought as I turned around and left the drugstore. *I hope Manny's faring well at the hardware store.*

The noise of the street hit almost as hard as the warm air, filled with exhaust and gasoline fumes from traffic.

"Excuse *me*," a woman said when I walked into her path.

"O-o-oh no, I apologize," I flubbed, but she disappeared into the passersby on the sidewalk.

I did have better luck at Adler's, but the owner was nosey and eyed Levi's dark, oversized topcoat that I wore.

"Why do you need so much?" he inquired when I asked for a pint.

Lowering the hat below my eyebrows, I responded, "Science project for school."

He nodded. "Wait here."

I tapped my fingers on the counter to expel some internal pressure, and he returned after a few minutes, carrying a glass container.

"That'll be seventy-five cents, fella."

Reasonable. I handed over the change.

He held out the acid, then pulled it back. "Now, see this here wax seal on the lid? It's to prevent leakage. You can't spill it, or it'll eat your clothes and skin," he cautioned.

"Don't worry, sir, I'll be careful."

When I got back to the Willys, Roman sat in the passenger seat, whistling a tune, his hand outside the window, slapping the side of the auto.

"Gee, what took so long, Babe?"

I didn't answer, just got in the car, and passed him the container. "Put this on the floor between your feet, but don't spill it." He took it, and I started the engine. "I had to go to two pharmacies. Did you buy the hammer?"

He held up a brown bag and made a hammering motion with it. "Sure did. Now, let's go to your place and type up the ransom note."

* * *

"Would you like me to help, Master Babe?"

Margaret stood in the kitchen wringing her hands as Roman carried meats, cheeses, and a jar of pickles back to the refrigerator.

"No, thank you, we're finished here." I slapped a thick slice of rye bread on the second roast beef sandwich I was making. "Grab a couple of root beers, will you Roman?"

"Sure, sure. Here."

I looked up in time to see a bottle flying at me.

"Oh!" Margaret shouted, but I caught it before it hit the wall.

"Thanks," I said through gritted teeth and handed him his plate.

He tucked his drink under his arm and took a huge bite of the sandwich. "Bye, Margaret," he said around a mouthful and walked out. "I'll be upstairs, Noah."

I shook my head and turned to the maid. "Final exams in all of my law classes, and I'm stuck with Roman helping me! Two other guys were supposed to come and cram tonight since the family is out for the evening, but one won't make it, and the other, Martin Bergen, isn't sure. At least, Roman can quiz me, in case he doesn't show." I secured a tray from the cabinet and placed my plate and drink atop it. "Send Martin up if he comes. Otherwise, please leave us alone."

"Of course."

I found Roman in my study sitting in the chair, his feet on the desk, empty plate resting on a book. He sat up and planted his feet back on the floor when I entered.

"Ah, great grub, Babe. Maybe you can work in the chow hall if we live."

"Amusing."

"Seriously, do you think we can get good eats brought inside the pen?"

"I did some research on Joliet, and our families can bring three-course meals during visits if we wish."

"We can probably buy power from some mugs in the Big House if we spread the wealth, eh, Babe?"

"Yes, but we'll be imprisoned for a long bit, Manny. Don't lose sight of this fact. Try not to romanticize it too much."

"Ah, you're nuts."

I walked through the connecting door into my bedroom. "The Underwood's in here."

He followed me. "Are you sure your family's gonna stick by you? Because you'll need their money for special privileges and stuff. Mine will."

"Of course. Although it'll be a difficult matter for them to deal with."

He sat on the edge of my bed. "Why're you acting so sore?"

I wasn't going to answer because I knew he wouldn't be able to comprehend my feelings, but I did so, nonetheless.

"I received a letter today from a taxidermist I use. An exhibit I've been waiting for, the Kirtland's warbler, which should have arrived by now as promised, has been delayed further."

"What do you mean?"

"It won't come until the fall. The reason I was fine with tomorrow's date for this, this thing"—I didn't know how else to phrase it in my state of mind—"is because I was under the impression that I would have some time to enjoy the display."

"Geez, Babe, I'm sorry. Do you want to move the date? Do this later?"

Is it possible he wants to back out of this? Has he changed his mind, and is he ready to give it all up?

"I can wait," he said and then winked. "Of course, I can't make any promises for sainthood if you go to Europe with Heinzie this summer."

I sighed. *I thought not.* "No, everything's set for tomorrow." I sat at the small table that housed the Underwood and ate my dinner. For once, Roman didn't get impatient. He just looked around and waited, drinking from his flask.

When I finished, I went into my study, returned with law books and composition notebooks, and spread them over the bed.

"What're these for, Babe?"

"Props if anyone comes home early or if Margaret should find her way upstairs for some unfathomable reason." I went to the table and opened the case for the Underwood. "Convenient that this machine drops the lowercase *t* and *f* keys, making it easier to identify."

"Did you make sure to use it for your study group?"

"Yes, a few times. Hopefully, Martin's friend, the reporter, will ask to see our notes once he finds out that we're being held for questioning. Guy will get some credit for 'solving' the case." I slid a sheet of paper into the machine. "Okay, Manny, you wanted to do the ransom letter, so start dictating."

He began pacing. "All right. Dear Sir. Unless you want to type in 'Mister' and print the name after?"

"No, sir is fine."

"Sure, sure. Okay, here goes. As you know, your son has been kidnapped. He is being treated well and is, at present, unharmed and safe. If any of the following demands are not adhered to strictly, these pleasant conditions can and will change in an instant." Roman snapped his fingers. "Resulting in the ultimate punishment for your son. Death."

I typed as fast as possible.

"Now, number the next few paragraphs, Babe. One. Do not contact the authorities, either official or of the private sector. If you disregard this directive, your son will die. Number two. Procure no later than noon today, the sum of ten thousand dollars."

He stopped and drank from his flask. "*Used* bills. Emphasize *used*, Babe." He burped into his hand. "The money must be in small denominations, seven thousand in fifties, three thousand in twenties. Do not mix in newer or marked bills. If you disregard this directive, your son will die. Number—"

"Slow down, Manny," I yelled, stabbing every other key in frustration.

Roman kicked my calf. I looked up, and he flashed his grin. "Guess you're not an expert in everything, huh, Babe?"

I fumed but held back a retort. "Continue," I said when I caught up.

"All right. Number three. Place the money in a box, wrap said box in brown paper, and seal it with wax. Keep the box at your side and stay in your house near the telephone. Make sure no one uses the telephone, and that the line stays open. I will contact you at precisely twelve forty-five in the afternoon, at which time I'll give further instructions. If you disregard this directive, your son will die.

"If these mandates are followed, your son will be returned to you six hours after receipt of the ransom. However, if you choose to veer from these explicit instructions, your son will die."

He waited while I finished typing.

"How shall I sign it?" I asked.

"Well, how about yours truly, Jim Johnston?"

"Fine." I pulled the sheet from the Underwood. "I'll place this in my notebook with the envelope. Now it's time to cut down the hammer and tape the end."

"Sure, sure."

Something in his tone made me check one last time. "Are you certain, Manny? Before we go ahead with this, you realize we can be betting wrong and hang."

He didn't say anything, just paced back and forth.

"Well?"

"Fantasy or not, Babe, I'm aware that life in the pen will be horrible, better than being in a bug house with crazy people, but still terrible. Joliet's old and dirty. Even the new hoosegow, Stateville, if we're transferred there after it opens, won't be much better. But hopefully, with our fathers' connections, we can serve our time together, do some good inside so we can be sprung one day. Alive beats dead."

"We can stop, Manny. No more crimes, killings." I stared at him from the small table where I sat.

He shook his head, wearing the most serious expression I ever saw on his face. "No, we can't."

Then his mouth morphed into his grin, and he walked around my room, eyeing everything.

"What are you gawking at?"

"First time I've been in here, Babe."

"Yes," I replied, finishing my root beer.

"No one's home."

I couldn't mistake the familiar shine in his eyes.

"Margaret is downstairs in her room, Manny."

He went to the connecting door, closed, and locked it.

My chest rose and fell quicker. The air being sucked into my lungs thickened, and my groin tingled.

"Yeah, but the story you fed her about Martin and studying is baloney. And tomorrow…can't you feel the excitement?" He pulled his shirt out and unbuttoned his trousers.

By the time he stood there, naked, my breathing was labored, and my heartbeats drowned out all sound. He pushed the books aside and lay down on my bed. I joined him.

I gazed at his body, so artistic in its perfection, and ached for the one thing he robbed me of time and time again.

"What will you do for mushy?" I asked, willing to risk his wrath and any punishment he might inflict. "You know, when we're locked up."

He grinned, so close to my face I felt the wisp of air as his lips moved. But they didn't touch my lips.

"I'll adjust, Babe."

Chapter 27

> Mistrust all in whom the impulse to punish is powerful.
>
> —Friedrich Nietzsche

Monday, 21 July 1924

BERTRAM HAWKE JUMPS to his feet as loud gasps and not-so-whispered chattering fills the air.

"What game is counsel playing with the people of the great state of Illinois?"

"Game?" Maurice Milton says, turning away from the bench to stare at a crimson-faced State's attorney. Without looking at us, he points to me and Roman. "Does Mr. Hawke view my clients' lives as some type of sport? Is he under the impression that we're withdrawing our not-guilty pleas and pleading guilty merely for some sort of recreational purposes? A show for the newspapers?"

The spectators go quiet again, most leaning forward, ears tilting toward Judge Castaner. A few of them gawk at us.

"Malarkey!" Hawke's chin is trembling, and his bulging eyes behind the thick lenses make him look deranged. "You're trying to put something over on the People, and I won't stand for it."

Milton waves a hand at Hawke, the other is secure under a suspender strap. "Nonsense. Due to my clients' youth, their mental condition at the time of the incident must be considered. The statute allows for evidentiary testimony to determine said mental conditions, and so we ask the court"—he turns back to address the judge—"to allow Babe and Manny to change their pleas to guilty so that we may present evidence on these young boys' mental conditions at the time of the crime."

"Huh, Babe and Manny. Such sweet boys," Hawke says.

"Our desire is to diminish the harsh outcome Mr. Hawke would see my clients' receive, that they hang by their young necks until they snap, and so we—"

"Objection!" Hawke screams, and reporters trip over each other, trying to move closer to the front.

"This isn't a trial," Judge Castaner yells over his banging gavel. Flashbulbs pop and burn. "Sit back down, Mr. Hawke. And I'll have order in this courtroom, or I'll clear it! Now finish, Mr. Milton."

"Thank you, Your Honor. We throw ourselves upon the mercy of the court." Milton walks back toward us, but he's glaring at Bertram Hawke. "And *only* the court."

"Defense cannot have it both ways! Counsel is trying to save his clients from hanging, they, who committed a heinous and brutal murder upon an innocent boy, a child, and whose parents they tried to profit from. The law does not permit an insane man or woman to plead guilty to facts. An insanity plea must be heard by a jury. If Mr. Milton wishes to submit evidence that particular circumstances led to a motive, then I have no objection, but for him to declare his clients have a mental condition that led to their actions falls outside the purview of the rule of law."

Hawke throws both arms up in the air, fists clenched. "These slayers bow before the court for mercy, and the State will forcefully demand their hanging!"

Newshounds rush out of the courtroom, likely to get notes to editors in time for the afternoon edition. *I can almost write the copy*, I think, trying not to smile and failing. An insanity plea in Illinois must be heard in front of a jury. A jury will slaughter us, something Hawke made sure of while he held us without benefit of counsel, so no one will believe that we're insane. But a mental condition, coupled with our youth? This can be used to mitigate our punishment. And Milton needs only to convince one person: a judge with more liberal views on capital punishment. No wonder Hawke is raging.

"I'll have quiet in here!" the judge demands as the murmuring increases. "Defense counsel, both of you, approach the bench with your clients."

Mr. Milton looks at us. "Let's go, boys." Lowering his voice, he adds, "Trust me."

Walter Rachben nods.

Roman is blinking more than usual, something he does when he's nervous, and the two of us rise and stand before the judge.

High on his bench, Judge Castaner towers over us. His face is stern. "With a guilty plea in case number 33623, the indictment for murder, you, Noah Freudenthal Lieberman Jr., and you, Roman Alfred Loewe, can be sentenced to death by hanging, imprisoned for the remainder of your natural lives, or imprisoned for a term no less than fourteen years. Knowing the ramifications, do you still wish to change your plea to guilty?"

"Yes, sir," Roman says before I can open my mouth.

"Yes," I repeat.

"Please, so enter the record," the judge directs the clerk before turning back to us. "With a plea of guilty in case number 33624, the indictment of kidnapping for ransom, you, Noah Freudenthal Lieberman Jr., and you, Roman Alfred Loewe, can be sentenced to death by hanging, imprisoned for the remainder of your natural lives, or imprisoned for a term no less than five years. Knowing the ramifications, do you still wish to change your plea to guilty?"

We answer in the affirmative.

"All right, we'll suspend until Wednesday the twenty-third of July. Ten in the morning. Sharp. I'll begin hearing evidence on mitigation then.

"Adjourned."

With one last bang of the gavel, court is dismissed.

* * *

10:00 a.m., Wednesday, 23 July 1924

The atmosphere in the packed courtroom this morning is a curious mixture of enthusiasm and tension. Roman is next to me, and we're in our usual seats. Misters Milton and Rachben sit at the defense table in front of us, both attired in their typical style and as different as a farmer and a banker. Mr. Hawke, Sever, and two other men sit at the prosecutor's table. My father and Levi are here again, as are Roman's brother and his uncle. Mr. Rachben told us that Roman's father is unwell and cannot attend the hearing. I feel Levi's eyes burning into the back of my head, but I don't turn around.

"Babe," he pleaded when he came to visit me in jail yesterday. "What's this guy doing by withdrawing your not-guilty plea? Why, the judge can just hang you!"

"With the coverage this case is receiving," I had replied, "a jury will hang us for certain, whereas a judge, a jurist, will take everything into consideration."

He and the rest of the family continue to worry about our chances.

As do I. I never anticipated the intense sensationalism of the case.

I sigh, pull on my collar, and look around me. Hats and jackets crowd every hook lining the far wall. A large fan on the judge's desk—facing toward the gallery—tries to complement the slight morning breeze coming in from a dozen tall windows a bailiff opened, but the fan's blades aren't suited for the task and only move around the curtains, stirring the odor of overheated anxiety.

Today's scene is much the same as every other court appearance, except for the metal file cabinet next to Hawke's table. I've no time to wonder about its presence before the bailiff announces the judge's arrival.

The sound of chairs scraping against worn wooden floors fills the air as everyone stands up. Judge Castaner strides into the courtroom and takes his seat behind the bench.

"The hearing before me today," he says after the bailiff makes his announcement, "is for case numbers 33623 and 33624 on the indictments for murder and kidnapping for ransom." He gestures toward the gallery. "Everyone be seated. If you can't find a seat, leave. My bailiff is instructed to remove anyone who causes a commotion or who disrupts the proceedings."

I catch Roman's eye and we smile at each other at the exact moment a flashbulb goes off.

I imagine that the newspapers will have fun with this photo. Cold-blooded killers laughing in court.

"For the record, Mr. Bertram Hawke and Mr. Jim Sever are representing the People of the State of Illinois and Mr. Maurice Milton and Mr. Walter Rachben represent the defendants." He nods at Roman and me.

"Now, I'll repeat my request once more. At the behest of the fire marshal, no one shall remain in this room who is not seated." He points to the remaining stragglers not quick enough to obtain a chair. I spy more than a few others sharing seats. "Bailiff, if these men don't leave voluntarily, show them the way. The ladies as well."

Roman chuckles.

"You may begin, Mr. Hawke."

"Thank you, Your Honor." Hawke uses his hands to push himself up from the table and rises with dramatic flair. "The State wishes to proceed with evidence in the murder case first. Once all our evidentiary material is presented, we'll continue with the kidnapping for ransom indictment."

"I object, Your Honor," Walter Rachben says from his seated position.

"Object to what?"

"On why the prosecution feels the need to present evidence on either indictment when a guilty plea is on record."

Bertram Hawke gestures around with his hands. "Does the defense think this is a mock trial? A dress rehearsal? Should the State charge admission for tomorrow's performance?"

Mr. Rachben doesn't budge from his seat, and unlike Hawke, no sweat pools on his forehead. "I don't think Mr. Hawke need be so theatrical. We merely object to wasting the court's valuable time on facts which we do not dispute."

"Nor do we wish to delay this *hearing*," Mr. Milton says, "by continuing the case for kidnapping."

"They're two different cases," Hawke insists.

"And both have guilty pleas attached," spits out Milton.

"Well, the indictment for murder should take the longest time. Do you agree Mr. Hawke?"

"Yes, Judge."

"We don't have to delve into the corpus delicti—the boy's death—in the kidnapping for ransom case," Sever adds.

Hawke nods his head vigorously. "Two separate and distinct cases."

"All right," the judge says. "We'll hear evidence on the murder indictment. Begin your opening statements, Mr. Hawke."

I listen with half an ear, picking up on words like *privileged* and *entitled* but tuning back in with *colluded*.

"...colluded together as far back as November of 1923, to kidnap the child of wealthy parents."

As if by muscle memory, Bertram Hawke faces the jury box even though no jury members occupy the benches. Instead, rapt-eyed newshounds listen to every word spoken, watch every move the State's attorney makes.

"In the next few days, I intend to bring forth witnesses and lay out irrefutable, concrete evidence of their guilt." He turns to us and points our way. "Most of it collected with the assistance of the arrogant defendants themselves. Proof of the meticulous planning of the ransom when they intended to kill the child all along, bludgeon little Bennie and then jam a rag down his narrow throat when three vicious blows to his skull didn't kill him. Proof of how they drove around with his body in the back, wrapped in an automobile blanket, waiting for it to be dark enough to dump the corpse. And you'll hear testimony from some of the most highly regarded alienists in *Illinois*." He curls his lip and glares at Milton.

"The defense would have these 'boys' given a slap on their bottoms. So naughty. Well, I say no!" He holds up one arm, fist clenched. "I say they walk the gallows like every other monstrous deviant before them. This is a hanging case if ever I handled one, and I promise the good people of the city of Chicago that I'll be satisfied with no lesser verdict. Their children and mine must be protected from these fiends!"

With this, Hawke spins around and takes his seat at the prosecutor's table.

"Who is opening for the defense?" Judge Castaner asks.

Milton rises. "I am, Your Honor." He stands in front of the bench, hands under his vest, and rocks on his heels. "The State desperately wants my clients to hang from the gallows. In fact, I believe if given the opportunity, Mr. Hawke would wrap the cord around them himself, kick out the stool from under their feet.

"We don't dispute the facts Mr. Hawke is so rabid to present with the mindset of turning the community into blood-lusting vampires who crave such an outcome. My clients have confessed to this horrible crime and have cooperated in every way with the State's attorney's office—"

"After they could deny it no longer," Hawke yells and springs from his seat.

"Enough shouting out!" The judge bangs his gavel. "I'll thank the State's attorney to remember where he is. This is not a Chicago White Sox game, sir. Sit back down and let counsel finish his statement."

Hawke does but taps his fingers on the tabletop.

Milton opens his mouth to speak, then closes it and just stares down at Hawke.

"Mr. Milton?" the judge says.

"We're prepared to concede every piece of physical evidence that the prosecutor admits, but if the State insists on dragging out this hearing with validated facts and demands the right to parade in a multitude of witnesses to waste the Court's time when we deny nothing, then we should let him." He returns to his chair behind the defense table. "We're ready to present testimony from respected alienists as well, who happen to be from the East Coast, which will shed light on how neuroscience affects the behavior of an immature but overly intellectual brain."

"Is counsel finished?" Castaner asks.

"Yes."

"All right, then Mr. Hawke, you may proceed."

"Thank you, Your Honor. I call Florence Frisch to the stand, please."

Gasps resound in the courtroom, and then it goes silent. The tension in the air is so thick it's oppressive, making it difficult to breathe. I loosen my collar. No one speaks, but pencils scribble as the bailiff walks down the aisle, his footfalls echoing.

When he returns, he's escorting Bennie's mother.

Chapter 28

Wednesday evening, 21 May 1924

"Your son has been kidnapped," I spoke into the handset. Roman stood next to me in the phone booth in the rear of the drugstore, his body heat mingling with mine. A large phonebook swung from a cord beside me.

"Who is this?" the woman who identified herself as Florence Frisch asked in a small voice.

I trembled from Roman's nearness and from our time spent in Washington Park after we dumped the body.

"Jim Johnston. Your boy is fine for now. Do not contact the authorities. You'll hear from me further in the morning." I hung up, turned to face Roman, and pushed him against the door. "Let's buy a special delivery stamp and drop the letter in the mailbox. I want to go to your place, burn the clothes, and clean the auto. I saw blood on the carpet and on the seat." I checked my pocket watch. "It's nearing ten forty-five, and I promised my father I'd be back around eleven to play cards with my aunt and uncle before driving them home at midnight. I'll have to use Father's car if Erik hasn't repaired mine."

"Sure, sure, Babe," he said, flashing his quick grin as we walked toward the front of the pharmacy. "But aren't you excited about tomorrow? Man, him scrambling to get us our cabbage and us waiting to collect the dough! Damn, I wish I could spend it."

Outside, we headed for the rental parked down the street. "Well, Manny, maybe the clues we're handing the police will go unnoticed by their subpar detecting skills, and we'll never even be accused, let alone be tried for the matter."

When we reached the touring car, he grabbed the handle and opened the passenger door.

"Then we're going to hang some day for sure, Babe, because after tonight I won't quit. No way." He winked at me, climbed inside, and closed the door. "You're right. Enacting prison fantasies will have to be my reality until we're released."

He threw the hammer out the window somewhere on Fourteenth Street. When we arrived at his garage, he tossed the clothes in the furnace and filled a bucket with soapy water. We gave the inside of the auto a rudimentary cleaning. Faint stains remained, but now it was impossible to determine their origin. They could be red wine. After we parked the Willys in front of an apartment building a block away, we walked to my house. My sports car sat at the curb, washed and waxed.

Erik fixed the brakes. Odds are good that he'll remember this day and that I didn't drive my automobile.

* * *

12:45 p.m., Thursday, 22 May 1924

I sat alone in another phone booth in a different drugstore since Roman and I were careful not to frequent the same establishment when dealing with this matter. He had left as I was telling Jonah Frisch where to await our next call in one hour. Distracted because Roman was upset, I hung up on Mr. Frisch while he was still speaking.

Manny and his love of scavenger hunts.

Fate intervened earlier when we arrived at the sanitation box on Lexington Avenue, only to find it overfull, so we decided to eliminate the note and just tell Frisch where to go.

Roman was standing on the sidewalk when I came out. Shading his eyes against the bright sun, he looked at me and said, "Let's go buy the damn tickets and board the train."

When we finished taping the final instructions to the last seat on the train, we disembarked and drove to a newsstand to get more cigarettes. I stayed in the car while Roman made the purchase. After a few minutes, I noticed that he was reading a newspaper. I got out, curious about what had him so interested. I lit a Lucky as I walked over to him and almost choked on hot fumes as a full double-decker Chicago Motor Bus drove by, its horn blaring at pedestrians trying to cross in front of it.

Why's he taking so long? I wondered, about to tell him that we needed to get moving. Jonah Frisch would be doing everything on his end, and we had to be ready to call him again and go collect the ransom, but Roman looked up, a curious expression on his face.

"What's wrong with you?"

"A fluke, Babe, a fluke if ever there was one," he said, shoving an early edition of a Chicago newspaper in my face.

BODY OF BOY FOUND IN CULVERT screamed the headline. I scanned the short piece, amazed that an immigrant railway laborer had spotted the body on his way to work.

"They haven't identified him yet, Manny, we can still get the money."

"Best we can do is call the pharmacy and ask if someone named Frisch is there, but I doubt it." His eyes narrowed as he flicked his cigarette into the street and started walking to the car. "Let's go to your place, make sure the auto is clean enough, and return it. I'll drive your Willys."

I couldn't tell how he really felt about the ransom falling apart, but he must be disappointed.

I never imagined anyone would find the kid so soon.

* * *

Friday, 23 May 1924

"Can you believe the news?" Dick Renford said between bites of his sandwich. "Boy's name was Bennie Frisch." He nodded at Roman, who sat next to him in the busy dining hall. I sat next to Owen Gregory, eating my lunch. "Did you know him? He lived in your neighborhood."

"Oh sure," Roman said around a mouthful of food. He wiped his face with a napkin, sipped some soda, and burped. "He was Thad's friend. Why, he played tennis at our place just a couple of weeks ago."

"Damn," Owen said.

"Hey, think maybe he beat my brother and Thad slugged him a few times with his racket?"

Dick and I groaned.

"How'd the little monster bring him all the way out to the swamp by the tracks?"

"Well, Owen, Thad's got a wagon."

I thought about restraining Roman, but what was the point? The goal was getting caught—so, no stressing over what he might say to implicate us later unless it hurt our chances of survival.

And Manny will appreciate what a hoot it'll be when Owen and Dick remember this conversation after our confessions.

The guys talked amongst themselves about how Thad might have lugged the body so far away. Idiots.

"Well," I said, gathering my plate and utensils to return them with the tray. "I'm heading to the law library. I have finals next week to cram for as well as my Harvard entrance exams and—"

"Hey, Roy," Roman yelled across the crowded cafeteria. He jumped up and waved his arms.

It took me a few seconds to place the fella walking over. Roy Rhoader, alumni of the University of Chicago. The anemic-faced guy interviewed me for the school paper last year when he wrote an article about one of my professors and the man's philosophical teaching styles as they related to the study of law. The two of us agreed to disagree on his interviewing prowess.

"This is Roy, a friend of Emil's," Roman said when the vulture-like man reached our table, his shoulders in their perpetual stoop and lost inside a comically large jacket. "Roy, these are the guys."

Dick and Owen said hello, but I merely nodded up at him, unsure and unconcerned about whether he remembered me.

"So, what're you doing here? Didn't you graduate last year?"

"Yeah, Roman, but I'm working for the *Tribune* now, out here scouting for a story from someone who knows the Frisch family." He dropped his chin to his chest. "No dice. Got no story."

Roman snapped his fingers. "Well, hey, now, I have an idea. Why don't you do a little sleuthing yourself? Try to find the pharmacy that the kid's father was supposed to go to according to all the rags." He grinned, and it reached his eyes, making them shine. "Whadda you say? I'll take a ride with you, and we'll hit all the drugstores on Thirty-Second. Can't be more than four, five on that stretch. We can ask if the killer called looking for Frisch."

"Wait until three. Dick and I have class now, and we want to go too, right Dick?" Owen said, standing up with his tray.

"Yeah."

"No," Roy said. "I don't want to risk someone who works at the pharmacy remembering the call and contacting the papers. I'm going now. Come on, Roman."

"Want to join us, Noah?"

I remained the only one seated. "No. As I said, I'm going to the law library to study. But happy hunting."

Almost twelve hours later, I sat in my Willys, parked down the street and around the block from Roman's house. The moist, humid air caused sweat to pool in the back of my shirt despite my not wearing a jacket. I drummed my fingers on the steering wheel and checked the time again. Nearly midnight.

"He's now forty-seven minutes late," I complained aloud. Reaching into my pocket, I grabbed a fresh deck of Luckies, tore off the foil, and tapped out a cigarette.

It started raining. Droplets at first, but by the time I smoked the stick to ash, water was pouring into the auto. I cranked up the window most of the way to keep some air in and leaned over to do the same with the passenger window.

"I'll get it, Babe," Roman said. Dripping, he opened the door and got in. He took off his wet cap and threw it in the tonneau. His drenched jacket came off next, and it landed over the Underwood in the back.

"You're late." Relief infiltrated my piqued tone.

"Ah, not much."

"Well, where were you? I called your house earlier, and the maid said that you hadn't been home all day." My hands gripped the wheel as rain pounded the auto, making it shake.

"What're you talking about? You were there, you heard. I went around with Roy, checking out drugstores. I led the stupe to three pharmacies before going into the right one. 'Ah, yeah, a man called here asking for a Mr. Frisch, and I told 'im he wasn't here,' some worker claims. Boy, Roy was happy for the scoop! 'I found the place! Thanks, Roman,' he said." Roman laughed and held out his hand. "Butt me."

I gave him a cig and lit it.

"Ole Roy was so tickled he took me out for some drinks." He winked. "Filled my flask too."

"Oh. I thought that maybe you were out with that flapper again."

"Geez, Babe, cut it out, would ya? She's just a girl I date sometimes. Besides, you're going out with Sally this weekend. She finally dumped her boyfriend and is willing to give you a spin."

"Yes, because you and I agreed to keep up appearances, and I'm going to have a pleasant time. I won't, however, be necking and petting her all night."

"Ah, why're you getting so mad? Do whatever you want to do on your dates and leave me alone. I can't spend all my time with you. After all, what do you think it'll be like in prison?"

There it was.

Neither of us spoke. The only sound was rain beating around us. The streetlights—dull, glowing orbs—provided the only illumination. No other cars appeared to be out. It felt like we were the only ones in the world. I took one last draw and pushed my cigarette through the open crack of the window. I longed to roll it down more, but doing so would only invite the downpour inside.

How to answer him? Did he even want me to?

"I won't lie, Manny, it will be difficult. The loss of freedom, of privacy, privilege…well, these things will be hard to adjust to."

His leg bounced. "Yeah, and what about booze, cigs, and good food?"

"Cigarettes are readily available in prison; matches are the issue. As far as food is concerned, our families can bring meals during visits, like I told you. For alcohol, we'll have to pay off the guards, but it's a viable option."

"Ah, how do you know this stuff, Babe?"

"I pretended to be interested in writing a dissertation on the behind-the-public-eye view of prison life. One of my professors candidly spoke to me at length about things that his relatives who work at Joliet have told him."

"So, you think we can buy favors?"

I nodded. "Some, yes. Don't forget that my father's lumber mills are supplying material for Stateville. He has many connections that can aid us, but we'll have to give a lot as well."

"What do you mean?" Roman said, rolling down his window and tossing his butt. "Crank down that glass, Babe, and let some air in here. Rain's letting up."

He was right. I hadn't noticed that the roaring in the car had stopped because the roaring in my head hadn't. I leaned back in the seat.

"Well, we'll likely be the most intelligent prisoners in the joint. Smarter than the guards too. We can use our intelligence, do some good, and earn rewards. If our behavior in the penitentiary is exemplary, this will go a long way toward parole when the time eventually comes."

I jumped when he slapped his hand on the side of the door.

"Hell, if this is what we're facing, then I say we go another round. Find some sap to bop off."

"You can't be serious."

"Why not, Babe?"

I sighed. "We've been over this before."

"Sure, sure, getting pinched for one at our ages might save us from the gallows, but more than one, no matter our youth, will hang us for certain."

"That's right, and the cops will already be trying to pin whatever else they can on us after we confess. They always do that. We can't take the chance, not after that guy in November."

"Which is why we play it smart, Babe, and off someone far away from Chicago like we did with the church rummy in Michigan. They're not going to try to pin something out of town on us."

"I'll consider it," I said but had no intention of doing so.

"I think you're forgetting that if I want to do it, you'll go with me if only to 'protect' me from myself."

I recognized something in his tone, and in the look in his eyes. He knew I couldn't refuse him. However, something had changed, shifted in the dynamics of our relationship over the last few months. Our usual king and slave roles became intertwined, mingled.

He flashed his quick, infectious grin.

"Pass me the typewriter." I pointed to the tonneau of the auto. "It's under your wet jacket. You'll find a pair of pliers and a small bag back there as well."

I held the Underwood in my lap while Manny twisted and pulled some of the white glass keys off.

"All right, the rain stopped," he said. He held up the bag and shook the keys. "Let's go dump this and head to the clearing in Washington Park, where we can discuss a repeat performance before we get nabbed."

Warmth in my stomach radiated throughout the rest of my body at the look in his eyes.

How could I, after all, refuse my king?

* * *

Sunday, 25 May 1924

"Babe, wake up."

I opened one eye. My father stood over my bed.

"What time is it?" I yawned, tired after staying out until the wee hours of the morning on my date with Sally. I had an enjoyable time; she was knowledgeable in many topics, and we talked after we went dancing.

"It's nearing noon. I'm sorry to disturb your sleep, but a police officer is downstairs, and he wishes to speak with you."

My stomach tightened. *Already? I thought we'd have more time.*

"Did he say what about?"

"No, but he's from the south side. You aren't shooting birds out in the preserve again, are you? I'll have to pay another fine."

I shook my head and sat up. "Tell him I'll be right down."

The officer identified himself as Captain Timothy White and asked if I would mind following him to the police station.

They can't know about the glasses yet, or he wouldn't let me drive myself.

The station was busy and noisy, but when he led me to his office and shut the door, the sound muffled.

"Have a seat, Noah," Captain White said.

I obliged and lit a cigarette.

"I got your name from the game warden over at the preserve."

I nodded. "Edwin Sanders. Affable man and quite knowledgeable about birds."

"Yes, Sanders says you're in the area a lot."

"He's correct. I frequently take my bird-watching classes to Fox Lake and the surrounds, but I go alone and with friends as well."

"When did you go there last?"

"Last weekend, as a matter of fact. I have a new class I'm teaching." I rolled my eyes and flicked ash into the receptacle on his desk. "Girls, this one. Quite the giggling bunch."

White chuckled. "Yes, well, I don't envy you." He shuffled papers and folders around. "Ah, here's my notepad. Now, can you give me a list of names of people you've seen out there? Some you know, maybe someone you don't that you can describe? Also, I'll need the names of the students in your birding class."

I did as he requested and then checked my watch. "If we're finished here, well, I have a lunch date, so…"

"Oh, sure, Noah, but before you leave, do you wear eyeglasses?"

"No, Captain White," I replied, going for honesty. But all I could think of was that Roman and I were running out of time. It wouldn't be long before they connected me to them.

I returned home less than an hour later, and after reassuring my father that all was well with the law, I phoned Roman. He wasn't available but called me back shortly after.

"You're right," I told him. "Things will likely move fast now, so maybe a discreet, farewell road trip might be in order."

The other end of the line was quiet, except for his breathing.

"We'll be careful," he promised. "When do we leave?"

"Better go tonight."

Chapter 29

> To live is to suffer, to survive is to find some meaning in the suffering.
>
> —Friedrich Nietzsche

Monday, 28 July 1924

I'M SITTING IN the same chair I've sat in every day since the hearing began, except for yesterday. No court on the Lord's Day, which is absurd. Instead, Levi and Emil visited the jail, bringing thick steaks, endive salad, roasted potatoes, and a delectable rice dish I didn't recognize. No one spoke of the case, and the four of us dined as if in a restaurant sans fancy plates and cutlery. Or ambiance.

But at least it hadn't been as sweltering then as it is now in this packed courtroom, I think, running a finger under my collar. I look at

Roman, who has the same bored expression on his face he's worn since the proceedings began this morning.

I glance at the big clock over the judge's bench. It's getting late. I've lost track of how many people have given testimony to date, but Mr. Rachben tells me that Bertram Hawke and Jim Sever plan to present over eighty witnesses in total. Yesterday, a woman who worked at the ice cream parlor across from the car rental place where Roman went to use the phone testified that he bought a cone and sat inside for fifteen minutes. This occurred while he waited for me to sign out the Willys-Knight. Trivial.

Very few witnesses have been cross-examined by Mr. Rachben and none by Mr. Milton.

"I'd like to call my last witness for the day," Hawke says when one of the reporters who rode with us in the Marmon finishes giving his statement.

The person who gets on the stand is a police officer. He testifies under direct examination that after our confessions, I stated that, of course, I preferred prison to hanging and hoped to have a "friendly" judge.

Gasps and exclamations of surprise and disgust rise from the gallery at the officer's inflammatory testimony, implying that our families would try to bribe the judge or anyone else.

"Order!" Castaner yells.

Milton whips his head around, and his sedate eyes are blue flames. "Did you say this, Babe?"

I shake my head. "Hell, no, I didn't!"

This is categorically true. I never would've tipped my hand.

"You're sure?"

"Positive."

When it comes time for cross, he gets up slowly and ambles to the witness box in his typical slumped-over position. He proceeds to ask the man innocuous, innocent queries, and then he straightens to his full height and hammers out questions faster than a woodpecker pecks at bark:

"Where were you when my client said this?"

"What time was it? Was anyone else around?"

"Did you reiterate this conversation to another person?"

"Who? When?"

"Do you take notes?"

"Let me see your notebook."

By the time the man produces and opens his notepad, his hands are shaking.

"R-r-right here."

Milton grabs the pad from the detective and studies it. "Aha!" he says, stabbing a finger on the open page. "This entry here where it states, 'If not hang plead guilty.' Is this the memo to which you refer in your testimony?"

"C-c-correct."

"Well, please tell me where it says anything about a 'friendly' judge?" He shoves the notepad at the red-faced man. "You can't because Noah Lieberman never said it, that's why! You made it up, likely coached to do so!"

He spins on his heels and strides over to the prosecutor's table, raising his hand and waving the detective's professional journal before slamming it down in front of Hawke and Sever.

"Don't bother to object. I withdraw the question."

Mr. Milton made his point for the day.

*   *   *

Wednesday, 30 July 1924

"The defense calls Dr. William Black to the stand," Maurice Milton says after the State finally rests its case.

Papers shuffle, and a chair scrapes loudly across the floor when the doctor rises and approaches the bench. But I don't watch him, my eyes are on Hawke and Sever.

The two are leaning forward. Hawke's protruding chin is rigid, and he's gripping a file with both hands. Sever's forearms are resting on the table, but he appears to be pushing down on them, straining his veins. Each man is tense and poised as if ready to act.

"What is your name for the record?"

"Dr. William Arthur Black, sir."

Milton nods. "And where is your place of domicile, Dr. Black?"

"I reside in Washington, D.C."

"Would you mind stating your age, Doctor?"

Chuckles ring throughout the room.

"Not at all. I shall turn fifty-four in three months' time."

"Lovely. What is your profession?"

"I'm a psychiatrist, Mr. Milton. Or an alienist, whichever term you prefer."

"Objection!" Hawke springs to his feet. "Irrelevant."

Sever rises slower. "Immaterial," he barks.

"Why?" Judge Castaner asks, peering down from the bench.

"These deviant 'children,' as the defense would have you believe, already pled guilty. The only reason for any references to psychiatrists is to build an insanity defense." Hawke is pacing back and forth. "Why, just the very mention of the word *insane* means that Your Honor has a legal obligation, a duty, to withdraw the guilty plea of the defendants and call a jury to order immediately!"

The judge's face turns purple.

"I don't need a lesson in the law from the State!" he shouts.

"I...I...I apologize, Your Honor. I didn't mean to infer that you—"

"My esteemed colleague meant no offense," Sever adds, wiping his sweaty forehead with a handkerchief that he stuffs back into his trouser pocket. "However, Your Honor, Illinois law is quite clear on the issue. There is no ambiguity in the matter. The Supreme Court ruled that any arguments regarding the sanity of a defendant must be heard in front of a jury."

"Who's claiming the boys are insane?" Milton says, jumping into the argument. "They are intelligent young prodigies who possess their sanity but have mental issues that must be introduced for the Court to assess the proper punishment. Why, if a defendant were to ingest an illegal substance and, say, shoot his wife when he mistakes her for an intruder, would not his mental state at the time be a factor in his punishment?"

"Punishment! Defense counsel talks of 'punishment' for these murdering monsters who sit in court with smirks on their arrogant faces." Hawke turns to us and points. "Don't think I haven't been noticing. Why, poor Mr. Frisch"—he points again, this time behind us and to our right—"sits here every day. Robbed of the privilege of ever seeing his son grow into a fine man, marry, have children. The only retribution for these slayers is hanging!"

"And there it is, Your Honor," Milton drawls, "the State's attorney's thirst for retribution. Paint every defendant with the same brush as you prepare the gallows for another meal. How many in the last year alone, sir?"

"Objection, Your Honor!"

"You can't object to an argument against your own objection." It's clear by Judge Castaner's tone that he's had enough. He glances at the clock behind him.

"If I may, Your Honor," Mr. Rachben interjects in his gentle manner. "We never said that the boys are insane. They are not.

But their mental condition, as well as their physical condition, is relevant in terms of mitigation of punishment. We're adamant in our position on this matter and are backed up by an Illinois statute that makes it mandatory for a judge to hear all evidence in a guilty plea when he holds the sole discretion in sentencing."

Hawke begins arguing, but Castaner bangs his gavel. "Court is adjourned for the day. We'll pick this up again in the morning. Ten o'clock sharp."

One more bang, and our guards shuffle us back to our respective cells.

* * *

Monday, 4 August 1924

Today is another scorcher. Heat seeps into the full-to-capacity courtroom; humidity strips the occupants of air as body odor and tension blends.

Wish I could light a cig, I think, although smoke will add nothing pleasant to the lack of air quality. Roman is sitting next to me; our guards are in the chairs on either side of us.

Mr. Milton just called Dr. Henderson to the stand. I shake my head, remembering last week. Bertram Hawke and Jim Sever argued for three days against allowing our side to introduce alienists. They tried presenting cases for precedent, but each one was knocked down by the esteemed Misters Milton and Rachben. The judge ultimately agreed.

"Thank you for your testimony, Dr. Henderson," Milton says when he finishes his direct examination.

"Does the prosecution wish to cross-examine this witness?" the judge asks.

"Yes," Hawke shouts, rising from his seat. He heads for the filing cabinet next to the prosecutor's table, opens the top drawer, searches around, and pulls out a file. "I have your report right here, Doctor."

The State's attorney's sarcasm drips off the word doctor and lands on the floor in plops.

"In the report is a section regarding a certain pact."

This is it. The part Manny is dreading the most. Our relationship. Two perverted boys doing vile, disgusting things to each other.

"I'd like to discuss this compact the defendants made when they drove home from a robbery that they committed at Mr. Loewe's old frat house." He turns to face us and the gallery of spectators, waving the thick report in his hand. "These two naughty boys, who, according to defense counsel, deserve nothing more than a spanking or perhaps the loss of privileges for snuffing out the life of a promising tot, spoke of a deal they made on their way home from stealing the very typewriter they composed the ransom note with. I would like you to tell me about this compact they entered into."

"Yes, well, I spoke with Babe and Manny separately, and they detailed a rather juvenile alliance that would satisfy both of their needs."

"Such as?"

"I'm uncomfortable about speaking of the matter in open court."

"Nonsense! I insist on discussing the details of this compact. After all"—Hawke sneers over at the defense table—"the judge needs all the facts to make a fair decision on mitigation for poor Babe and Manny."

"If it pleases the Court," Milton says, "I suggest that we retire to chambers."

"I object!"

"Of course, you do, Mr. Hawke," Rachben mutters, but the State's attorney ignores him.

"This is a public hearing, and all statements and evidence should be presented in front of the public with no prejudice."

"All right," Judge Castaner says. He looks around the room. "I want every woman to exit now. Clear out."

"Wait, what?"

"That isn't fair!"

Cries from the few female reporters fill the air, but the men look too excited about the testimony to come to their coworkers' defense.

"Bailiff, escort the women out."

Roman is grinning when the ladies are gone, but his face is pale, and he's bobbing his knee. There's no way I can reach out and touch him, so I do the next best thing and slide my foot over and tap his.

Stay strong, I think, trying to convey the thought to him. *This is the part that will almost ensure we don't hang.* Now, they'll be convinced we have mental issues that played a role in the crime.

"The following testimony is not for the newspapers," Judge Castaner says. "Continue, Mr. Hawke."

"Thank you." He turns back to the witness stand. "Dr. Henderson, explain the 'juvenile' compact as you call it, as told by the defendants."

"Yes, well, Mr. Lieberman, despite the enjoyment he receives from dating the opposite sex, possesses strong homosexual tendencies and is particularly attracted to Mr. Loewe."

I look around. Every eye is glued to Dr. Henderson, but I sense my family's eyes on my back. The short hairs on my neck tingle as I realize that I never considered how uncomfortable this revelation would be for me. I only thought about Roman's uneasiness.

"Mr. Loewe, however, is prone to criminal activity. This is his excitement. He derives a sexual thrill comparable to an orgasm when he commits an offense. The two boys decided in the early morning drive home from Ann Arbor one weekend—"

"After committing burglary," Sever interjects.

For the record, no doubt.

"Correct. Mr. Lieberman complained about not getting enough out of their crimes, while Mr. Loewe reaped the most rewards and satisfaction. Therefore, they made a deal, a pact, outlining the number of sexual deeds for each criminalistic act committed."

An audible gasp rises in the courtroom.

So untrue. Some head doctors don't know when they're being fed information like a baby bird from its parent.

The reporters are writing so fast and furious that I can hear the words being scratched on paper.

"Newspapermen put down those pencils!" the judge demands. "This should not be for publication."

"What kinds of perversions did they promise to perform after their lawless and felonious behavior?" Hawke demands.

"Mr. Lieberman was permitted to undress a drunken Mr. Loewe and place his erect penis between Mr. Loewe's legs and thrust in and out until ejaculation. This is how Mr. Lieberman's fantasies play out. Mr. Loewe, for his part, claims that although he has a strong passion for girls and a healthy sex life, being taken advantage of is an exciting experience for him."

Manny wanted to save face, but it still stings to hear this aloud.

This time, Roman's foot taps mine, and the hurt in my stomach loosens.

Hawke glares at Dr. Henderson and then over at the two of us.

"This type of testimony, I do believe, is in concert with a sexual crime." Hawke raises his arm and points at us. "These two cold-blooded murderers assaulted that child, that tot!"

"Objection!" scream Milton and Rachben.

"Your Honor," Milton says, shaking as he rises. "I direct the Court to read the coroner's report. There isn't a scintilla of evidence of molestation either antemortem or postmortem. I demand that this be stricken from the record and the prosecution barred from mentioning it again!"

I chance a look at Roman, and he's staring back at me, his face white. I must be pale too because I'm cold. If the judge believes that we molested the boy, he'll hang us for sure.

* * *

Wednesday, 10 September 1924 – Verdict Day

I sit on the edge of my bunk in the cell, smoking, waiting to be escorted into the courtroom for the final time. My hand shakes as I raise the cigarette to my lips. This will all be over soon, one way or another. Manny and I will know what our fate is. Die now or live decades behind bars until freedom can be achieved.

"Neither outcome will be pleasant, but death will at least be quicker," Roman said a few days after the long, grueling, contentious hearing concluded. We were in the yard, him playing baseball with other prisoners and myself reading. Both of us agreed that after the State's false accusation of sexual assault, our chances of avoiding the gallows narrowed.

"Let's go, Lieberman, it's time."

I look up and see my faithful guard unlocking the cell door. Putting out the cigarette, I say, "Already?"

"Yeah, and it's a damn mob scene! Streets are cordoned off a block away from the building. Gotta be a thousand people out there waitin' to find out your fate." He chuckles as we head for the bridge that connects to the county courthouse. "Guess you and your friend are celebrities."

"Amusing."

The trek seems to take longer than ever. Roman is already seated next to his daily chauffeur.

I stop in my tracks at the sight of him. He's wearing a light blue suit, and his hair is slick and parted on the side. His head is turned, and he's speaking to one of his brothers a few rows behind him. For a second, I can't breathe; the air gets stuck in my throat.

"Move it, Lieberman," the deputy holding my arm growls.

I gather myself and continue, reaffirming my mission to save Roman from himself.

I'll chance swinging next to him on the gallows and will happily rot in jail to keep him alive.

Mr. Milton and Mr. Rachben turn around when I'm seated.

"Don't be nervous, boys," Milton says, his craggy face wearing a soothing expression. "I feel positive about our outcome."

"No matter what happens this morning, sir, and I think I can speak for Roman on this topic as well." I turn to him, and he nods in agreement. "Your closing argument was nothing less than brilliant, Mr. Milton."

He smiles, and Rachben pats him on the shoulder.

"The passion with which you defend your clients, the intelligence with which you present your case, your empathy, combined with your outstanding use and understanding of the English language to support your abhorrence of capital punishment is tantamount to nothing." I hold out my hand for him to shake, and he does. "Thank you, sir."

"All rise," the bailiff says, and then the judge enters and sits down at the bench. "Hear ye, hear ye, court is now in session with the Honorable Justice Jack Castaner presiding."

Cameramen rush forward, taking pictures as the judge opens a folder before him. The stenographer is seated to his right.

"I'll have order in my court, and anyone who doesn't abide by this rule will be escorted out." He looks down and adjusts his spectacles. "This has been a grueling case that reached the ears of the public worldwide.

"Although tragedies are inflicted every day, the brutal murder tied into a kidnapping for ransom of a child by two individuals barely out of childhood themselves, contains all the sensational elements. Two privileged young men whose every whim was provided for decide to kidnap a child for ransom and kill him regardless. And for no apparent reason.

"The Court's intention is not to reiterate a case that has been laid out in minute detail, and one that has a confession attached to it.

"Sentencing as a result of a plea deal between the People and counsel for defendants is nothing unusual in a criminal matter. This case is different in that a plea of guilty has been entered with no agreement or recommendation of penalty. Therefore, the decision is up to this Court.

"Evidence and testimony were presented on both sides in favor of and against mitigation of punishment."

Judge Castaner is speaking in a monotone voice, and none of his sentences are making me feel confident. Although now I'm not sure what I'm rooting for. Death might be the wisest choice. I steal a glance at Roman, but he isn't looking at me. He's biting the inside of his cheek, and his leg is bopping up and down.

I want, more than anything, to reach out and touch him. Perhaps for the last time.

"The laws are clear for the crimes of murder and kidnapping for ransom. I won't quote the statutes, but in each case the punishment in the instance of a guilty plea lies with the Court. It is at my discretion to impose a death sentence, life imprisonment, or imprisonment of a term no less than fourteen years.

"Sentencing these boys to die is the easiest decision to make and the one that will satisfy the lust for vengeance harbored by the majority of the public."

My gut tightens, and Roman's foot connects with mine. It doesn't leave.

We lost. I played this wrong, and I took Manny down with me.

"However, this Court will not be swayed by calls for blood. The defendants and their attorneys will please stand."

My legs are shaky as I rise. I want to look at Roman, but I can't move my head. I can't swallow or even blink my eyes.

"All of the exhaustive testimony aside, the defendants' ages when the crime was committed, eighteen and nineteen respectively, dictate this Court to impose the following verdict:

"Noah Freudenthal Lieberman Jr., for the crime of murder, this Court sentences you to be confined in the penitentiary at Joliet for the rest of your natural life. For the crime of kidnapping by ransom, this Court rules that you serve the term of ninety-nine years in the penitentiary at Joliet.

"Roman Al—"

I don't listen to the rest, don't need to, because Manny's fate and mine are entwined.

I did it. I pulled it off. The true "crime of the century."

Chapter 30

Tuesday, January 28, 1936

"Never thought I'd say this in prison, but great sweet rolls, eh, Babe?"

I smile and bite into the sugary treat that we bought at the commissary. Roman doesn't call me Babe anymore, not since the early days at Joliet—before they separated us for years—and it's nice to hear the nickname again.

We're alone, but I glance around anyway to make sure that we're not overheard. Other than the guard at the tower, the circular cell block is largely empty, and both of our respective cellmates already left for their jobs. Metal doors are open in every cubicle, and I can see Roman's cell across from mine.

He takes his last bite and licks his fingers. Then he looks right at me and smacks his lips.

Ah, our signal that he wants to meet in our private spot in the library—the library we helped rebuild after rioters destroyed the old one in 1931.

"Ready to go grade those papers now, Babe? Pile is building."
Another of our codes.

I nod. "Sure, Roman. Give me a few—"

"Hey, Lieberman, Loewe."

I turn to see a friend of Roman's walking over. Johnny Daley. He smirks when he reaches my cell, grabs the last roll off my small desk, and stuffs it in his mouth in one piece.

"Looked for you in the mess hall, Roman," he mumbles around the mass. "Want to talk to you."

Roman squirms, just a little, but I notice.

"Sure, sure, Johnny, I'll see you later, though. I'm going to work now."

The con swallows in a noisy gulp. "Yeah, all right. Catch you at noon."

"Okay," Roman says, and Johnny leaves, wiping his hands on his shirt as he goes.

I sit at my desk, stomach queasy, no longer interested in the treat.

"So, he's the new..." I can't finish.

"Don't do this, Babe." He stands up and brushes crumbs off his chest. "We've talked about this. Seven years was a long time to wait."

"I never imagined the public outcry would follow us inside prison, never dreamed anyone would continue to care about us once we were out of the news." I hang my head, which suddenly feels heavy after almost a dozen years behind bars. But the last five at Stateville, being around Roman so much, makes it all worth it.

He touches my shoulder, albeit a brief contact. "Look, Babe, I give you everything that I'm able to give, but..."

"I know," I say. "It's just that I don't trust Johnny."

He smiles the quick grin even prison hasn't been able to dull.

"You don't like or trust any of my 'friends.' So, come on, what say you, Babe? Wanna go grade some papers?"

I laugh despite my mood.

Later, back in my cell, I sit at the desk and work on the new algebra curriculum Roman and I discussed adding to our courses.

I smile. Life is funny the way it works sometimes. On that tenth day of September in 1924, while we awaited our fate, I believed that we would hang. But Maurice Milton accomplished what I hoped he could do—he saved our lives; however, even he, an aging jurist, couldn't predict the vast publicity our case received.

Mr. Milton wrote, and when he visited us in Joliet, before Roman and I were separated, Roman begged him to tell us if he thought we would ever be free.

"Yes, I do," he'd said, and I read truth in his eyes. "Unless you die young, I predict you'll spend not much more than two decades behind bars." He had stared at us, one at a time, and gave his last bit of advice. "Do some good, build up a clean record."

So, we did, individually, and together once allowed.

To date, by my calculations, Manny and I have served over half of our time.

We talk about the future. "Later," we call it. One thing we agree on about "later" is that we'll live together. No one will dictate our relationship. But mostly, we discuss the school, our accomplishments inside. Roman is proud of himself, as he should be. He took to prison life like he takes to everything—with ease. Everyone is victim to his charms, and the residents of Joliet and Stateville have not been exceptions. At one point, he held one of the most coveted prison positions—he worked for the deputy warden. A very cushy job indeed.

A chirp gets my attention, and I glance over at my pet bird, Flea, in his box.

"Ah yes, I forgot something, didn't I?" I rise and reach into my pocket for the small piece of sweet roll hidden in a napkin. Unwrapping the treat, I feed the horned lark I rescued from the yard as a fledgling.

"Noah!"

I look up and see Tiny running over. He stops at my cell, bends over, hands on his knees, panting. Tiny is huge and grossly out of shape.

"What's wrong?"

"R-R-Roman."

"He's taking a shower," I say, conscious of my head shaking back and forth by itself. I try to stop the motion but can't. "I just left him half an hour ago."

"He's hurt, bad, Noah. They took him to the infirmary."

As he speaks, a couple of screws come into the blockhouse and go straight to Roman's cell and start shaking it down, tossing things around.

I head for the exit.

"Here," Tiny says, throwing me my jacket and hat. "Cold out there today."

"Thanks."

When I reach the gate, the keeper won't let me through.

"Please," I beseech. "I just got word that Roman's in the hospital. I have to go to him!"

He doesn't relent. Finally, I convince him to call the warden. No answer. Desperate, I'm about to rush the gate and risk bullets in the spine, when Father O'Leary approaches.

"Noah," he says, "I just heard." He turns to the guard. "I'll escort Mr. Lieberman to the hospital ward."

"All right, but it's your head if the warden gets angry," the guard says and lets us through.

Frigid air slaps my face, numbing it as we run across the grounds. Three more gates and accesses to pass before I push through swinging doors, ripping off my outer garments, and stop short.

Roman is lying on the operating table, naked and bleeding from dozens of areas all over his body. An ether mask covers his face, and he's breathing through a rubber tube inserted in his windpipe. Four doctors surround him, two working on his throat, which appears to be cut so deep it's a wonder he hasn't been decapitated, and the others moving from arms to thighs to torso. My feet propel me forward in slow motion, and I stand to the side, out of the way.

His pale skin makes the ugly wounds stand out vividly.

"He was stabbed, slashed with a straight razor in the shower."

I turn to see Paul Perry, an inmate who works in the pathology lab.

"B-b-blood, I can give him blood. See if we're a match." I roll up my sleeve, but Paul is shaking his head.

"Already taken care of, but they can't staunch the wounds fast enough. Keeps pourin' out."

Sick, all I can do is stare with a lump in my throat and what feels like an automobile parked on my chest, constricting my breaths and crushing my heart, while the doctors do their best to suture every cut so Roman doesn't bleed out.

Time moves so quick, but it drags on, and he gets whiter; his breathing becomes more labored.

The doctors talk among themselves as they work, giving instructions, suggestions.

"His temp is rising, get warm blankets, hot water bottles!" someone yells.

"I'll do it," I say and rush out to find the items. The doctors are busy when I return, and they've been joined by a fifth doctor who is attending to the deep gashes in Roman's neck. I place the blanket over his feet, the bottles between his legs.

"A throat specialist from Joliet is here," Father O'Leary says before I can ask who the newcomer is.

I can't speak, just nod at him and step back out of the way.

"I'm sorry, Noah," the prison physician, who happens to be tremendously fond of Roman, says. "But we're losing him."

I stand, helpless, next to the person who was not only my biggest blessing in life but also the worst person I could have met. Still, I love him and would do it all over again to be with him longer.

The doors swing open, and three men rush inside. I recognize Roman's brother, Emil, along with two other men whose faces are familiar, but I don't recall why. My greatest emotional accomplishment is keeping burning tears from spilling over when the oldest man's face registers.

The Loewe family doctor. I know him because he ministered to the Lieberman family as well, along with most of the families in our neighborhood.

The old physician strokes Manny's cheek and picks up his hand. With one last rise of his chest, Manny stops breathing, leaving this world holding onto the one who brought him into it.

This is when my world ends.

Epilogue

But it is the same with man as with the tree. The more he seeks to rise into the height and light, the more vigorously do his roots struggle earthward, downward, into the dark, the deep—into evil.

—Friedrich Nietzsche

Friday, April 30, 1971 – San Juan, Puerto Rico

"Let's go, Sadie. Do your business," I coo to the nervous old dog, who seems to be deeming this patch of greenery unworthy of her waste. Although, perhaps her anxiety this morning is more of my doing. I'm not feeling well, which makes me irritable. Additionally, the animal senses that I don't care for her and never have. I much prefer birds. I give the leash a tug. "Come on, find another spot." The beige-and-cream-colored Chihuahua that I adopted ten years ago when I married her mother, Geraldine—Gerri to family and friends—moves about a foot and begins sniffing around again.

I gaze up at the sky. It's been raining lightly all morning, but the clouds have finished emptying for the time being.

"Hola, Noah, Sadie. Buenos días!"

I turn my head at the greeting. "Good morning yourself, Enrique," I reply to the young man jogging by. I sigh. I despise being called Noah, but when I was a child, I hated being called Babe. I eventually got used to it. However, in prison, I was "Noah," "Lieberman," or "Inmate." I miss being Babe.

Mostly, I miss the people who called me Babe, the majority of whom are dead.

Oh, I have a few friends from the old days back in Chicago—first and perhaps the most important, the attorney who ensured my freedom—and some peers who I correspond with regarding ornithology and other matters who still use the nickname but everyone in Puerto Rico, Gerri included, calls me Noah.

I stop next to a mighty palm tree to lean on it and catch my breath. I've been having trouble now and again, more frequently of late, with getting enough air into my lungs despite quitting the Luckies a decade ago. Except when I drink. And I tend to drink often. Gerri and I have our most interesting spats while I'm imbibing.

I chuckle. Our last one had been a doozey.

"I'm sick of looking at this, this…monstrosity!" she'd yelled, pointing to the large portrait hanging in our living room before throwing her glass at me but missing. "I don't understand why you keep it."

A pang that never dulled in the years since his murder grips my heart. Roman. The portrait is of Manny.

"I keep it because I treasure it," I tell Sadie, who continues to fuss around. Damn dog.

Thinking about Manny releases a plethora of emotions, and I'm grateful for the tree supporting me.

Running wild. Nasty bums. A boy named Bennie. Prison. Life with Manny. Despair. Dealing with ignorant, sadistic, bigoted motherfuckers. Rebuilding. Hope. Redemption. The never-ending void.

Thoughts crowd my head, and desperate for a distraction, I check my watch, a nice Timex with a blue face and red stripes that Gerri bought me for my last birthday. It's one thirty-nine in the afternoon, but the date is what grabs my attention.

The thirtieth of April. I met Manny fifty-one years ago today while touring the University of Chicago. Also, on a Friday.

No wonder I feel off. This day typically creeps up on me, not like his birthday in June or the day he died in January. On these days, I'm skunk drunk for seventy-two hours straight. Twenty-four before, during, and after. A man needs buffer zones.

Sadie finally squats to urinate as memories flood my mind. I accomplished what I set out to do—save Manny from himself while not letting on that I was also ensuring that I would never lose him to a wife and children, that I'd have him relatively to myself. I never dreamed he would find the kind of trouble he found in prison. I should have known better.

Everything went as planned. Maurice Milton worked his magic to spare us from the gallows, and we each received life sentences for murder plus ninety-nine years for kidnapping. Twenty to twenty-five years, tops, is all the time we should have served. However, the notoriety of our case, something I failed to anticipate, attached itself to us like glue.

The sensationalism of the crime sparked outrage during certain periods. Like in 1927 when we were paraded in court for the ridiculous trial of some taxi driver who accused Manny and me of mutilating him and leaving him for dead years before, and when someone from the Department of Corrections made a name for himself by claiming that we could potentially be paroled in eleven years. Although I suffered weeks in solitary confinement for minor infractions throughout my decades of incarceration—more so after Manny's murder—my prison record was commendable. Manny and I founded a correspondence school, the curriculum of which was copied, and the program was used in prisons throughout the State of Illinois. I taught English to multiple foreigners—Polish, Italian, and German immigrants. I ran the library at Stateville and worked as an X-ray technician in the prison hospital. In 1944, I volunteered to participate in an experimental malaria program and offered my arm willingly to be stabbed with the Anopheles mosquito.

A guinea pig inflicted by a bug, causing me serious medical issues that I suffer from to this day.

Once our mitigation hearing ended in 1924 and we were sent to Joliet, things pretty much went the way I imagined. The other inmates only cared about our characters, and so Manny made friends fast. The ones I made warmed up slower, but they were loyal. The two of us got jobs right away, me weaving the bottoms of chairs and Manny woodworking. We took advantage of the Jewish holidays and were excused from work and allowed to mingle with other Jews in a large room behind the auditorium. Being in prison gave us a freedom we could never enjoy out in the real world. No one cared how close we were because all the long-timers had relationships at one point or another during their stints.

Our families' money and status bought us a little comfort. We enjoyed pints of gin to share with other fellas, snuck in by a guard one of Manny's brothers had a connection to. Family visits were scheduled together, giving us even more time to pretend that we lived a normal life. And the excitement Manny craved was fulfilled in prison.

When Stateville opened, I was transferred, and Manny stayed behind at Joliet. It took seven agonizing years for him to join me there, and when he did, he told me that he had stayed sexually active. He needed to live his fantasy since it was also his reality. Although I had waited for him, I understood. And I loved him, would take him however he offered himself to me.

If I insisted on fidelity, maybe he'd still be alive! This is my mistake, my biggest regret, I think, unaffected by Sadie tugging on the leash to go home. I stay where I am, head and shoulders resting against the tree, tears streaming down my face as I remember that horrible day in 1936.

The next few years after his murder were the worst of my life.

I shake my head to rid the thoughts. Life has been tolerable, if not good at times in the decades since. Once the sitting governor commuted my sentence to eighty-five years, making me eligible for parole in 1953, my goal has been to tell my story. For Manny. Our story, the real one and to be published after my death. However, writing about the truth is proving difficult to do. And I've been busy since I finally earned my freedom in 1958.

It occurs to me that I've lived almost thirty-four years behind bars—about a dozen more than I anticipated—and, so far, in total, I've been a free man for about thirty-two years. Before I left the joint, though, I had my cellmate give me a prison tattoo. Gerri hates that the name Manny graces my hip even more than she hates the painting.

The frenetic dog's twitching and squirming catches my attention.

"Okay, Sadie, I see that you're ready to go home." I make a tsking sound and smirk at the arthritic cur that doesn't like me ever since it had an accident licking peanut butter from a knife.

Poor, yappy thing needed to have its tongue amputated. "Shame you can hardly bark anymore."

I straighten, and we start walking home. Handsome Enrique jogs by again, smiling, and I nod and smile back. I can't see his dark eyes behind sunglasses, but something about his quick grin stirs familiar feelings in this old man.

Coughing into my hand, I take a moment to let my lungs fill before we continue home.

"I believe I'm ready to write my *real* memoir, just as soon as we return from our trip to Chicago this summer," I confide in Sadie. "The tale even Manny didn't know." The dog doesn't respond, just keeps all four legs pumping, heading in the direction of her water bowl and comfy bed. "After all, Roman left me once. If I didn't do something drastic to keep him, he would've eventually left me again." I shake my head. "Although, he did leave me in the end, didn't he? Left me stuck to endure prison without him." I turn to admire the back of the jogger's fit legs, calf muscles bulging as he runs. "I know. I'll hire an assistant. Enrique is always looking for odd jobs, and typing has never been my strong suit. I can even buy a new Underwood for him to use. I've read that the newest models are wonderful. What do you think, Sadie?"

She doesn't pause in her quest toward home.

Yes, well, I think it's a great idea. Time for this Übermensch to prepare for his posthumous bow.

The End.

About The Author

D. L. SCARPE has always had stories rattling around inside her head, locked up tight, only set free on those endless childhood nights spent swapping tales with her best friend. The story-weaving continued into adulthood—her little secret. However, raising a family; managing a household; building retaining walls, patios, or fire pits from stones (rock "jigsaw puzzles"); refinishing oak floors and furniture; or helping her husband on a roof—although she tried to pay attention when on a roof—kept her too busy for that other side of her to come out. So, it remained a secret.

But kids grow up and bodies get too tired for physical labor, and now it's time to chase her own passions and dreams. Working on her bucket list, Scarpe picked three things that make her happy, and she's pursuing them all with no apologies:

Writing.
Shoes.
Tattoos.